THE WONDERFUL STUFF

A H RAJA

For Polly
and the boy on the hill.

1,946 km east of Jakarta, INDONESIA - 2018
Two years, 36 days after Mutation 3
One day until Mutation 4

Ears ringing, eyes swelling with tears, Aydin was only now becoming aware of the numbness in his legs as he knelt on the rubble clenching the hand of his dying mother. The sunlight shone on her light brown hair, giving it the appearance of strands of gold. She was always the most beautiful thing in the world to him, but now as she lay beneath shards of glass and chunks of cement, he loathed the sight of her. He wanted to be as far away as possible, and yet he knew this was exactly where he needed to be.

His finger was now partially lodged into his mother's open wound. Aydin could see her mouth moving but barely paid attention to it, for the bone he could feel against his own hand consumed his thoughts. It felt like a cold set of dice, the kind he took out of his pillowcase every Saturday morning just as the sun came up. His mother's bones felt like those dice. He never wanted to play with them again.

Feeling a quick pulse within the wound, Aydin came to. Wiping the tears with his untainted hand, he tried to focus on his mother's voice rather than the grotesque feeling trickling its way up his finger.

He was failing.

With the ringing not subsiding, and his vision blurring once again, Aydin could do nothing but rock back and forth watching his mother slip away. Lifting his head and turning right, then left, he faintly caught glimpses of other people frantically shouting through the haze. Why was she so calm?

He saw her smile fade and eyelids close. He would never know what her final words were. And so that became the last memory Aydin had of his mother, since the team sent in to clean up the damage of the explosion never bothered to separate or identify any of the casualties. Living below the poverty line, separated from common society, definitely had its perks.

1,946 km east of Jakarta, INDONESIA
Two years, 36 days after Mutation 3
Same day

Approximately two kilometres away, Salar stood in the doorway of his home fixated on the growing cloud of dust at the opposite end of his village blending in with the rising sun and the immaculate shades it produced. The shades were tainted today; dullness accompanied them, one that the young boy had not seen before. Goose bumps began to rise on his skin as he deduced that if he had not been running slightly behind to meet his cousin for a quick game of dice, he would have been in precisely that spot. Unsure as to whether moving towards it was the best plan of action, instead he took a step back and entered his kitchen, which happened to be empty at the time, though not for long as he heard his father's footsteps getting close.

Being the son of a particularly violent man, Salar had learned from a delicate age how to judge his father's approaching presence. It was a beastly combination of dragging slippers' dense thuds that managed to somehow echo on the concrete, and the deep wheezing that set him apart.

"What was that?" boomed the aged man's voice, not so subtly implying his son had had a role to play in it.

Not wanting to get in the man's way, Salar quickly stepped to the side and pointed towards the disseminating cloud of filth, all the while keeping his gaze firmly on his own bare feet.

Shuffling to the door, the man looked upon the event just as a softer set of steps sounded in the room. If it was not for the noise of the wooden leg, the individual may have come in undetected. Salar looked up at his mother as she came towards him and gently settled an arm around his shoulders. Although she was not placing any weight on the boy, she always appeared to like the idea of him being someone she could lean on, so to speak. Or at least that's what Salar had deduced. Thus, the motion had become habitual when one was in the vicinity of the other.

A sharp intake of air came from Salar's mother as her eyes fell upon the sight outside.

Looking up at her expression, it was evident to the boy she wanted someone to rush over, not being able to herself. But he also knew from exponential experience she was too terrified to ask her husband. Requesting something of a man was not a woman's place—no matter how far the world had come.

Speaking for the first time all morning, Salar said in a barely audible whisper that came out hoarse, "Can I go see if they're okay?"

By "they," he had meant his aunt and her two children. It wasn't curiosity that motivated his actions, but rather what he believed was the right thing to do. Neither empathy nor concern resided in the boy's heart by nature.

Minutes later, Salar found himself rushing towards the area where a dust cloud had been moments ago. With the sun entirely above the horizon now, he squinted during his approach. The closer he got, the more he tasted dust and sand in his mouth. More so than average in the heat of his desolate town.

Nearing what he figured was his destination, Salar stopped just short of the first batch of debris. Not out of concern or awe, but simply obstruction. Rolling across his line of vision and gradually forming a barricade were military tanks.

The sound from their chain link navigating over the rough terrain would make you or me cringe. Fascinated, Salar saw the tank casually roll in front of the marketplaces, not caring about the blood in its way.

The scene reminded him of his ventures through the hallways of his father's clinic and seeing, for the first time, human blood spilling over an operating table and dripping to the floor. How natural the scene was, how calming for him: we were all messes in the end.

Peeling his eyes from the soiled ground, he noticed others waiting to cross following the tank's departure. He needed to see someone's face. He needed to see what expression this was supposed to provoke. Looking up towards the face of a lady he recognized as a vendor from the market not far from his home, Salar found what he was looking for. Concerned was the look she had. But with tears. This was a rare combination to lay eyes one. Salar felt pleased with himself for having witnessed it in such a circumstance. Well done.

He noticed others making their way towards the explosion, if he could call it that prematurely, all with the same concerned looks. Salar attempted to imitate the expression physically. Tears were never really something he could re-create, though not for a lack of attempt. So those were out. Crease the forehead, draw the eyebrows together, bring down the corners of the mouth, and part the lips slightly as if you forgot to close them. He felt he was pulling off "concerned" impeccably.

1,946 km east of Jakarta, INDONESIA
Two years, 36 days after Mutation 3
Same day

Aydin had not let go. He could not bring himself to release his mother's hand, on the contrary, he had developed an attachment to the feeling of his hand in hers, even with the one finger lodged in a wound. She cannot leave him if he does not let go. He had shifted his position to sit cross-legged, subconsciously planning on being there indefinitely. The screams and cries of people nearby seeped through him, leaving no residue. The staggering amount of blood littered in varying degrees around him began to be mentally blocked out. He did not care for other people at this point, or so he thought.

It was then that amongst the constant stream of shouts, a new voice was added that caught his attention simply because of its familiarity.

"Mommy!"

Turning his head slightly to the left, Aydin saw his younger sister curled on the ground, surrounded by various rubble and grasping her torso awkwardly.

Aydin stood up, still holding his mother's hand, afraid he would lose her, and stretched as far as he could towards his sister.

"Kivran!"

Noticing her relentless sobs, he called out her name again. This time locking eyes with her, but only momentarily for it appeared her degree of pain was increasing.

Closing his attention on her and her alone, Aydin caught her murmur in a quieter voice than before. "Help, Aydin."

He turned back to look at his mother, her head had shifted in the movement and her hair no longer caught the sun. Her light was gone. Rocking back and forth on the balls of his feet, unsure of himself, the boy wiped away his tears with the free hand. Looking back over to his sister, he noticed her tears.

It's funny, the things you remember at the weirdest of times. The day Kivran was born, Aydin being five years old then, sat with an off-duty nurse in the waiting room of the local clinic. He was waiting for his mother to be okay. He doesn't remember the screams his sister made as she stepped into this world, but he remembers the deafening silence from his mother. He wanted to hear her voice above anything else. As the nurse sat there congratulating him on becoming a brother, Aydin didn't want to be congratulated. He wanted to be told he could go see his mother.

Finally, a woman bearing a kind expression and blood spattered garments exited the room just left of where he was and caught Aydin's eye. He didn't like the sight of her with all that blood.

"Would you like to meet your new sister?"

Aydin didn't move or respond. He felt the damp hand of the nurse sitting beside him on his back.

"You can come in now."

Aydin stood up and made his way to the room he knew his mother was in. Letting the doctor guide him through, he found himself in a small room with a wooden pen against one corner underneath a noisy heater and a bed in the opposite corner. There lay his mother, smiling.

"Would you like to see your sister first or your mother?" This wasn't a question he needed to think about.

Understanding what he had to do now, Aydin knelt back down and gently released his mother's hand and rested it on her chest. Bending lower, he wiped away the debris on her forehead and tenderly kissed her. As his nose began to run and tears continued to spill, the young boy turned around and made his way over the rubble to Kivran, the only real family he had left.

Akureyri, ICELAND
2 years, 36 days after Mutation 3
Same day

Shifting in his seat out of pure impatience, Garrett crossed his arms and swung his legs, hoping his father would miraculously realize his frustration at being told to stay put. Seated at a table close to the window inside a bookstore, the young boy glared at the bus stop across the sidewalk where his father stood. Having driven together four hours straight from the capital, Garrett wanted his father to let him be. He felt naive, not that he knew what that feeling was called at this point in his vernacular, why would his father change his demeanour after eight years of treating him like scum? The truth was the man had no place else to physically dump his son whilst he conducted his business, which is precisely why the two disjointed family members found themselves in downtown Akureyri—one disgruntled in a bookstore, the other standing out in the sleet and fog.

Realizing his father was deliberately going to ignore him, Garrett turned his gaze indoors. His vision settled on a dark-skinned woman sitting at the table across from him, immersed in a paperback version of *The Viking Sagas.*

Tourist.

Having sat through countless dinners with his parents, Garrett knew people like her—people who still travelled for the sake of travel, or worse in their opinion, cultural enlightenment—were the sole variable in Iceland's inevitable succumb to the fourth mutation. Whatever that was and whenever it was. Moving up here was meant to establish a sense of isolation in order to prevent his family being afflicted with the disease. But as his father repetitively mentioned: until the World Health Organization recognizes the lethality of the strand, there was nothing his father nor his company could do about the matter.

Turning back to the window, Garrett watched a man slightly older than his father approach the bus stop, he could tell this simply because of the man's gait. Sitting up in attention, the boy craned his neck in order to see the stranger's face, but the fog was drifting away from the water and towards the city's inclined main street. He could barely make out his own father, let alone the unknown figure now.

Alternating his leg swings, the boy gazed around the store. It was commonplace for him to be left to his own devices. However, it was not commonplace for him to be left to his own devices in such a place. Looking at the two teenagers working behind the counter, he observed as one was occupied on her phone while the other was hunched over the counter reading something.

Reading. That's what he would use this rare opportunity to do. Read.

One last glance to his right out the window confirmed two vague figures still stationary amongst the fog. Jumping down from his seat, Garrett already knew what he was headed for. Subject: Nonfiction; topic: Military. Iceland didn't have a military, but the United Nations did.

Garrett knew he had more than a long way to go prior to actually stepping into that realm. But the idea of it wasn't a flame he could easily put out. He had spent his whole life, all eight years, on this one island. Told endless tales of how the mainland was, and to quote his own father, "a wasteland of infected human beings and livestock that would eventually wipe out all traces of life as we know it." The only problem was, Garrett wanted to see this wasteland before it was gone for good. He wanted to see what sort of being would still choose to live there, knowing what they do.

289 km northwest of Beijing, CHINA
2 years, 37 days after Mutation 3
0 Days until Mutation 4

"Thank you, Han. I am here on location at one of the few remaining, fully functioning pig farms in the world. The Xiang family has owned this land and livestock for five generations now and they will be the first ones to tell you just how daunting this task of keeping up with demand has become for them alone. As you can see behind me, with just under a dozen pigs, this farm is home to the largest pig population in one confined space. Though many would argue such conditions for confinement are no longer ideal, if we are to remove these animals from the endangered list that is, the Xiang family believes with growing trespassing and attempted livestock theft on the rise, they have no other choice. When taking into account the ever-growing demand for pig meats and the skyrocketing prices accompanying them, one can't say these reactions are unwarranted. I attempted to contact members of the Agricultural Committee in Beijing last week, and although they officially declined my requests for an interview, there have been clear signs of government intervention in order to regulate these types of farms. However, following China's induction into the now-functioning Trans-Pacific Partnership, such regulations have been heavily condemned, with most regulations falling to the wayside. Few advocates outside of China have asked the World Health Organization to investigate living conditions for such rare animals that are most likely to end up on the dinner tables of the rest of the world. However, the WHO has denied such requests, going so far as to release a statement in which it makes its stance clear: the World Health Organization does not have significant actionable data indicating life-threatening diseases are manifesting or originating in such livestock conditions. Han."

"Thank you, Emile. And it looks like one of these livestock is quite taken with you there."

"I'm glad you noticed. This little pig here has been nudging my knees this whole segment! I've been trying to pat him away, but he's taken with me indeed."

"That must be so fun, splashing around with those wee piglets! Thank you again, Emile. We go now to Iwan for the Asian market. How's everything in those stocks today, Iwan?"

HONG KONG AIRPORT
~~2 years, 39 days after Mutation 3~~ - data no longer relevant
2 days after Mutation 4

Awaiting a flight yet to begin boarding, a gentleman in his late sixties occupied a seat in the waiting area. Checking the screens a couple of rows ahead, it was determined he had at least a few minutes prior to boarding call. Just enough time to catch up on key international headlines.

Familiar with his desired site, he wasted no time in switching the tablet adjoined to his seat on and scrolling through their alphabetical site map. Stopping on International, he proceeded about his business. Had he stopped a few lines above this, under Editorial Comments, he would've seen something only a handful of people bothered to browse that day:

"Our final word for today is a somber one as we say our goodbyes to one of our own, Emile Zui. Most of you knew her from field pieces throughout East Asia, we remember her as a wonderful human being and a generous colleague. Ms. Zui passed from rapid pneumonia. Her family is proud to say their beloved Emile donated her organs; she always looked to help others above all else. You will be missed, Emile."

1,946 km east of Jakarta, INDONESIA - 2035
17 years, 26 days after Mutation 4

Drawing wet doodles in the dry sand, Mica stood in an alley towards the rear of his home, emptying his bladder.

Looking right upon hearing his neighbours, Mica quickly finished and made his way towards the main street while zipping himself up. The main road wasn't much to look at, it consisted of near identical-looking shacks meandering in each direction with no logical pattern. The only reason this particular street was referred to as "main" was because the primary grocery store was located here—Mica's home. Half of the bottom level functioned as a store, while the other half along with the courtyard in the back functioned as living quarters for him, his mother, his two older sisters, and a cousin. All girls.

It wasn't the store that seemed to be the most interesting aspect of this street to Mica though, in fact, it was a different house many didn't even register in their peripherals. From its appearance, it wasn't anything out of the ordinary. From its residents, it wasn't anything out of the ordinary. From the items lugged in and out of it, however, it was anything but ordinary.

Having grown up in the same home all his life, Mica knew the area like the back of his hand. He could tell a complete stranger the backyards to cut across when trying to reach a particular spot, or how far the damp smell of the Pit reached in each direction, or where each resident worked. Hell, he could even give you a pretty educated guess on what each person did in their spare time. His neighbours, however, remained a mystery.

Approaching his mother, who was multitasking her way through a conversation with said neighbours while sweeping the two steps at the front of her home, Mica attempted to eavesdrop. It should be noted: subtlety is a characteristic Mica believes he possesses, but actually lacks.

"How many litres do you need?" his mother asked, not looking up.

"Two litres for the time being, if you have them. If your source is going out to get it, we'll take six."

The elder of the three neighbours answered, his name was Salar, as far as Mica had figured. There was something off about this one, he never seemed to be at ease. Always behaved as though he was pretending to be someone else.

Not realizing a pair of eyes on him until now, Mica looked to his left to find the younger of the two present men smiling at him. The neighbour came over and ruffled his hair. Mica was only a few years or so younger than him, albeit scrawny for his age, but that was no reason for his hair to be ruffled. He was the man of the house, dammit.

"How's it going, Mica?" the neighbour asked. Aydin, he believed was this one, the generally nicer one of these two. But no comparison to the single girl neighbour. Single, as in there was only one girl who lived there, not that he knew whether she was single or not. Not that Mica cared. That much.

Sidestepping to keep the ruffling to a minimum, Mica bypassed the men to enter his front door only to be stopped by his mother's raggedy broom on his chest on the way.

"Why are the empty bottles still there?"

Sighing for dramatic effect, the boy turned back around towards the alley, dragging his feet along the way. He knew fair well his mother would get in trouble if the gasoline bottles were found anywhere near her property or the neighbour's, tagged as they were, Mica couldn't genuinely get angry at her. She'd only told him at least three times. It's just that he hated the Pit. That dreaded swamp that reeked of God knows what. Though he loved the smell of remaining gasoline in the cans, he hated the smell of where he had to take them. You'd think living so close to the place he'd be used to the smell.

Swiftly picking up the items by the neighbour's ajar door, he began cutting through the family's courtyard in the rear. Mica carried two large bottles over his imaginary trapeze line, replaying a comedic sketch in his head, both upside down so he could make wet doodles in the dry sand. Reaching the Pit, he looked around. With his own courtyard within earshot behind him, and the children on the football field on the opposite side of the Pit, he looked down at the thing.

Terrible at math and unable to tell us how massive this Pit was, know it was taller than him and wide enough to fit that football field. Did we mention it reeked? It was a mixture of the community's daily garbage, delinquents' urine, and something generally unknown. The last one being an eerie blue substance that seeped through the ground. Rumour had it there was a leak in the underground storage of a factory of sorts that used to be in the Pit's place that had never been properly taken care of. Or it was just their island sinking into the ocean. Take your pick.

Holding his nose against one of the gasoline bottle's openings and taking in a deep breath, he held it. Tossing the bottles rapidly on top of the rest of that junk, Mica legged it in the opposite direction as fast as he could.

1,946 km east of Jakarta, INDONESIA
Same day

"We can just push the experiment back a few days, at least until we have the gas."

"No, Salar, that heart won't survive a few more days in that junk icebox and this weather. We'll just have to hope that gas will be enough."

Standing in the doorway dusting off her uniform, Kivran overheard the other two farther inside the home accompanied by a distinct clang, someone had kicked the icebox in question.

"The whole experiment is going to be botched. We'll be stuck halfway in-between with no lights and a warm heart."

"I'd like to apologize on behalf of all living things that we can't all have cold hearts like yourself, Salar."

Inadvertently letting out a chuckle, she let them know she was in the vicinity.

"I heard that, Kivran!"

Unwavering in her smile, she saw Aydin and Salar standing in their lab across the courtyard. That was just what they referred to their cluttered room in the back of the home. Latex lined the floor, walls riddled with sketches, diagrams, and torn pages from textbooks that she had deliberately avoided looking at in detail: this was their lab. It was her brother's pride and joy.

Hearing their bickering in the background, Kivran continued about her newly formed routine. After washing her hands under the low-pressure lukewarm water, she retrieved a metal bowl from underneath the sink and filled it halfway with the same water.

Gingerly walking towards the now-hushed tones, both hands on the bowl to keep it steady, she stopped short. One step into the courtyard to be exact. Setting down the bowl, she took a good look at its recipient: a goat. Tied up with a fraying rope to a vertical pipe running the height of the house, the goat's appearance made Kivran's stomach churn. Running her hands through its carob-coloured fur on each side of the neck as it lapped up the water, she tried to calm herself. It wasn't working.

The animal no longer made any noises, it had stopped doing so after the third consecutive day of being kept in this state. Instructed to give it less and less water each day, and under no circumstances to get attached to it by naming it, she couldn't help herself. Not the naming part, but the attachment part. How could she not feel something towards it? Its entire purpose was to make the two young men in the next room better understand transplanting organs so they wouldn't botch it when it was her turn for the operation.

Having drained the water now, the goat nudged its face against Kivran's forearm, seeking out more. Sinking deeper in her kneeled state, she wrapped her arms around the creature, attempting some form of apology. She tried to remind herself of the silver lining as the animal continued shifting in her arms: it has to die soon.

Precise location unknown, UK
17 years, 37 days after Mutation 4

Holding steadfast against the gust, Garrett stood on the only remaining gravel path on the island looking out at the approaching boat. That time of the month again: the mandatory supply run.

Having been here for nearly nine years, the young man had etched himself a peaceful routine. Wake up at six thirty am. Go for a walk around the easily accessible side of the mountain whilst checking up on the only other residents of the land mass: sheep. Go around to the shop, find something of sustenance, bearing in mind not to indulge. Re-angle the solar panels to not lose electricity. Head over to the lighthouse, the only place equipped with Internet, and catch up on the vast world's affairs. If at least a dozen people had died, it would be your average kind of day. Re-angle the solar panels to not lose electricity. Go for a run the length, then the height, of the mountain. It should be clarified, it wasn't really a mountain so much as the tallest hill on the island. Re-angle the solar panels to not lose electricity. Continue building a useless wall of limestone around the shop in order to retain upper body strength, oh, and in order to retain sanity to a degree. Rummage through the shop again, this time for dinner and multiple bottles of filtered water before walking back to the lighthouse. Making sure to check up again on our, currently, only friends: the beloved sheep. Re-angle the solar panels to not lose electricity. Confirm the beacon is operational. Settle in for a night of bingeing through old, long over and forgotten television series while listening to the waves thrash and sheep's whatever-you'd-like-to-call-that noise. Re-angle the solar panels to not lose electricity. Call it a day and remind yourself: he has to die soon.

Now, the man stumbling off the boat was not Garrett's usual point man. The usual would bring him necessary, and only necessary, supplies, have the courtesy to stay for a cup of tea, knowing he was the only company the young man would get for another month, and be on his merry way. If only Garrett could go on his own merry way. He'd be lying if he said he'd never daydreamed of knocking the man unconscious and stealing the boat to go his own merry way. The only thing that ever stopped him was knowing, but having nothing to support this, that the man was a prisoner in his own right. For this, he held an ounce of sympathy for him. His usual man was not this man.

Hands tucked in the pockets of his windbreaker, Garrett waited patiently for the stranger to approach. After shaking his legs one at a time, similar to a wet dog, and gingerly making his way around the one sheep witnessing this spectacle as well, the stranger approached. The suit stood out in a horrible way, this was no place for tailored items or ties. Oh look, dress shoes to match. Someone was definitely in the wrong neighbourhood.

"Are you Garrett Asher?"

Slowly moving his neck to look over his right shoulder, then slowly over the other, Garrett raised his eyebrows. Either the man didn't know where he was, or Garrett's father hadn't bothered to tell him.

Noticing the condescension in his expression, the man continued his approach as well as his speech.

"I'm sorry to have to be the one to tell you this, Mr. Asher, but I'm afraid your father has passed."

Drifting his gaze from the man towards the sheep still loitering in the vicinity, Garrett allowed himself a smile as two things crossed his mind:

1. Well, sheep, it looks like I'll get to leave before you, after all; and

2. His daily reminder: he has to die soon.

1,946 km east of Jakarta, INDONESIA
17 years, 44 days after Mutation 4

Allowing the breeze to freely course through his papers, he watched them lazily flutter on the walls and spread across the floor. The rhythmic storm was audible upon the courtyard's metal haphazard roof. Aydin was consenting to his frustration running amok over his rational. He was trying to help his sister, and failing.

The mutilated animal lying next to him on the surgical table reeked. Upon the host rejecting the allograft—fancy word for the transplanted organ, Aydin and Salar cut her up again to figure out the plight. Out of sheer frustration at not being able to piece the issue together, Aydin had slashed everything in sight. Luckily for everyone in the house, with momentary tunnel vision, that meant the sight was confined to the creature's corpse, while the downside was he had inadvertently butchered the intestines. Hence the nauseating stench. The storm's humidity was doing little to air it out either.

Knowing when to step back from him, Kivran and Salar left the house shortly after his massacre, allowing him to fester in silence. Which is exactly what he had been doing for the last thirty minutes or so.

Aydin couldn't figure out what he was doing wrong, and he didn't have the luxury of endless time and opportunity to cushion his various falls any longer. Turning to his fellow companion, blood still dripping down the edges of the table and its limbs, Aydin looked at Goat Number Four hoping to get some blatant answers.

Though pigs bore the closest semblance to human anatomy in terms of livestock, there was no logical or even subtle way to obtain a pig for experimentation, let alone multiple, so he couldn't change the general subject. Every goat obtained carried Mutation 4 without a scientific doubt because he checked each one himself. Lastly, he knew Kivran carried Mutation 4 in her bloodstream without a scientific doubt, because he checked himself.

On the day his mother had died was also the day his sister received a blood transfusion, there was a silver lining to Salar's father's existence after all. Even with his stern demeanour, the man lost no time is aiding Kivran before many others at his clinic. Many who arguably needed help more immediately. Regardless, no one could have foreshadowed the biblical humour that the blood now coursing through Kivran's veins belonged to an elderly farmer who had spent his entire life among livestock, soaking in the Mutation on a daily basis. It was easy to abhor the man he would have no circumstance to cross paths with. However, as Aydin grew and pondered over his anger, he began to move on. There was no reason why he couldn't try to save her. He had enough time to study his obstacle and find a way around it. It was only now that Aydin was starting to realize time was eminently running out.

Tuning into the rhythm of the rain in time with the blood droplets, Aydin's eyes followed the blood's trail down the animal's limb once more.

Limb.

What if it took more than just a singular organ to filter out the Mutation? Like a limb must be detached in its entirety in extreme cases. What if the kidney or the liver or the spleen alone weren't enough? What if they all needed to be replaced simultaneously? Sure, graft versus host disease had a higher likelihood to occur in hosts with allogenic spleens, but that margin was minimal. So minimal, in fact, to Aydin's current state of mind, that it appeared to be worth a shot.

1,946 km east of Jakarta, INDONESIA
Same day

Having left Salar at the clinic after one of the doctors pulled him aside, Kivran made her way back home. Not thinking well enough in advance to grab an umbrella on her way out, she tried her best to walk fast in the rain but couldn't pick up too much pace for the stitch in her side wasn't ceasing, and neither was her cough.

Rather than ponder what the Mutation was doing to her insides, she instead thought of her brother and the innocent creatures in his care.

Was she worth this? Aydin would answer in a heartbeat, "Yes," but Kivran wasn't sure she could.

She didn't believe in a divine being or divine fate, but in spite of her rational mind-set, Kivran believed in a bastardized version of divine intervention: you are exactly where you need to be; what's happened could not have happened any other way.

Maybe she was meant to have this disease. Maybe she was meant to never give birth to a healthy child. Maybe she was meant to live a short life.

This was something she couldn't explain to Aydin for the life of her, though. She could see what this obsession to fix her was doing to him. If she didn't die soon, or he didn't find a cure soon, he would lose his sanity. Then again, if the former occurred, she wasn't altogether convinced he wouldn't lose it regardless.

"Hey, Kivran!"

Not realizing he was there, she stopped just short of her neighbour's front steps. Mica looked up at her, light from within his home casting an eerie glow around his seated figure.

"Hi, Mica. What're you doing up still?" She stopped in front of him, holding her breath to refrain from coughing.

The boy seemed to plan his answer before proceeding. "Oh, nothing really. I just saw you coming now, so I figured I'd say hi. Hi."

Kivran smiled down at him, he was stumbling over his words. "Hi, Mica. How are you?"

"I'm fine, thanks for asking. I saw you that day I came into the clinic, but you looked busy so I just stayed with my mum."

"Well, I'm glad to see you're getting over that cold." She ruffled his hair as he cringed under her touch.

"You're glad?"

"Uh-huh." She began walking to her door, the boy was getting ahead of himself.

"Okay, bye, Kivran!"

"Good night, Mica." She waved behind, not looking. The boy could be heard running back inside.

Clutching her abdomen with increased strength, Kivran inhaled deeply long enough to put on a strong face and open her front door. Ready to face Aydin and not expose him to something that would only make his state worse.

"Aydin? Is it okay if I come back in now?"

Cautiously entering the house, not yet closing the door behind her in case she needed to leave again.

"Yeah, yeah, Kivran!"

She entered, following the voice back towards the lab.

"Don't come in here, though. I don't want you seeing this."

Stopping just short of the courtyard's entrance, she watched Aydin swing the door behind him but not shut it entirely. She waited for him to say something else, still not convinced it was okay for her to be here.

"I think I've got it, Kiv!" He held a smile in his approach. Good sign. "Where's Salar? He needs to hear this, too."

"He's held up at the clinic. What is it?"

"A diseased limb!"

"I didn't know I had that too…"

"No, no! You don't have it, Kiv. That's our solution!"

Following him through to the kitchen where he began pouring himself a glass of water, Kivran couldn't help but think about the goat in the other room.

"I'm sorry, Aydin, I don't follow."

Grabbing a box of matches from beside the stove, Aydin spilled a handful on the table and began to move them about, forming a stick figure.

"Okay, so if you have a diseased limb, you may have to cut it off above the infected area, correct?"

Kivran nodded as he flicked one of the stick figure's arms aside.

"Now, what if your whole body's haematopoiesis system…" He rearranged the matches into a circle.

For those of us who don't remember tenth-grade biology, haematopoiesis is the process of making blood within our bodies.

"…is like a diseased limb. This whole time we've been trying to cut off and replace one part and expecting everything else to function the same. The kidney, then the liver, neither worked!"

Again nodding, Kivran took a seat opposite him. She waited for him to practically inhale the water before proceeding. There was a part of her that saw where this was headed. She didn't like the idea.

"What we have to do is chop off the whole thing and start new. Like a wooden leg. It takes time, but because you've chopped off the entire problem and gave it something new, a clean slate of sorts, your body can learn to walk with the wooden leg. And before long, it starts to feel like a phantom limb, something that's always been there."

Moving wet hair off her face, her throat began to swell. If this is what he wanted, she needed to hear him say it. "So what you're saying is… you want to 'chop off' my bone marrow…?"

"No! God no! That would kill you, and I don't have the equipment to do something of that scale. Bone marrow transplant, no, no. I'm saying we should replace everything else in the circle." Flipping three of the matches in his circle so all the heads faced one direction, Aydin looked up at his sister. "I want to replace your kidney, liver, and spleen. Give your body a relatively clean slate to work with."

Looking across the table at his excitement, Kivran didn't have the heart to preach divine intervention to him. But she'd be hypocritical as well if she didn't see her own brother's intelligence as divine intervention in disguise. Regardless of how absurd his idea really was.

A H RAJA

Budapest, HUNGARY
17 years, 45 days after Mutation 4

Garrett watched his father being put into the ground. Morbidly, he found himself smirking at the notion. His mother looked on, tightly grasped around the shoulders by her twin sister. His educated guess told him she was shedding crocodile tears.

If isolation does anything to you, it's making you reanalyze everything that has ever happened in your life to get you to this point. Though not much thought was ever handed to the relationship between his mother and father, there was an afternoon during which young Garrett came to the realization that his parents simply tolerated one another. Nothing more. The realization didn't have a significant effect on him, his inability to catch this earlier, however, did.

He observed his mother bring a crumpled tissue up to her eyes, making a show of it all. He was glad nobody had picked up on his presence yet. Standing towards the rear of the gathering, he watched over the various strangers accumulated around the grave. Many mingling amongst themselves as the priest read a lengthy passage at Garrett's mother's request most likely. Another stranger, really.

For a man who was terrified of physically interacting with others for the sole reason that they could potentially transmit a fatal virus to him, there was a respectable number of people present. Granted a majority of them seemed to be impatient to make their egresses—judging by the incessant chatter, weight shifting and dry eyes, that is.

Garrett didn't want to be here. Hunching lower than usual, he had instantly decided he'd rather take that bloody island over such humans any day of the week.

It's funny, the things you remember at the weirdest of times. Though this memory might've been a little more fitting than most. The last time Garrett had seen his father's face was the night Garrett had left for the island. The order was made for him to pack his belongings into one bag. Nothing excess, only necessities. Clearly a common rule in that man's life. Not in the mood to argue, the sixteen-year-old had done just that. He was then personally driven by this father to the Egilsstadir airport, which was three hours away from their then-location. Silence the entire way there.

Upon arriving at the airport, Garrett gazed out the window as his father placed the car into park. He was told to proceed inside and look for a man displaying his name, accompany that man on a flight to Wales, then on to a boat that would take him somewhere safe. Never did he explain what the implied danger was. This explanation was never expected, Garrett had learned that early on. The young man looked at his father in the dim florescent lights surrounding the airport. Dark circles prominent enough to be visible beneath the glasses, protruding vein pulsing at his temple, both hands fidgeting against the steering wheel. The man displayed no emotion. Internally angered, yet believing his father was not worth his emotions, Garrett exited the vehicle with his luggage and did as he was told. The final words his father ever spoke to him were then uttered, "Good luck with everything, kid." A few moments later, when the two-passenger airplane took off, two thoughts crossed Garrett's mind:

1. What a strange thing, to not believe his own father was worth such emotion; and

2. Those beautiful grey mountains, he wished he had spent more time lost in them.

He was only in attendance now to prove to himself he didn't feel any different towards this paternal figure. That the years he'd spent maintaining an emotional distance from his father had been warranted. Watching the people around him standing in the spring breeze, Garrett straightened his posture, ready to leave just as the priest concluded his speech.

He didn't feel different at all. And, in that moment as he glanced one last time over the small gathering of people, no longer burdened with an unidentifiable weight, he came to the conclusion that his mother wasn't worth his emotions either.

1,946 km east of Jakarta, INDONESIA
17 years, 47 days after Mutation 4

Aydin paced the courtyard, allowing the rain an attempt at soothing his thoughts. He loved monsoon season. The rhythm of each droplet, the musty odour, the literal electricity in the atmosphere, it all made him feel invincible. The macabre element of the situation evidently was lost on him, our little Frankenstein.

It was well past midnight and he had to leave in a few hours for a shift at the clinic, but he couldn't sleep. Nearly an hour had passed since the intruding event had awoken him: the sound of his sister seizing in her sleep.

Though now used to the noise, he instinctively couldn't ignore it. Spontaneous, random grunts, ruffling sheets, blunt-fingernailed hands clawing at flesh, and the occasional thud against the headboard. Having rushed over from his lab in which he had fallen asleep amongst the tattered textbooks for the umpteenth time in his life, he had found her on the bed convulsing.

Kivran had lived with the condition long enough to embrace her own habit of placing an ad hoc retainer in her mouth to prevent herself from biting her tongue. Aydin knew she didn't like carrying it around during the day since she ran the risk of advertising to the rest of the world what she suffered from. She refused to take his advice of simply stating she suffered from periodic, run-of-the-mill seizures. She didn't like lying much either. The point was, he wasn't afraid of her harming herself in this unmanageable state.

But he also couldn't bear the singular possibility of the alternative—maybe tonight was the night she'd pass. Thus, he needed to see her through each one. She hadn't found out yet.

As he paced now, Aydin attempted to conclude whether or not a variable had changed in his sister's life to cause her seizures to increase exponentially. And he didn't like the idea of concluding it was simply because her condition was worsening. Not in the least.

This was the ninth consecutive night, the third one of which the seizing occurred twice in the night.

The rain was failing to soothe him at such an irritated level now.

Looking upwards at the sound of a branch scraping against the metal sheet roofing, his heart paced faster. A thought crossed his mind that hadn't reared its irrational head in quite some time. He let it consume him.

He needed to see how the person who had given this condition to his sister now lived. It was only fair that man should suffer as Kivran now did. And Aydin needed to see that, to satisfy the darkness that remained in the depths of his mind.

Before long, Aydin found himself dragging a borrowed dingy ashore on an island northeast of his own. Against the backdrop of scattered fireflies and crickets, he traced the same steps he'd taken about two months short of eleven years ago. He'd been searing with anger that time, now it was curiosity that drove him. Coupled with just enough anger to keep his guard up.

Reaching the end of his path, Aydin slowed the few remaining steps, not wishing to attract attention. Though who would be alert at this time of night, he couldn't say. Regardless, he observed a single light flickering from within the house across the small barren patch of land.

Aydin was overcome with a nauseous case of déjà vu. The last and only previous time he'd stood in this position amongst the tree line was so debilitating, it had pushed this currently surfacing thought far into his mind's depth. The house in question had seemed alive then, a focal point for the lives beneath its roof. Two small boys, uncertain in their own infant footing, had been chasing chickens around the fenced yard, both boys barefoot, red in the face from exhaustion, and bursting with uncontainable laughter. A man and woman standing side by side with their backs to Aydin pointed towards the house's roof, planning something.

This man had a family, a happy family from the looks of it. The man had tried to act in kindness. It was simply Kivran's bad luck that she had received this particular man's blood. Simply bad luck.

Aydin had bolted from the house, wiping tears along the way, afraid of what he would've done had he not come to reason. What could he have done?

A figure opened the door, flooding the ground with light. Aydin remained still.

"You can come in if you want."

The voice was of a woman, yet husky. Aydin again remained still.

"You, in the trees. There's no one else out there."

Hesitantly stepping forth, out of the shadows, he slowly walked towards the voice. Remember: it was curiosity that compelled him to come this time around, not anger. Not so much anger.

Nearing the door, she stepped aside to let him through. Aydin looked around the small house smelling of must, clutter everywhere his eyes wandered. Feathers scattered around. The woman closed the door and gestured for him to sit at the table a few feet away. Rubbing his wet hands against his wet jeans, Aydin sat down.

His host appeared to be no older than himself, albeit worse for wear. Wrapped in a stained night robe with strings jutting out, hair hastily pinned away from the face, pupils shrunken. She asked if he wanted coffee, to which he refused before she sat down opposite him, mug in hand.

"I remember you, when I was young. You stood outside my home one day. Never said a word, never came forward, stared at my father most of the afternoon."

Aydin hadn't realized anyone was watching him back.

"I was afraid, that's why I remember."

He felt a pinch in his stomach. Curiosity was receding, only to be taken over by guilt.

"Also because I realized who you were and why you would be here." She spoke over the cooing chickens in the backyard. "He never told my mother about… the problem, if he had even known, that is. We found out when my youngest brother died seizing. He'd never had one before, a seizure, that is."

She pointed to the bottom right of the ajar back door. Aydin followed her hand towards the floor where he saw three urns in a line, sinking atop a stack of cloths.

"My second brother went next, then my father a few weeks later."

Moments passed as they each gazed at the urns, the sound of water dripping somewhere into her home echo between Aydin's ears.

Taking a sip, she spoke again. "We weren't allowed to bury them. The town wouldn't allow it, afraid putting them—putting it—into the ground would taint the soil. They did let me bury my mother; she killed herself after my second brother died."

Without explanation and within a heartbeat, Aydin found himself hastily fleeing the home, nauseous once again.

Reaching the dingy, he began to push off just as the fireflies' glow died down. It was dawn. Heading back home, Aydin calmed himself against the warm rain and cold sea water both splashing against his skin.

The rationale in him couldn't help but wonder if he'd done the right thing by letting Kivran have the transfusion. Would it have been better for her to just have died the same day as his mother?

Looking behind from whence he just came, Aydin let the mental image of those two young boys, playing with not a care in the world, overcome him.

Children, of all beings, didn't deserve death.

He looked back towards the island he was heading to. Even if he could just buy his little sister some time, just a little more time, it would be enough.

St. Petersburg, RUSSIA
17 years, 359 days after Mutation 4

<BREACH 0442HRS>
Log: security breach detected 0442 hrs - 0443 hrs;
Location LAOS;
Affected files 1176;
Patch initializing…
<REMOTE ACCESS>
Duplicating: file 1005/…

Christchurch, NEW ZEALAND
18 years, 0 days after Mutation 4

Sheep. The irony wasn't lost on Garrett. Upon signing up, he didn't really expect to be back on an island with the same animals again. Thankfully, he wasn't the only human this time around.

He tried to keep his nerves calm, scratching around the bandage on his left wrist, as the situation was sinking in. In shambles with member nations performing a mass exodus, his childhood dream of becoming a United Nations trooper hadn't quite panned out. However, from the crumbling mess that was its Peace Corps, came forth the World Health Organization's military branch. Viewing it as a feasible alternative, Garrett set out to see the world his father had envisioned as an apocalyptic wasteland. Surprisingly, he found himself more eager to see the people inhabiting it. A notion he had held on to. The surprising part kicks in when you consider the people he most interacted with were pretty poor representatives of the human race—his parents.

Keeping his head down and following the officer in form, Garrett jogged towards a wing on the military base marked K1. He was about to meet his new unit.

The officer in front held the door open for Garrett to go through first. Taking one last look up at the handful of stars shining in the dusk sky, he entered. Once inside, he found himself surrounded by unmarked jet-black crates on either side, stacked well above his own height. A singular trail was forged among the crates down which he now followed the officer as the man spoke.

"This is a temporary holding facility for your unit. Your missions will all be deemed classified until explicitly stated otherwise. There are no ranks within the unit, however, you have one designated leader, think of him more as the wise old man than your superior. You also have The Akureyri Base which manages your assignments but for the most part, you have free rein to pick and choose as the situation arises and presents itself to you—the collective unit."

Switching views from left to right among the monotone crates, Garrett wondered just how big the wing was.

"I myself am not authorized to disclose anything further, thus, I'll leave you in the capable hands of your wise old man."

The officer stepped aside to let Garrett through, if he hadn't said so, Garrett might have missed the destination altogether. The path abruptly ended but to the left, an opening wide enough to fit one man at a time appeared. The officer was evidently not going forth; Garrett followed the man's hand gesturing him in and passed the threshold. Within, again surrounded by crates on all four sides, was an ad hoc room approxi mately thirty by thirty feet. An indeterminable amount of cots were haphazardly stacked against one side while the remaining space was occupied by three men surrounding a single table upon which were spread various detailed black-and-white maps. All three men stood mid-motion looking his way.

Garrett saw and heard one of the men approach, but he couldn't hear the officer outside leave. He finally realized his hearing felt heavy, as if under water, and also that he knew this approaching man.

Shifting his eyes down to the man's gait, Garrett tried to place him. Firm footing, knees continuously ever so slightly bent, one hand tucked in a pocket. This was his usual point man—from the damned island.

The man seemed to realize just as Garrett did. Locking hands, the man visibly relaxed his posture. "I see you made it out in one piece. Nice to officially meet you, Asher, I'm Marek."

"Marek, you as well."

"Step on through, let's get you acquainted."

Garrett followed him towards the table. Before getting there, one of the men spoke while measuring up the new one.

"You're the lab coat, yes?"

Unsure of the question, Garrett shook his head regardless, and realized the other two were watching him in the same manner.

"So you're not the one from research division?"

Again, Garrett shook his head, beginning to feel he might be in the wrong place.

The man at the opposite end of the table began to make his way around. "Ah! You must be new Tactee then!" He outstretched an arm. "Walcott, fellow Tactee."

He was using the same wording as the initial deployment officer: Tactee. From what Garrett had gathered, it was a colloquialism for someone assigned to tactical duties.

"Garrett."

The final man came forth. "Odeli."

Garrett nodded, unsure of what to do with himself. Feeling Marek's hand on his shoulder, he turned. "Glad to see you finally made it, your father had been telling us for years we should be expecting you."

He stiffened.

"Not too happy about the idea to say the least, felt more of a threat."

Walcott chimed in with a wide smirk. "Which is why we are greatly looking forward to this."

He couldn't bring himself to be at ease still. "Is that sarcasm?"

Marek emitted a belly laugh beside him. "Gods no! Are you kidding? Kept saying we'd rue the day you'd decide to join for a solid two years. We're expecting apocalyptic measure failure from you, good sir, and I for one can't wait!"

"No offence but your father was a piece of work, all right," said Odeli, eyeing Garrett's hesitant expression. "We weren't fans. Thought WHO's military unit should be armed to the teeth, an extension of a state's armed forces in a way and what-not. Going out and killing the incurable rather than helping them. Blood hungry son of a bitch who never wanted to get his own hands bloody. Irony, I think that's what that's called."

Garrett let the bag over his shoulder drop to the metal-sheeted floor with a thud. He'd never cared enough about his father to delve into what the man did. And because he believed if he let that curiosity overcome him, he'd be feeling something towards his father—the last thing he wanted—he never allowed it to.

Looking around at the men, their demeanour far from standoffish, he felt that curiosity could now flow. The man was dead, there was no way for his father to know now.

"Sorry, what did he do?"

This time Walcott let out a laugh. "You don't know? That man is responsible for us being here. Created the WHO military unit, didn't he?" A Scottish accent became prominent as the man spoke.

"Easy, easy." Marek held a hand up to halt Walcott. "If you're going to explain it now, of all times, at least start from the beginning. Look at the kid's face." The man gestured to Garrett's confused expression. "You know Asher wouldn't have told him a thing." Garrett felt juvenile at the wording utilized, but figured now was not the time to contest this.

As Marek spoke, Garrett could see Odeli grab his bag from the floor and fling it the remaining length of the room to rest on the stacked cots. The man then reached beneath the table and slid out a stool, pushing it towards Garrett, who gladly sat down. One by one the other men followed suit, Marek piled the maps in the table's centre.

Walcott clapped his hands once, evidently giddy at having this opportunity, and began. "Let's see here, the beginning. We're new to the whole WHO thing, research and health standards are what they focus on, as I'm sure you know already. Late twenty-twenties, your dearest father, head of WHO research at the time, decided to cry wolf with no proof. He went to the

Director and convinced him," at the last word, Walcott rubbed two fingers and a thumb together gesturing "money." "The Director, at the time, we were about to be hit by the next plague. Mass graves, every which way. So, the Director let him set up facilities to actually look into this forthcoming plague."

"Hang on," Marek interrupted him. "The plague was allegedly going to affect everyone's vital organs. Somehow, whatever the virus is, it'd transfer to all people, all organs at an exponential rate. Everyone assumes it'd be transmitted via bodily fluids, but we never got the answer because before Asher could find results, the Director had to step down after the fiasco with Zika spreading to Europe and the refugee cleansing across the pond, and so Asher lost all his facilities." Marek nodded back at Walcott to continue.

"These facilities were everywhere, classified shit, but we do know they were around the world. Anyways, as you know from basic training, hopefully, the main WHO military branch protects the docs and nurses doing work all over the place. Glorified body guards. But we, we are the leftovers of what Asher wanted as the bigger picture. There's about five of our type of units—"

"That's not confirmed." This time Odeli interrupted.

"Sorry, yeah, that's from what we can gather. We get the pleasure of tracking down any odd patients, people that might be on the brink of bringing about the plague."

Garrett shook his head, not out of contestation but trying to clear something within. "You made it sound like the plague wasn't a genuine thing, no? If the research was halted, how would you know for sure?"

The men all looked at each other, not jumping to answer. In the moment of silence, Garrett realized the reason his hearing felt off. This room was so enclosed, noise seemed stagnant within, and yet he'd never heard an echo.

Marek leaned forward to rest his forearms on the table. Garrett could deduce from the man's simple demeanour and the way in which the other two men interacted with him, this was the proclaimed wise man of the group.

"Garrett, us three have been together only two years in this unit. By many people's standards that's not a long time, but for us, it is. Each unit only has four or five people, so you end up being close. My preamble is for the sole reason that what you hear here, cannot leave. Understood?"

A part of him was attempting to revert back to an isolated state: we don't need these people, better without them than with them. And yet a part of him wanted to remain as these people had lived through the stuff he'd only read about, the stuff that made him want to join in the first place. He'd kept his isolated persona intact throughout basic training despite a few trainees' attempts to break him. None of them qualified as genuine enough under his eyes to warrant such connections, regardless of how mundane he considered the connections.

He let the latter choice win while the former remained a voice of skepticism in the back.

"Understood."

"Odeli here, has been with a doctor for a while now, like with with."

Walcott whispered something on the opposite end, making Odeli chuckle. It sounded like "female."

"Her team gets stationed anywhere and every-where, willy-nilly. They find a case sometimes, one unit goes in to find and secure said case, or odd patient, and or handle relevant intel, a separate unit has to go in right after and handle the aftermath depending on the situation's severity. So, Odeli crossed paths with the doc as we were coming in, and long story short, the plague is most likely real. It's just not something of biblical proportions. Just yet."

Odeli leaned forwards now, looking around Gar-rett towards the small entrance. "Shouldn't we wait for the lab coat to get here so we don't have to do this twice?"

The Scottish accent chimed in. "No, he probably knows more than we do. Not that he'd ever disclose that. Lab rat." Walcott then proceeded to chuckle at his own pun.

Shaking his head at Walcott, Marek continued. "You'll remember from basic training Mutation Four is not a classified thing, regardless of what media outlets state. Unless WHO states otherwise officially, Mutation Four is not a problem. But it is. The reason they're keeping it under wraps though, is they haven't found a way to figure out who is affected, who isn't affected, and who carries the mutation, and who doesn't. Don't want to cause mass panic with nothing to back it up. But it's there, because we've seen it. People who've died with no evident cause, full autopsies and nothing.

There's no pattern of symptoms or visible conditions, none that match across the board anyways."

Garrett nodded, believing he'd finally wrapped his head around this. "So we follow up on unusual intel that might help us find or figure this out."

"Bingo!" Walcott seemed pleased with his quick pick up.

"How is this part of Asher's picture though?"

Odeli nodded now, expecting the question. "The units are exempt from state laws. If WHO has authority to go in, we have authority to conduct our own business on their coattails. With little to no oversight, we make the call on what happens with each case we handle." Garrett could finally pin down the man's accent as his speech picked up, South African. "Asher's big picture: we do whatever the hell we want."

This sounded like his father. "How would any state agree to give WHO authority then?"

"Aha!" Marek pointed at Garrett. "An established institution tells you your citizens are dying and more will die when they don't need to. We can help you find the problem and eradicate it, all you have to do is let us in. What do you do? Let your citizens potentially die? Bear the potential public outcry in its wake? And if WHO has the right countries on their side, ignite international public outcry? Place sanctions? The possibilities are endless. Not giving authority is almost worse."

Garrett nodded as a moment of silence fell around them. Tucking his head to his chest, scratching at his wrist again, he thought back to the two islands he had spent his entire life on. His father had been running from something after all. And now here he was, again on another island, his father's shadow still cast in front of him. From his peripherals, he noticed the other men looking at each other, a shrug or two exchanged amongst themselves. They seemed to regret saying anything.

He tried to piece together the information he had just been privy to:

1. His father had created this unit in the hopes of fighting off the next plague, which may be running rampant right now;

2. The plague was a certainty, at least according to these men, though the details of its existence were scarce; and

3. This unit had free rein to find such details by any means they so wished.

It was the second point that Garrett had some difficulty with.

"Does the plague really spread through bodily fluids? Or even organ transplants, as you said?"

Walcott answered as though this question was expected. "First off, I think 'plague' might be the wrong word for this, at least for now. For the most part, we refer to it as Mutation Four. Back in the two-thousands, we found it would take five mutations of a particular strand of virus to basically kill off the human race. People somewhere with microscopes glued to their heads, scalpels to their hands, with far greater IQ than myself, have determined we have definitely already hit three, and that was back in the two-thousands! Fifth is supposed to be when the virus goes airborne, hence we refer to this as four, if the thing was airborne already, we wouldn't be here having this conversation. Mutation Four is carried in the bloodstream."

"So organ transplants would be okay then, right?" Garrett was now mirroring everyone else's stances, leaning in with elbows on the table. Immersed in a foreign realm.

"Well, not exactly. We've never found a living subject, hence why we can't be sure of anything. For the deceased we've found though, they carry something in their bloodstream that kills the host, not entirely sure how. It seems like each host has a different reaction to it. But, as the tainted blood is filtered through the organs, some residue of sorts is left behind in each one. Which is why WHO is trying to convince everyone allografts are a no-go. Until we can pinpoint the virus, that is."

His hearing was finally beginning to feel normal. "Why is it so hard to pinpoint? You know what Mutation Five is, and definitely what Mutation Three was, couldn't you figure it out from there, genetically speaking?" A part of him felt an unease, placing these men under an inquisition of sorts. However, the feeling was easily overshadowed by his need to know what he had been made to run from all his life.

Odeli whispered "uh-huh" before Walcott continued. "We thought that, but this mutation comes from livestock, and because the state of livestock has changed so drastically, it's making it quite difficult to do so."

"And you can't even find this 'residue' in the organs?"

Odeli spoke again, this time louder. "You sure you're not our lab rat?"

Not wanting to seem standoffish, Garrett replied. "No, I just… want to know what we're in."

In response, Odeli nodded with a quick wink.

Walcott, however, ignored him. "Negative. Because every subject we've come across has already died, we can't study it as a living virus. We can't even tell if this is just a natural abnormality the host has or the virus itself."

"You also have to understand," Marek now chimed in, a somber look across his face. "It's not like we have subjects flooding in left and right. We'll find one every six, seven months, if we're lucky. We don't have much to go on."

"Which is why," Odeli pointed an index to Garrett's bandaged wrist. "We're setting up a universal database: everyone's DNA sample all in one place, supposed to be some sort of baseline. So if you ever wound up dead or sick, we could cross-reference the DNA at that time to when you gave us the sample and eliminate anything that could be deemed your natural anomaly."

Garrett nodded, understanding the idea better.

Another moment passed, he watched the others' expressions, they were waiting for him to ask anything further. He had no more questions, at least not now.

Realizing this, Marek moved his stool back with a screech against the floor. "Now that that's out of the way, we'll get back to what we were doing, shall we?"

Walcott nodded before sliding the maps back open, motioning for Garrett to grab the opposite ends.

Using magazines, Odeli helped hold down the corners as Marek picked up a blue marker from beneath the table.

"Just a quick question, mate," Odeli whispered to him, well as much as could be whispered in those confines. "If you had to choose, which gummy bear flavour is your favourite?"

Garrett hadn't even realized he was smiling until the answer came out with a joyous tone. "Green, I guess. Why?"

"Brilliant!" Odeli placed an arm around Garrett's shoulders and squeezed... affectionately? Was that what that was? "You're gonna fit right in, pal."

The map they had chosen to unfurl displayed both hemispheres, cutting just at the start of the eastern hemisphere, which meant Iceland was tucked away in a corner. Garrett's smile spread wider as he noticed the island. Grey mountains.

Small blue and red circles were hand drawn at various locations. A handful of blue circles were concentrated around the western and southern Russian borders, one red circle near Mogadishu, one red circle in central China, one red circle in northern Singapore, and approximately seven other blue circles littered across Africa and southern Europe.

Marek automatically offered an explanation. "We're hoping a geographical pattern exists, help us narrow down what cases to take seriously out of the ones that get passed on to WHO authorities. Red means a genuine case, from what we can gather." He pointed with the marker to the three in question. "The blue mean cases that have been flagged but generally undetermined to be genuine or not. Still need our attention though."

Garrett nodded, leaning in closer. Eager to finally get answers to questions he never had the courage to ask his father. Hell, he didn't even know what to ask for back then. He allowed himself a faint smile again.

He didn't pay it much attention, why would he, but if he could look back in hindsight, Garrett's eyes would have drifted towards the group of islands not terribly far from his current location, Indonesia to be exact. Where he would notice, no red or blue markings existed. No one had reason to pay attention to that corner of the world.

1,946 km east of Jakarta, INDONESIA
18 years, 4 days after Mutation 4

Head tilted, lost in her trance, she felt a pull on the sides of her mouth as Kivran watched the woman seated in the examination room. The woman was just a month pregnant, and already she was glowing.

The woman smiled back beneath Kivran's gaze.

"You'll have to excuse our nurse-in-training here, she's still bright-eyed and bushy-tailed." Dr. Thi was standing by the window, making note of the vitals he had just measured.

"That's okay," the woman replied, rubbing her swollen hands together. She was doing her best to hide the swollen feet beneath the chair itself, but the discoloured skin remained visible. "How long have you been here, love?"

The woman couldn't have been more than a handful of years older than Kivran, who wondered if the pregnancy was making the patient more prone to such jargon.

"Officially, two months." The doctor answered for her; he had voluntarily fallen into the habit. "And she's still like this, it's a miracle."

The woman smiled again, however, by now, Kivran had come to. The doctor's need to speak on her behalf was difficult to ignore.

"We'll see you in a couple of months then, Ms. Tileski. The girls will help you change back." He made his exit promptly, evidently not one to spend any moment past necessary with the patients.

Girls.

Upon hearing a dramatic exhale, Kivran turned to find the nurse she had been assigned to primarily shadow slouching by the entrance.

"Sometimes…" Innaya trailed off while her hands gripped an imaginary neck, at least from the looks of it. The nurse came forth to help the woman up, motioning for Kivran to lend a hand. Together, they began to undo the gown now spotted with sweat. There was no fan in sight in the middle of a sweltering summer.

"Are you going to be okay, walking home?" Kivran noticed Innaya took the time to talk to patients whenever she could.

The lady smiled with a nod. "This one seems like a calm one. My first one drove me up the wall all nine months and still does!"

"You didn't bring the munchkin with you?"

Though the smile faded in the slightest, the woman didn't look upset. "No, she lives with her father, for good now, over in Turkey."

"I'm sorry about that, dear."

The woman shook her head. "No need to apologize, it is what it is."

Kivran thoughts wandered, hopefully the woman would be all right; hopefully she was happy—being a mother, that is.

She knew she was staring, but she couldn't help it. At least she could help the tear ducts from swelling, the staring, not so much. She'd never get to do this—be pregnant.

"Remember what I told you, Kivran." Innaya wasn't even looking at her. Was Kivran's demeanour that revealing?

Don't get attached.

That's what she had told her. Innaya knew her instantly enough to know she had difficulty with that, it might also have been revealed when Kivran took to crying upon a patient's discharge earlier that week.

She was trying. She didn't enjoy investing so much of herself in strangers, but look at it this way: Kivran knew, in the depths of her mind, that she wouldn't live much longer, let alone experience the colourful things other people iterated to her. She wouldn't come close to experiencing the things many others did, these patients were her only opportunity to see a bit of everything she would leave behind. A world she would never see. Lately, her temporary existence had been weighing more than she was prepared for. Kivran cried—she got attached—because she lived vicariously through their eyes, and their eyes alone. And she couldn't explain this.

She nodded, acknowledging the other nurse's request, and yet still, she looked down at the woman's belly and felt a pang of jealously. Hopefully this woman was happy. Kivran wanted to believe she was.

Christchurch, NEW ZEALAND
18 years, 18 days after Mutation 4

He found himself to be happy. The feeling had crept up on him as he meshed and found a pattern with the other men. He wished he had known them earlier on in life. He wished all those years hadn't been wasted pushing himself away from people. The only ones he knew simply represented a skewed, shitty sample of the human race.

Beads of sweat continued to trail down Garrett's back even as his shirt vented the breeze in and out. The formerly glorious, or so he'd been told, skyline lay out in front of him.

He remembered a month back on that island during which all major headlines focused on the destruction of Australian and New Zealand states. Ebola had reached epidemic levels more than two decades ago, leaving residents with two options, only one of which really seemed viable:

1. Stay put. Wait for the entire crisis to blow over or for someone to find a cure, no need to leave.

2. Migrate. Evacuate the country and find the next piece of solid ground that can support you.

As anticipated, the majority chose option two with a good one-third of them choosing New Zealand as their destination.

Poor New Zealand.

Ill-equipped, the country buckled under the weight of health care, and unfortunately also under the weight of tectonic plates. The earthquakes gave the epidemic a run for its money—losses on all sides. Finally, and oft criticized for taking too long, WHO quarantined all of Australia and New Zealand, though they did eventually internally lift the quarantine on Christchurch in order to erect a permanent base. To global knowledge, however, both countries remained quarantined for the sake of the general masses. You're probably thinking the same thing Garrett was upon hearing this is where he was going to be deployed: why set up a base within the quarantine zone? The public relations answer: the area has been deemed fit for habitation. The real, albeit complicated, answer: the quarantine wasn't altogether warranted, WHO just needed to keep a close eye on the situation.

At least that was the combination of theories he'd heard so far. Walcott and Odeli had no shortage of them, perhaps they had even stumbled across the truth already without realizing so. For the time being, however, Garrett required no explanation. His father had never offered any, and yet, he had itched for one. And now, with every explanation at his feet, he didn't want them.

Garrett wished he could've witnessed this place in its heyday.

He turned his head right at the sound of an abnormal splash while continuing to jog. Skimming the water with his gaze, he finally found the source: a family of orcas. Most of them lazily emerging and submerging without a sound along the shallow waters beneath the cliffs.

He let out an unadulterated laugh, alternating his gaze back and forth between the trail and waters. For a change, Garrett was happy.

**1,946 km east of Jakarta, INDONESIA
18 years, 147 days after Mutation 4**

Waiting his turn, Salar stood behind an elderly woman making conversation with Mica behind the counter. The boy was fidgeting with his sleeves, mouth taught when not speaking, and short answers given when he was—Mica clearly didn't want to participate in this conversation. The woman's back was to Salar, he was not able to determine her expression and emotions.

He found it exhausting, to always have to determine a being's demeanour. He simply didn't care.

Eventually, the woman began her shuffle towards the exit and Salar moved up to take her spot. Without a word, the boy motioned that he needed one minute. Waiting again, he watched the boy jog out from behind the counter to take the lady's right elbow. Maintaining her slow pace, Mica walked the woman all the way down the front steps before returning. The expression he held was no longer the same, his eyes didn't look heavy, and a faint smile now pulled at his lips. Watching the slight changes, Salar determined it was a minor expression of pride.

"Hey!" The boy's tone had changed as well.

"Hello." Salar placed the small bag of onions on the counter.

"How's it going? Everything cool at the clinic?"

"Yes. Thank you for asking." Salar added the final part knowing, after experience, this was a more sincere communication.

"Pretty good. My cousin's now up at the hospital, did she tell you?"

Salar shook his head, there was no reason for that woman to be telling him anything of the like. Why, then, was the boy telling him this?

"Yeah, it's pretty cool. She says she's around guts and brains all day, kind of like you guys."

Salar stared back; that was an awkward statement to make.

The boy stuttered beneath Salar's gaze. "I mean, like you guys at the clinic. That's all."

He nodded as the boy gave his change back. Leaving the conversation at that, Salar made his way towards the exit, not acknowledging the "See you later!" called out from behind him. Walking the short distance back home, he entered to the stench of blood.

Storing the onions in a cabinet beneath the sink, he followed the smell towards the lab, finding Aydin hunched over an organ, dissecting. They stored extras in the lab in the event that they needed to determine something prior to experimenting it on a living subject.

Joining his cousin, Salar went to the opposite side of the table to view the, now determined, liver beneath the spotlight. "What're you looking for?"

"I'm not quite sure yet," Aydin mumbled beneath the surgical mask he donned.

In silence while Aydin maintained the concentrated look in his eyes, Salar waited. In that time, he contemplated the last conversation he had just had. Strategically, the information could be vital, however, it was the emotional aspect he needed to confirm. He was doing his best to abide by his mother's dying wish: he was trusting himself to good people. If his deduced definition of "good" was admissible by everyone's standards, that is. Only when the other man had removed his mask with a sigh of frustration and arched over, his elbows upon the table did he begin.

"Some information has just come to light."

Head angled down, Salar couldn't determine the other man's expression. If no verbal prompt was given, he couldn't proceed — something he'd learned from his father, the hard way.

Finally, Aydin's voice echoed against the floor. "What's that?"

"One of the women next door now works at the hospital."

Letting out a chuckle beforehand, Aydin replied, "Every other person around here works at the clinic, Salar."

"Not the clinic. The hospital."

He had his attention. Aydin tilted his head up, allowing Salar to read the expression. Pupils slightly dilated, eyebrows raised, mouth slightly ajar. Aydin was curious.

"The hospital. As what?"

"That I don't know. The boy made it sound as though she might be a doctor."

Aydin straightened up, crossing his arms. Though many people translate this physical expression as disinterest, Salar had seen this on enough occasions on this particular individual to know the body gesture did not supersede the facial expression. Which at this point had shifted to… enlightenment, perhaps.

"I'm assuming you're thinking what I'm thinking."

"I was thinking we could get her to obtain the organs we need." As he finished the sentence, Salar watched for subtleties in Aydin's expression to determine if they were, in fact, thinking the same thing.

It wasn't necessary though, as a smile spread across the man's face opposite him. Aydin nodded enthusiastically, gladly substantiating the idea of even asking the woman. However, just as suddenly, the smile disappeared.

"We can't ask her now, though. We're nowhere near ready, none of them have survived." Aydin panned one hand over the table between them. He was referencing the things that had lain there.

The subtleties kicked in. Salar watched as the man's expression went from hopeful to distraught. The shoulders bowed into his chest, the neck came down just as he exhaled.

It's funny, the things you remember at the weirdest of times. Obviously, Salar couldn't tell you what fixing Kivran meant to Aydin, he didn't understand the nuances of the relationship. But he could tell you what he saw, the physical manifestation of that need to fix her. The night before they were about to complete their first year of medical school, Salar had found Aydin in a near empty room towards the back of their home, tucked into a corner, he was tearing out pages from an anatomy textbook. Though the room had no artificial light, the sun was going down, shining through the only window, illuminating Aydin's face distinctly. Salar observed the determination on his cousin's face.

"I have to get started; I know enough now," Aydin had said.

"Get started on what?"

Aydin had paused his frantic movements to look up at Salar, an urgent glow in his eyes, bloodshot cheeks. "Kivran. I can do this; I can cure her. I know I can." It was curious, the young man was smiling—a genuine smile—and yet, there were tears streaming down his face.

His eyes hadn't focused on Salar while he spoke. He was distracted. Looking down at the torn pages, Salar saw diagrams of transfusions, spleens, and kidneys. In his peripheral vision, he saw shaky hands continue to flip through the book. As long as Salar had known him, Aydin had been the most composed individual. So composed in fact, that Salar rarely looked to him to determine what his own expressions and emotions should be, the man didn't give anything up easily. However, as he watched him in this feverish state, Salar saw something he hadn't witnessed before. An unmatched selflessness and a resolve oozed in the man's tone and gestures. Salar had grown up in a home where the former was quite rare, he was never sure how to handle it.

As he looked across at his cousin now, Salar saw that same expression beginning to creep into Aydin's expression. The desperation was still there, and though the resolve hadn't faded in all these years, it was as though fresh kindle had just been tossed in.

Finally, he could interact with people of his own intellectual stature. Finally. Those imbeciles at the labs were only holding him back with their nuanced views on ethical behaviour and moral standards. Mikael knew why they fired him: he was putting the rest of them to shame and they couldn't keep up. Good riddance. Transferring him to a field unit would be the best decision made by anyone in that department.

Right?

Legs involuntarily twitching, he waited for the commanding officer to sign him into the unit. That's how it worked.

Right?

Turning towards the gate scraping open, Mikael looked over in anticipation. Marching through was a troop of exactly twenty men, he counted, exhausted expressions emanating on every face. Leading them was a man dressed slightly different, jogging backwards and keeping the troop in line. Mikael focused on them as they went straight through to the opposite end of the hangar.

Sixty-three steps. Sixty-three steps from the entrance to the exit. Please don't let him be one of those idiots marching along in unison. Please.

One hundred and twenty-two. One hundred and twenty-two times his right heel had tapped the ground in the time the twenty men had taken the sixty-three steps from the entrance to the exit.

"Mikael Keuhl?"

He hadn't even realized anyone had approached him, but he shot up the moment his name registered. "Yes."

The man before him stood at the same height, neatly ironed white t-shirt on him contrasting Mikael's own head-to-toe, standard-issued and required military uniform. In the back of his mind, he felt superior to the other man for this sole occurrence already. In the remaining portions of this mind, Mikael was infatuated.

The man before him was as close to perfection personified Mikael could ever dream of. Chestnut-coloured eyes, soft hair to match, bottom lip slightly larger than the top, prominent Adam's apple. The longer he looked, the deeper the infatuation settled. The only thing he could fault him on was the hunched position, hands jammed into his pocket. This man needed to stand up straighter and own his presence.

Instinctively, Mikael stood taller himself, finding the right position to look down at the other man. His superiority complex swelled, and with good reason.

"That's me, Mikael Keuhl."

A hand came forth from the pocket. Warm, yet soft to the touch, firm grip.

"Garrett Asher. I'm here to take you through to the others."

Quickly picking up his bag off the floor, Mikael gestured for the other man to lead. By the time they were out of the bare confines of the hangar, this Garrett fell into stride beside him.

"You're coming to us from the research division, I hear." The voice had a beautiful drawl in its base.

"That's correct. I understand my deployment was unexpectedly delayed at the last moment, but alas, I am here now, hoping to expand my horizons. I mean, see the problem from ground zero that is."

"And what problem would that be?"

"I'd rather not discuss the matter at this point in time. At least not until I have spoken to my commanding officer. I take it you are not such an individual." The swelling increased.

From the profile, he witnessed Garrett's forehead crease. Was he surprised at Mikael's forwardness?

The tone he responded in gave no suggestion towards such a thing. It remained calm and comforting. "I am not such an individual. I'm relatively new to the unit myself, got here only a few months ago."

That might explain the attire, Mikael thought as the man opened the door of a different hangar.

Ninety-seven. Ninety-seven steps between the exit of the first hangar to the entrance of this particular hangar.

Twenty-four. Twenty-four times Mikael had peered over at Garrett's profile in those ninety-seven steps, fascinated by the image.

Zero. Zero times Garrett had glanced back at Mikael.

1,946 km east of Jakarta, INDONESIA
Same day

The sixth test subject lay limp over the surgical table less than fifty feet away as Aydin sat at the kitchen table, exhausted and shaky. The creature was still alive.

Kivran had deliberately been requesting over-night shifts at the clinic. Initially he had believed she'd done so to prevent him from witnessing her exponentially deteriorating state. It was only a couple of days ago that she had, inadvertently mind you, revealed the worse spasms only surfaced while asleep. Her solution to the degenerating condition was to not sleep at all.

At least she was here less and less to see his failings. Aydin couldn't get the various organs to pull together and filter the mutated blood enough to make the other organs not attack their own system. Barring a singular exception, he'd tried everything he and Salar could conceive:

> - Transplanted a spleen, only;
>
> - Transplanted a kidney, only;
>
> - Transplanted a liver, only;
>
> - Transplanted a spleen, kidney, and liver in one operation; and
>
> - Concocted medicine in an attempt to find a non-invasive approach.

The second to the last one was his most recent attempt and the only one to have ever left the subject in a living state, hence his shakiness. He wouldn't know anything until after it woke up and continued about its business. The reason he wasn't jumping for joy: Aydin genuinely didn't believe the animal would last the night. He needed to come up with another plan.

The only item he hadn't attempted was a full blood transfusion. I know what you're thinking, this should've come up sooner. What can I say, Aydin's not much of a big believer in "the simplest solution is the best solution." Regardless, when he'd finally been persuaded by Salar to pursue this avenue, they'd hit too many insurmountable obstacles.

Say what you will about the condition of the Indonesian health care system, its blood bank program is sealed tight. Every donation is tagged scrupulously, every bag is tracked at all times, whether en route or not, every blood batch is input into the World Health Organization's Universal DNA Initiative. As is the donated blood of every other country, if given under legal circumstances.

With three separate failed attempts at obtaining donated blood, and Kivran's fits of rage that wouldn't allow them to donate directly, Salar and Aydin had to cross this option off their list.

So here we are with Aydin's frustration and dwindling time.

Walking around the courtyard amidst the empty home, he tried to not let the creature's bated breath monopolize his concentration. Finding an alternative was much more important in the event this didn't pan out. Salar was due back soon enough; he had volunteered to collect human organs from the cousin at the hospital, Eshaal. Human organs, Aydin was still frightened at the idea of going through with the thing he had been planning most of his adult life. What if he failed? What if he put Kivran into a worse state? What if he could never have access to human organs again? If these newly obtained organs were all utilizable, he couldn't store them for an infinite number of days. If he didn't perfect the procedure in the next few days, they would have to find a whole new batch of organs. Each trip would inevitably become riskier than the one preceding it. This could be his one and only shot.

Kivran's face remained swimming about on the surface of his mind. She had cried—begged—him to go through with it.

"No more experiments, Aydin. I don't want to wait any longer, wait for something… something worse. I trust you; you can do this, if anyone can, it's you. Please, Aydin."

He couldn't concentrate inside with the animal wheezing. Shutting the door behind him more aggressively than necessary, he stepped outside. He didn't get too far in peace however, as he stepped out of his home's shadow, he found his neighbour, Ines, leaning discreetly in the small alley separating their two homes.

Nodding, he was going to continue onwards, but then she spoke.

"Aydin?"

"Hi, Ines, how are you?"

Ignoring the question, she stepped towards him, arms crossed against the night chill.

"Do you have a moment?"

Willing to allow himself a distraction, then soon after kicking himself for wasting time, Aydin nodded whilst stepping forth. Ines motioned for them to walk.

In silence, he followed her down the road towards the island's eastern shore. Her footing seemed hesitant as she kept looking behind to make sure he remained following suit. The still night accompanied them on their journey. It wasn't until they were a dozen homes away that she finally turned to him, ready to speak.

"I've never asked what you do."

Aydin nodded, confirming her statement. Ines had been his mother's friend for a long while, Aydin had never had a reason not to trust her. That being said, he'd also never told her what he was trying to do in a small room at the back of his home. He'd simply asked her for resources, to which she had been more than obliging. He figured her complacent behaviour was strictly based on her friendship for his late mother as well.

He waited for her to continue, mouth still ajar.

"But I can take a guess."

Aydin inadvertently took a step backwards. Why had she made him walk this far away from home?

"Nothing to worry about, I'm not going to tell anyone." Her shaking voice made it difficult to determine the believability of her tone.

Remaining where he was, Aydin questioned, "What do you think I do?" He needed to know how his behaviour was interpreted to those on the outside.

Cautiously, he waited for her to utter *the* word: farm. If she was about to insinuate what he believed, she was preparing to accuse him of operating a farm—a place where illegal transplants were conducted on a regular basis for those willing to dole out enough. Aydin differed from this, he didn't prefer to dabble in something that would jeopardize his ability to secretly find his intended cure. And his conscience wouldn't let him take money from people that desperate.

She stood up straighter now, sure in her footing.

"You do organ transplants. Actually, more like you're trying to."

There it was. Aydin shook his head, testing how much she'd reveal.

"Organ transplants are a common thing, Ines. They're not illegal, just restricted."

"I'm sorry, Aydin." She went down, resting her hands on her knees, head bowed.

He himself knelt down to her eye level. It was in this moment he realized why his mother must've chosen this woman to be her friend. There was a vulnerability palpable in her presence.

Upon feeling his hand on her shoulder, she looked up. "I don't mean to come off as confrontational, sorry. I'm just…"

As she trailed off, he watched her swollen eyes in the dim moonlight. A sense of guilt began to prevail within him.

"Ines, what's wrong?"

"Mica. He's not well."

"What's happened to him?"

"He's…" She stood up again. Aydin mirrored. "He's… his… kidney's failing. We took him to Jakarta a few weeks ago, the doctor wanted to put him on the donor list, but you know them. Most hospitals and clinics don't even allow donations anymore, afraid of the disease, and the rich just buy their way up the list. He'd never get one from there. At least not in time." She took a deep breath, biting back tears.

The disease in question is what we know Aydin refers to as Mutation 4. No universally utilized manner of identifying this Mutation in living humans, coupled with the spike of a phobia that anyone at any time and any place could suddenly be infected, resulted in a drastic decline in organ donations and more importantly, organ donation acceptance.

Involuntarily, Aydin looked towards the east coast, beyond the water where a woman with four deceased family members lived. He looked back at Ines.

"How can I help?"

"Could you perform the transplant? I obviously can't take him to a clinic, too many questions."

Before he could ask where the kidney would come from, she continued.

"Eshaal says she can get a kidney, a clean kidney. She can find a deceased patient who will undoubtedly be clean… and she'll take it out herself. All I'm asking is for you to perform the surgery. Eshaal can't, she's not qualified in that way. At least that's what she says, but a part of me thinks she's terrified to operate on her own brother."

Realizing she was done speaking, Aydin turned away once more. It was one thing to delve in the world of illicit medical behaviour to save his sister from something unknown, but something else entirely to blatantly go about doing something that could be done by legal means.

Contemplating, he gazed up and down the road. Cramped homes lined either side, the distance sound of lapping water came from down way, a handful of dim lights accompanied them.

Aydin turned back to Ines, he'd tried to approach this logically first. If that failed, he was already willing to let his emotions get the better of him.

"I'm not a surgeon, Ines. Like you said, I'm trying, and that's it. You'd put something like this in my hands? Knowing it'd be a risk still?"

She let herself display a faint smile. "There's a part of you that's just like Luana. I can't describe it, but you'd know if looking from outside. That part of you I trust."

It's funny, the things you remember at the weirdest of times. As Ines finished her thought, Aydin flashed back to a memory of his mother. Before Kivran had been born, when it was just the two of them, a memory that he found, only now, to soothe him. He'd been sitting on the bed, watching his mother comb out her wet, tangled hair by the only mirror. Dark when wet, he watched the hair slip through the bristles, down her back. Noticing his eyes on her, she had held the brush out to him, offering him the job. With delight, he nodded and stood on the bed as his mother came closer with her back to him. Gently, afraid he'd pull too hard, Aydin took a bit of hair in one hand and combed with the other. His mother had begun to hum as he got into a rhythm. It was one of his happiest memories—he had felt loved. He could've sworn it was raining in that moment.

Aydin smiled back. "I can't promise anything, Ines. But I'll damn well try.

Children, of all beings, shouldn't suffer.

Approximately 14 km northwest of Dubai, SAUDI ARABIA
Same day

This is what he wanted, he kept having to remind himself of that. He wanted to be a participant in this world. And if that world just happened to currently be confined to a relatively minuscule area of land devoid of all vegetation, surrounded by skyscrapers occupied by citizens looking no farther than their own shadows, so be it.

Garrett's back grazed the chain-link fence behind him at odd intervals—someone down the perimeter was moving it. It was starting to irritate him. Stepping a foot away, a bit unsteady in the newly acquired weight of his weapon strapped taught against his thigh, he turned to gaze into the confines he had been tasked with protecting. It wasn't in their general job description, but since their missions surfaced at irregular intervals, the unit members were often called out to fill in mundane blanks along the other WHO military factions. Through the links he skimmed over a compact sea of refugees in their own little world. From the looks of it, many had been here long enough to form permanent-looking residences under standard issue humanitarian tents. Garrett wondered what brought each one of them to this… this cage.

"Duck!"

Whirling around, he caught a glimpse of Walcott as he patted his crown just before the man continued his jog around the perimeter. A few laughing children, dirt smudged across their clothes and faces, paralleled him on the opposite side, all mimicking the soldier.

"Duck! Duck! Duck!"

As the dust settled in Walcott's wake, Garrett focused his attention on the city centre. "An oasis of gluttony," Marek had referred to it as while assigning this task.

"No matter what it looks like, Gar," the man had said in the process of escorting him to the helo. "Remember: we are tasked with protecting the refugees from the outside world, not the other way around."

The initial thought running through his mind was: *Why would that not be glaringly obvious?* However, having now stood sweltering for the better part of the afternoon, watching the lives roam both inside and out of those confines, Garrett understood.

A Range Rover sped along the closest road less than a klick east of his location, Garrett's eyes followed it unconsciously until it disappeared into the city, the mess of people.

Turning back, out of the direct sunlight, he saw the children again. They, in turn, looked passed him in the same direction the car had traversed. With their hands clinging to the fence and heavy panting, it was their eyes that unsettled Garrett. They looked on with a hunger meddled with disdain and jealously. He would know, it was often how he had looked upon his own father during juvenility.

"Son of a bitch!"

From his peripherals, he saw Walcott hysterically laughing while flat out sprinting, Keuhl nipping at his heels. The screeching belonging to the latter.

Garrett didn't turn around, the thick layer of curiosity that had compelled him to join the unit thinned in the slightest as he viewed these children—on the opposite side of the fence, amongst dislocated lives and subpar standards of humanity; Garrett knew why Marek needed to clarify this job. From this side of the fence, the world needed to be protected from these caged beings hungry for something unattainable.

He felt unsteady and unprepared.

**1,946 km east of Jakarta, INDONESIA
18 years, 149 days after Mutation 4**

She was glad everyone else in the house was asleep by the time she returned. It took a fair bit of internal arguing to even convince her to return tonight. Ultimately, the choice to come back after finishing her shift rested upon a singular simple, yet heavy, point: this may be the last time she would see home.

Taking her time, drinking in every step as though her first, Kivran entered the house and looked upon it with fresh eyes, albeit, the tears were quite effectively blurring the vision. The dark didn't help either.

She vaguely remembered entering the home the day she was released from the hospital after her transfusion. Aydin had begun to cry the moment he entered that day, but Kivran could only recall being happy. She never found comfort in that clinic, confined to that bed. And that day, Aydin had held her hand as they entered together. She was back home, and that's all that mattered. Though her brother had soon after left her side to lock himself in his mother's room, Kivran went about playing in her own room for the balance of that day.

Evidently, she wasn't old enough at the time to remember too much of her mother, that's not to say the little girl didn't cry upon learning the news, it's only to say the connection wasn't as strong. However, the way that Aydin had mourned that day and those days throughout his life where a shadow would come over him, that indescribable sorrow, Kivran knew her mother was an amazing human being.

Entering now, with her lease on life possibly about to expire, she tried to seek out the happiness tucked away in the home's corners. Like the morning of her tenth birthday when Aydin, with a little help from Salar's mom, endeavoured to make chocolate chip bread for breakfast. It had more chocolate than dough and rendered them both into a sugar coma by eleven am. There were still burn marks on the table where they had placed the hot pan.

Or like the day when Aydin had come bursting in the door, announcing his acceptance into medical school. The door handle imprint was still there in the wall, neither of them wanted to plaster over it. Or the engraved lines running the distance from the kitchen to Kivran's room across the floor, where Aydin would drag a chair every night to make sure she got through the night okay.

Happiness tucked away beneath all the lament.

By the time she hit the courtyard, Kivran was on her knees, unable to keep herself upright. The rope reserved for the animals temporarily awaiting death was still wrapped around the pipe in the corner. This was it. The accumulation of all the days, the years, she had held out a singular flame of hope, believing she could live through it, it was about to come to a standstill. All the days, the years, her brother had spent fighting through blood, sweat, and tears, to keep her flame alive, it was about to come to a standstill.

She looked up to the metal sheet roof and imagined the stars. Maybe it was about time she got to spend some time with her mother.

Keeling over right there in the courtyard, her head hit the cold floor, her limbs spread out, welcoming whatever was to come with open arms. Kivran cried the whole night through. Miraculously though, she felt a weight lift—she could stop fighting. Unprepared for something that she had been preparing for most of her life.

"I need you to count down from one thousand now, Kivran, all right?"

As he was finishing his sentence, his thoughts wandered from Kivran's eyes towards the crown of her head. It's funny, the things you remember at the weirdest of times. Aydin watched the artificial light reflect off his sister's hair, it appeared golden. Just like his mother's the last time he saw her. It was more than a simple rarity for anyone this far from the centre of Jakarta to naturally possess such a thing, but here it was: a physical representation of his mother's New Zealand heritage.

Aydin smiled.

This was finally it, his chance to save his mother in a way. A calmness washed over him, he had the potential to be content. Finally. As his pulse steadied, he allowed the singular thought that had been clawing at him to surface: he wouldn't let his mother down. The clawing had persisted from the very moment he realized his sister was sick.

Content, finally.

"I know how this works, Aydin."

Her voice shook, as did her lower lip. She wore the same expression as when she looked upon the test animals. With remorse, and a final good-bye.

Aydin used his ungloved hand to stroke her hair, touching her light.

"Maybe I should've been trying to cure your sassiness instead this whole time."

He watched her gift him a faint smile, she was only doing so to comfort him. He'd come to know the difference between her expressions. Aydin always figured if he could retain memories of the nuances of people he cared for, they'd never be gone for him. Which is why he could tell you how his mother would've appeared in this moment, he could tell you the expression of concealed weariness she'd display, from memory alone.

Looking across the table, he drifted his attention to Salar, trying to focus back on the task at hand. He hadn't made up his mind whether being emotionally involved in the outcome of this endeavour was an advantage or not. It hadn't mattered to this extent with the animals, the emotional distance somehow seeped through every time the animal wound up on the table. Still seeing Kivran in his peripherals, he found himself becoming anxious. Terrified of any outcome.

He wished it was raining. He could use the rhythm as an unbiased companion right about now.

Salar doused a cotton ball with antiseptic before rubbing it on a small patch of her skin just inside the left arm's elbow bend. He then injected Kivran with an anesthetic. As soon as the needle touched her arms, she began counting down.

"One thousand. Nine hundred and ninety-nine. Nine hundred and ninety-eight. Nine hundred and ninety-seven."

The men waited patiently, stationary, as they watched Kivran drift. Any natural sunlight began to dim, and the two lamps within the lab illuminated the three. Leaving the corners of the room in darkness.

Kivran's eyes glazed over as the anesthetic began to take hold, her eyelids began to slump and closed shortly afterwards. She didn't make it past eight hundred.

Without lifting his gaze from Kivran's face, Salar spoke. "Last chance."

Feeling the sweat accumulate between his palms and the surgical gloves, Aydin took another look at Kivran's hair. It no longer caught the light. But he realized he wasn't expecting or even hoping for it to do so this time.

Turning his gaze to Salar, who now looked back, Aydin took an audibly deep breath. "Ready."

As though it had been waiting for him all along, drizzle began to hit their sheet-metal roofing. Aydin smiled again, this time instinctively.

Content, finally.

1,946 km east of Jakarta, INDONESIA
18 years, 152 days after Mutation 4

With exponentially numbing lower legs, Aydin stared at the wall, in particular, at a magazine clipping Kivran kept above her headboard.

Upon hearing a wince, he looked towards his sister lying on the bed beside him. Sheets visibly drenched in sweat, thrashing at irregular intervals, she'd been like this for four consecutive days now. This movement was not anywhere similar to the seizures she experienced before. Those were violent, these made it seem as though she was simply experiencing a nightmare. An exceptionally petrifying nightmare. More than anything, he feared her body was rejecting one or more of the allografts.

The odd thing was, there were no significant signs of transplant rejection. With the exception of the fever, that is. There was no swelling anywhere that couldn't be accounted for by the actual surgery scars, no nausea. Hell, she hadn't been conscious in four days and that's what scared him the most; she had been getting by on an IV alone. Though he knew from the get-go this procedure wouldn't magically filter the Mutation out of her system, a part of him clung to that hope. Until yesterday that is. The blood test conducted thirty-six hours ago revealed the Mutation's presence still. He'd just have to hang on to his original intention now: if they filtered her blood, perhaps these "new" organs could make the rest of her body stop attacking itself. Fingers crossed.

Kivran's involuntary movements ceased just long enough for Aydin to place a damp washcloth on her forehead. And then it was thrown off again, thrashing about.

Sinking back into his chair, Aydin slumped his shoulders, reluctantly drafting a Plan B at the corner of his mind. It was going to be arduous.

1,921 km east of Jakarta, INDONESIA
18 years, 153 days after Mutation 4

His head was throbbing, not only because of the transport helicopter's machinery but from the incessant talking of the man seated next to him. There was enough room for two men to occupy the space in-between and it still wasn't a large enough expanse for the annoyance to be mitigated.

Having flown back to the base less than ninety minutes ago from a humanitarian border protection detail and then being ordered to board the next transport out in order to protect an unspecified package, Garrett was more than eager to set foot on solid ground. Hunching over to tuck his head into his chest, he tried to ease the pounding in the back of his skull. He tried concentrating on his scuffed-up boots, but deviated his gaze to be mesmerized by the nervous leg spasms of the man beside him.

Somehow noticing this, Keuhl apologized amidst his rambling and moved his legs closer together but continued to twitch nervously anyway. Garrett looked up at him with an agitated glare.

This particular mission seemed odd enough, the fact that this was the lab rat's first field outing only added to the mess. Judging by the sideways glance Odeli was giving Keuhl from across the way, it might just be his last.

With both of them being the newest members of the unit, they had often been placed on mundane assignments together. Because of this, Garrett knew

Keuhl quite well, it was beside the fact that he did not care to know him at all.

"I think I found the exact gene! I know for sure this time, I know it!"

Garrett saw Marek, who was seated across from him, jolt his head up at Keuhl. If this was worth Marek's attention, it had to be of some use.

"I mean, I obviously can't tell anyone. I mean, obviously. After what happened last time, obviously not. Have I told you I was nearly booked, twice?"

"Yes, Keuhl," Marek answered.

The researcher had mentioned this any chance he received—well more so any chance he concocted for himself—always the same tale of how he'd narrowly escaped being convicted on unethical behavioural grounds, in particular for his unauthorized animal experimentations. Unvoiced, the remaining members of his unit knew exactly why any actual conviction hadn't been handed down: if Keuhl had found anything of substance from these experiments, WHO could keep them contained until they were ready to address them at their own leisure. Convicting Keuhl would publicize much of his work, but as long as they kept him on the payroll, the WHO nondisclosure agreement could still tread water. So either Keuhl had found nothing, and WHO was simply taking precautionary measures, or Keuhl had found something significant and it needed to be contained.

"Well then, you know the details and what not, obviously. Anyways, so I think I found the gene for Mutation Four. It would mean that we wouldn't have to ban allografts altogether. You know, that's like a person-to-person transplant. But, I mean, we could just check for this gene, and those people wouldn't be able to donate or accept organs, but everyone else can. And better yet, it could even be recessive, and well, I mean, people had already reportedly found the gene, but I found a way to detect it. Without having to conduct a complete DNA scan."

"And how's that, Keuhl?" Marek asked, but Keuhl kept his eyes on Garrett.

The unit knew Keuhl held an unvoiced infatuation with Garrett, whereas the latter felt nothing in return and did nothing that could be construed as encouragement. He simply did not believe Keuhl was an individual who warranted his emotions. Not so unusual for him, as you've probably figured out.

"Well, I mean, it could be any variable, any visible variable on their being. I mean, you can't pinpoint it if the variable you're looking at is simply their birth trait just by a glance, bu—"

"Hang on!" Odeli slid down the ledge, moving away from the two strangers and continued with a lowered voice. "So you're telling us you haven't found *kak*? Is that it?" A smirk began to emerge.

Garrett watched as Keuhl's legs settled and he leaned back against the transport's interior, eyes rolling upwards.

"I knew it would be too complex for you to unde—"

"All right gents, ETA two minutes," Walcott shouted back into the carriage from his pilot seat. His deliberate interruption could not have been better timed.

Garrett straightened himself up and gently stretched his neck, taking care to not aggravate the pounding further.

Having no windows in the compartment, he wasn't able to determine precisely their whereabouts. The extent of his knowledge for this particular mission was confined to the forty-second long, one-way conversation he had had with Marek at the base.

Having been loaned out to a general WHO military unit to pick up slack on an overnight watch, Garrett was coming back alone on a transport, no other members of his unit with him. The door barely open wide enough for him to exit, Marek pulled him out of that transport, one hand on the shoulder guiding him through the courtyard towards another outbound flight.

"Just in time! We're on an escort to outside of Jakarta, guard duty of sorts, some package. I think. Not in charge of the actual package, we're just guarding the delivery men." At that point he pointed his chin towards two men entering the flight a few steps ahead. "We guard the men, they drop it off, we all come home. Easy-peasy, kid, yeah?"

Kid—the expression had grown on him. To his wonder, he found it endearing coming from Marek.

Having never said no to the man and not about to start, Garrett nodded while trying to blink away the haze before his eyes brought on by lack of sleep from the night before.

Watching the rest of his unit follow the other men inside, the only thing he replied with was, "Well that's new, isn't it?"

Marek nodded back, gently tightening his grip around Garrett's shoulders. "First time for everything."

Looking across at him now, he could see Marek still slowly shaking his head, playful smile across his face at Keuhl. Garrett found himself smiling in turn.

As the transport began its audible and ear-popping descent, the unit members double-checked their gear instinctively. While doing so, Garrett observed the two extra men on board. In stark contrast to his own uniform of black, head to toe, these men wore dry-cleaned suits. Ties clamped between clasps, solid cufflinks slightly visible beneath navy-blue suit jackets, collars miraculously not stained with sweat yet. The men appeared out of place yet simultaneously, Garrett believed this wasn't the first time they'd made this sort of run. He thought of that man he had met only once on that bloody island, the one so out of place.

Feeling the rattle of the touchdown, Odeli slid open the door and stepped aside for everyone to exit. Marek and Garrett brought up the rear with Keuhl and the two men ahead, Walcott remained inside.

Moving to form a low huddle, the men jogged the distance between their drop point and a clay-bricked building ten feet due north. Habitually, Garrett, Keuhl, and Odeli circled around Marek for guidance. The other two men followed suit. Definitely not their first run.

As he heard Walcott taking off behind him, Garrett could make out the various sounds amongst the civilian streets. Without drifting his gaze from Marek, he tried to take in what he could. The area they'd landed in wasn't urban by any stretch of the imagination. The building they found themselves beside reflected the other erected structures within vicinity, none of them above two stories in height. There was a stagnation in the air, a storm was coming.

"Destination is a hospital a quarter of a klick due northeast. Odeli, Keuhl, you two are stationed at the primary entrance. Intel only states one entrance, that's rural for you. Garrett and I'll take Repo Men here inside. Walcott's doing one sweep over head before pickup, in and out five minutes' tops, yeah?"

Marek honed in directly on the two strangers, each nodding on cue.

"I shouldn't have to remind you gentlemen: this is not a quarantined nor a potential-quarantined zone. We do not have authority here. No threatening behaviour. That being said," Marek stepped closer to Odeli and Walcott at this point. "Do not let anyone in. Deflect as need be, but no one enters or leaves the target building whilst we're inside. Acknowledged?"

These two men now nodded. Acknowledged.

As the unit fell into position to move, the new men naturally falling in without direction, Garrett brought up the rear with three thoughts now circulating in his mind.

1. He became very cautious suddenly of his concealed weapon beneath the uniform windbreaker.

2. What the hell were these men transporting that it warranted blocking access to an entire hospital by the actual World Health Organization?

3. Why did he want to be on solid ground so bad, again?

Understandably, we all have two kinds of selves. The kind we are when around those we trust, and the kind we are when around those we can't quite bring ourselves to trust. Eshaal deviated from this generality in the slightest: she was one person in front of those she trusted and those she didn't; and she was another person when in the presence of someone who, quite possibly, was just as sociopathic as her. Salar. I'm talking about Salar.

Eshaal's inhibitions were a missing thing. You could chalk it up to the fact that she spent much of her day in the company of cadavers. Or, and this is the one Aydin secretly preferred, Eshaal abandoned her inhibitions in Salar's company exclusively. It's as though she could pick up on his apathy and allowed her own to prevail above all else. However, unlike Salar's silent apathy, Eshaal was known to be quite verbal.

Let's take a step back and mention however, that all three of these individuals had only crossed paths a handful of times, if that. With the exception of the above-noted transaction between Eshaal and Salar alone, that is, during which the latter ventured to acquire organs for Kivran's transplant. The first few meetings had been amidst residency, during which Salar and Aydin, along with a trainee Eshaal, shadowed professionals. Her apathy had been well under wraps, as she wore a mask of professionalism in those interactions. The other singular correspondence occurred approximately three years ago, when they had come to this particular hospital looking for bags of donated blood—untraceable bags—and were unsuccessful. At that point, they had been attempting a cure via dialysis for Kivran. We already know the end result of that.

Today, our gentlemen cross paths with said woman for a specific, prearranged purpose: she happened to be the individual who had preselected a kidney for Mica's operation at the request of Ines.

Aydin and Salar made their way down the linear corridor. Smell of antiseptics and humidity hovered around them. Compared to the clinic they worked at, this was a bustling microcosm of Jakarta. Civilians of various ages occupied the hallways, military personnel haphazardly stood guard at varying intervals—doing their darnedest at keeping another civilian rebellion at bay, at least that's what their superiors would state. The primary difference between Aydin's home island and this place was the striking difference in types of civilians.

As the mass migration of New Zealand and Australian citizens reached its peak, many could no longer afford, or had the will, to go anywhere farther than Indonesia. Thus, a vast variety of immigrants descended upon the southeastern most islands. It wasn't bloody, but the conflict that followed resulted in a majority of the native Indonesian populous moving to the key main islands surrounding the capital region, leaving the refugees behind.

Consequentially, the hospital Aydin was now walking through, was populated primarily with natives, whereas his home was as diverse as a child's imagination.

His mother happened to be one of those immigrants.

Reaching the end of the corridor, they began descending a set of stairs on their left. Reaching the only door at the bottom of said stairs, Salar knocked.

"Come in," Eshaal's muffled voice replied from within.

Stepping through, the men found her hovering over a cadaver on the only examination table in the room. Examination table might be a misleading term, as Eshaal's legally granted job was to cremate all bodies, preferably immediately in order to prevent any further undesirable diseases. This hospital was one of many to implement the doctrine sweeping across Asia: do not donate organs, do not perform any transplants.

Fortunately for us all, the population this hospital primarily services wasn't large enough to warrant two people in Eshaal's position. Which meant no one else could witness their transaction. Clearly this system required better bureaucratic oversight, but it works in our favour.

"Nice to see you both again." She didn't look up and her monotone did little to purport truth in her words.

Closing the door behind him, Aydin waited for her to complete the work currently occupying her attention. Exactly what work that was, he couldn't make out.

Knowing she had minimal medical expertise, it could be explained why she was bent over the body with a set of household scissors in hand, of all things. But it didn't explain the fresh blood spatter scattered across the front of her apron and bare forearms.

Stealing a momentary glance in Salar's direction and seeing his undisturbed demeanour, Aydin acted as though nothing seemed out of place.

He felt something to the contrary.

Straightening herself while tossing the scissors on a tray to her left, Eshaal finally looked up, briefly acknowledging Aydin before focusing her attention on Salar exclusively. She smiled. It seemed off.

Salar remained stationary.

"How have you been?" Though monotone, this sentence exuded genuine interest.

"Fine. Do you have the kidney?"

As Aydin broke into a smile, he thought: there are moments I love Salar for exactly the way he is.

Clearing her throat, she nodded whilst muttering an "Of course." Reaching beneath the table towards the bottom shelf, Eshaal pulled up a duffel bag and placed it on top of the cadaver's legs. Upon unzipping it, a miniature cooler became visible. As she began to open this, Aydin stepped closer. Though this was a natural movement for him to make, and he did so almost instinctively, his mind wandered mid-step and he found himself eyeing the body first.

The entire abdominal region had been cut open. By "cut," we don't mean the standard operation of creating an incision and clamping the skin to the sides, out of the way. What "cut" actually means here is: a rectangular section of skin, running the length of the body's pelvic bone to the top-most rib and running the width of the body's ribcage, had been entirely removed—cut off, not clamped away to the side, removed altogether. Speaking of removal, by the looks of it, that's generally what had happened to the body's organs. The kidney was gone, the small intestine was gone, the lower half of the right lung was gone. With the exception of the initial dermal incisions, no precision was paid to any other cut. And why the hell were the ribs broken, nay, ripped apart?

"That's where it came from."

Eshaal was speaking to Aydin directly, though he recognized it, he couldn't reply. He was staring at the gaping hole on the table.

"Did you extract it?" Salar asked.

"Yeah, I did." The monotone was gone, she was proud of herself.

Aydin felt nauseous.

She continued. "The blood type is compatible, couldn't check the possibility of a Mutation but Ines said it didn't matter either way."

Aydin finally looked up at her as she spoke to Salar. He couldn't shake the feeling, this didn't seem right. She didn't seem right.

Oh God, Kivran. He had so willingly taken organs from her possession for Kivran.

Filling the silence, Salar spoke again. "We should be going then."

With no contention, Eshaal closed the cooler and zipped it back in the bag, handing it off to Salar. The body shifted under her movements. Did he just see the organs shift?

Not waiting for an invitation, Aydin took to holding the door for Salar, encouraging him out. Quickly following behind, they left Eshaal smiling over the cadaver, eyes glazed over.

It wasn't until they reached the top of the stairs did they speak.

"Are you okay, Aydin?"

Salar generally didn't ask questions of this manner unless there were clear visible signs of a distressed nature. Furthermore, he definitely didn't care for the answer.

"Do you feel okay about doing this?" He knew all the reasons why Salar was the wrong person to ask this question to, but Aydin needed to speak his mind. And Kivran wasn't here.

"We've done more difficult operations, if that's what you mean." He handed the bag to Aydin upon his nonverbal request.

The question wasn't interpreted as Aydin had hoped.

1,937 km east of Jakarta, INDONESIA
Same day

Following Aydin out the door, Salar tried to mimic his cousin's demeanour. Evidently this situation was supposed to be anxiety-inducing, inner-turmoil-igniting stuff. Thus, he kept his pace slightly quicker than average yet with sure footing, head angled down, eyes frantic. However, as Aydin's emotions likely legitimately hindered his ability to take in his surroundings, Salar faced no such blockade.

How fortunate for us, because he can tell us what happened.

The hospital's entrance opened up into a square, since cars were currently a luxury, people passed every which way at their leisure. The street to their far left would lead them back to the shore whence they had left their boat. Having no other business on the island, Aydin led them back. With his head still down, Salar caught sight of young children playing football down the right-hand street. With a mixture of furrowed brows and smiles, the children emanated sounds of joy.

It's funny, the things you remember at the weirdest of times. One of the first memories Salar had of this internal conflict of whose emotions should he mimicked, was during an argument between his parents. On a quiet afternoon with no patients occupying the rooms or halls, Salar had been sitting in the stairwell, hidden from plain sight, practicing his weekly vocabulary.

Hearing the event before seeing it, he watched as his father dragged his mother by the arm into the hallway. His mother's wooden leg wasn't latched in properly and she fell against the force. There in the middle of the hall with his father angrily shouting at her from above, his mother lay on the floor. Tears streaming down, face blood-red along the left side, her hands hiding the space between her own flesh and the wooden leg, silent.

Whose emotions would it be appropriate for him to reflect? His father's fury or his mother's despair?

Logically, you could argue that because his father was facing away from him, and he couldn't quite make out that expression, having not retained this variety of "anger" in his inner emotional repertoire, he behaved as he did. And yet, the illogical, unspoken explanation was much more comforting.

Salar had cried that day, and with ease.

As they turned the corner into the last street on the left, Aydin sidestepped so he was nearly dragging his left side along the wall. Beside them, headed towards the way from where they had just come were six men.

The first four and the last donned military-esque gear, minus guns. Visible guns, that is. The next two wore professional looking suits, both men's eyes followed them in the intersection until they had passed. Possibly longer, Salar didn't dare turn around to confirm. They all shared the same gait; it emanated authority.

Looking back at Aydin, Salar confirmed he hadn't taken in the sight of the other men and was still moving in the same manner. Speeding up, Salar nudged Aydin, catching his attention before picking up the pace, now leading the way.

Without a word, upon seeing their boat, Salar broke out into a run, hearing Aydin close behind. He untied their transport, visibly lost in the crowd going about their business on an average Thursday afternoon.

Tossing the bag in, they both pushed the boat away from shallow waters before hopping in. A subtle expression of confusion was frozen on Aydin's face—he had yet to determine the reasoning behind their urgency. Salar was just relieved his cousin acted accordingly with the absence of an immediate explanation.

What happened next happened so quickly, it was difficult to state which detail preceded which. Regardless, this is what occurred: Salar revved the engine, propelling them away from the shore; out of seemingly nowhere, a helicopter appeared over the island, its blades fracturing the sunlight; two well dressed men emerged from a rapidly parting crowd, their arms up towards the direction of the boat; and the sound of bullets being fired stood out against the noise of screaming people and crashing waves.

1,937 km east of Jakarta, INDONESIA
Same day

He heard the whizzing noise before he felt a thing, yet once he did, the hair on the back of his neck stood on end. By then, something else had whizzed past his ear.

In the motion to look behind, Aydin caught sight of Salar. Stark white, mouth agape, he was looking in the same direction: behind them. There, upon the shore of the island they had just so casually departed from, stood two men in suits, stationary with the exception of their trigger fingers as each one held a gun, firing in the direction of Aydin and Salar's boat.

He heard Salar cursing under his breath as he curved the propeller, attempting to thrust them on an angle away from the shore.

"Get down!"

Aydin didn't need to be told twice. Crouching to fit himself between two of the bench's wooden panels, he clutched the duffel bag to his chest, water spraying across his back.

As he heard Salar curse again, Aydin risked a glance. There were three men outfitted in black clothing, bulky jackets, military gear hidden beneath, rushing towards the shore; the two well-dressed men were exactly where he had last seen them. Except now, there was no whizzing.

He caught Salar's eye, who was steering from his own crouched position, mirroring his own expression.

With guns still drawn, why weren't they firing any longer?

That's when they heard the splintering sound. The noise wood makes once pierced through with an object traveling at a high velocity. That splintering sound. The noise occurred twice more, close to each other in time.

Aydin stretched down to have a look beneath a bench at the boat's rear. It was as though all three shots had been concentrated at this small diameter for there was now a hole approximately the size of a walnut six inches away from the motor. Water was beginning to splash inwards, albeit at a slow rate.

"Salar, there's a—"

An indeterminable number of shots were once again fired.

The way they had been trying to angle themselves, they inadvertently exposed the entire right side of the boat to the strangers.

Aydin didn't need to see the newly formed holes, he knew they had made a large enough impact, as his stomach began to submerge in the water now seeping in. And because he felt the holes.

One in his forearm. One in his side.

In the back of his mind, he registered Salar shouting his name from somewhere in the vicinity, he felt the bag now beneath him sway with the current, he felt the boat stop. Not having the strength to hold his head up any longer, he lowered it to rest on the bottom of the boat. As water dipped in and out of his nostrils and he lost his breath, Aydin's eyes lined up with the hole at the boat's rear.

He couldn't see the shore, just the magnificent blue of the ocean as it swayed. He couldn't hear anything except the tide lapping around him. Rhythmically. Like the rain. His left hand was tightly clenched, waiting for something, perhaps. He watched his blood stirring with the water. The red changed from dark to light with each receding wave.

Like hair, changing from dark to light. Beautiful golden hair.

Aydin couldn't help but smile as he released the grip of his hand. Content enough.

1,937 km east of Jakarta, INDONESIA
Same day

The crowd was making him anxious, hovering in small packs around them, talking amongst themselves more so than addressing or blatantly acknowledging them.

Briefly glancing over his right shoulder, Garrett saw Odeli positioned exactly as he himself was: back towards the centre group, a visual on the crowd at all times, forming a defensive position in the event that this particular situation was to escalate. He looked over his left shoulder to find Keuhl not following protocol. The man's entire body was angled away from the crowd, facing the centre group, the defensive formation was compromised. Unable to attain Keuhl's attention, Garrett left him as is.

The said centre group consisted of the two strange men and Marek, engaged in a hushed, yet heated conversation. This wasn't the best time or place to be conducting such correspondence. Not when these men had unholstered and shot their weapons at civilians. Allegedly.

The fleeting glance Garrett had paid the victims occurred on their walk to the target building, their first attempt, that is. They hadn't stuck out enough to warrant anything other than a fleeting glance, at least not for him. Evidently, they had for our two strangers. With the hospital entrance at arm's length, the men had forced the unit to a halt. They looked at each other as though they already knew what the other was supposed to do. Without a word, one of them thrust their parcel into Keuhl's arms, and with Marek's shouts to cease comprising the backdrop of the entire situation, Garrett had watched both men race down the path they'd come up on a moment ago. With momentary hesitation, Marek ordered the remaining unit after them as he relayed new instructions up to Walcott. With no weapons drawn between them, they reached their initial drop-off point. The men were nowhere in sight. Hearing a set of shots, quickly fired one after the other, Garrett had followed Odeli towards the shore where they witnessed the incident while running towards the men, unsure of what to do once there. Though his stint with the unit was still in its infancy, he had neither used his own nor was privy to an incident where another member had utilized their weapon in public.

The incident, from what Garrett saw, went something like this: the men gave chase to—with no communicated reasoning—the two civilians approximately three blocks in the direction of the island's eastern shore where they opened fire, standing on a populated dock, at said civilians from a distance of approximately sixty metres exiting on a motorboat. It should be noted that the victims did not return fire, or initiate it, neither did the civilians appear to be maliciously fleeing the island.

To Garrett's relief, the radio's static indicated Walcott's voice behind him as Marek stopped to take the call. Unable to hear that either from the increasing crowd around him, he figured it was for the best since just a moment later, Marek called out loudly, "All right, back to target building. Maintain current formation."

Taking another glance at Odeli, Garrett moved in reverse off the dock towards the dusty streets, the sun beating down on them as harshly as the malice radiating from the crowd. The latter now acknowledged them blatantly. The conversations abruptly ceased. He wasn't sure which was worse: the crowd's gathering or their gazes now in the unit's retreat.

Walcott's position became audible and clearly visible, he was hovering over the boat that had been the men's target. Glimpsing back in intervals to maintain appropriate footing, he noticed Keuhl behaving impeccably now. A real textbook G.I. Joe. As they migrated closer to their target, the crowd disappeared out of view, thankfully they weren't pursuing. Garrett genuinely didn't see that holding pattern lasting much longer.

Finally, they reached their destination. As previously instructed, Keuhl and Odeli positioned themselves at the entrance as Marek, the men, now reunited with their parcel, and Garrett entered. The men began to lead, and Marek let them.

Shifting beside him to keep pace, Garrett looked at his friend. The stern expression strewn across the latter's face prevented him from doing anything further.

Evidently the noise from the docks hadn't reached as far as said hospital, for everyone went about their business as usual. With the small exception that two men dressed in bulky black clothing and a heavy gait turned the usual number of heads. Alternatively, a fleeting reasoning dashed across Garrett's mind: these people are used to the sounds of violent interactions. The confinement smelled of urine. You would think Garrett had been to enough filthy places to not be irritated by such a stench any longer, but you would be mistaken.

Reaching the end of the corridor, the men began descending a set of stairs on their left. Reaching the only door at the bottom of said stairs, they found it ajar.

Marek halted at the entrance and motioned for Garrett to wait with him outside as the others entered.

In an attempt to bring Marek back from his irritated brink, Garrett spoke. Actually, let's be honest, Garrett was hoping the other man would enlighten him on what exactly was occurring right now, and whether he should be prepared for a repeat showing of The Dock Show.

"That's where you draw your morbidity overload line, Mar?" He pointed to the nameplate screwed into the wall beside the door reading "Crematorium."

"Yeah, it's just a little too Hansel and Gretel for me."

Marek faintly smiled.

Before Garrett could begin asking his intended questions, the hard clang of multiple metal objects falling emanated from within the room. The door was suddenly swung fully open from within.

The slightly shorter of the two men stepped out, blocking view into the room itself. "Does your unit have jurisdiction over illegally extracted human organs?"

Marek shot a look at his partner, the stern expression had completely vanished. "We do."

The man nodded before stepping aside, holding the door for them and gestured at nothing in particular within the room. Garrett now cemented the notion that had been swimming around in his head from the moment he joined the mission: these men had very different objectives than what this unit generally operated beneath. Not that his unit didn't have a long shadow cast behind it either.

"I think you might wanna see this." The other man now spoke. He was focused on something beneath a plain white sheet hastily thrown over an object on a metal table in the centre of the small confines. The area did have a silver lining: it didn't smell like urine here, just burned flesh instead.

Garrett moved instantly inside while Marek only angled himself in at the threshold, as the closest man gripped the sheet, ready for some big reveal. In the middle of the cold room stood a surgery table, on which lay a body with a noticeable sunken hole in the torso. Garrett nodded at the transporter standing on the opposite side of the table, who in response folded the sheet down from the shoulders to the waist.

In basic training, there was a whole section dedicated to determining where any specific organ rested in the human body, among other currently insignificant things. If you were going to work for the World Health Organization, you were going to learn the basics of medicine if it killed you. Stepping closer, Garrett now observed three critical facts as one significant law crossed his mind:

1. The object was a deceased male of Asian descent, roughly thirty years in age;

2. There was a gaping hole in the corpse's torso from which the kidney, the small intestine, and a portion of the right lung had been extracted;

3. The cuts and motions appeared frantic, done in haste, leaving the body in a butchered-like state; and

4. Organ extraction has been outlawed in Indonesia since 2032, four years ago.

1,946 km east of Jakarta, INDONESIA
18 years, 154 days after Mutation 4

Kivran's eyes shot open in an instance of immense, excruciating pain. She felt the bed sheets sticking to every inch of her sweating body and smelled the ever-present musty stench. Instinctively clenching her abdomen with both hands, she rolled over on the bed, allowing herself to lift her neck enough to look around much of the room. She tried to keep her breath as weight shifted within her. It felt as though her organs had come unhinged, just floating about of their own accord.

This was the second time she had woken up after the surgery. Or so she believed.

There was a vague image of Aydin sitting by her bedside rattling around in her head. If it was true, she had no idea how long ago that was. It could have been a mere hour ago, or a day ago, she genuinely had no idea.

"Aydin!" she shouted, hoping the image was recent.

Silence.

"Salar! Aydin!"

Silence.

Sinking into the old mattress, still heaving, Kivran contemplated her options. She could bear the pain and wait for Aydin to return. The clock near the sink told her it was 5:47 in the morning, but what day?

Or, she could get up and find a way to alleviate this.

She gradually rolled herself off the bed in to a standing, albeit severely hunched over, position. Better to fix herself than allow her brother to find her in such a state.

The back of her head began to throb, increasingly so as she moved, she couldn't see straight, the initial signs of a seizure. Kivran sat back on the bed, preparing to lose control.

Teeth clenched, back arched, goose bumps multiplying, she waited. And waited. And waited.

Frustrated by the haze in her view, she tightly shut her eyes. Ready to put herself through a test: she held out her left hand, palm down, using the right to gently rest the wrist on. She opened one eye just a tad. Her hands weren't shaking. She wasn't having a seizure, at least not right now. She felt weak, but nothing beyond that.

Unable to muster the strength to keep herself upright any longer, Kivran let her upper body tip over as she gently lifted her legs back up, attempting to keep the stretching of the stitches to a minimum. Drifting off, primarily unaware of her surroundings, only a part of her registered the red stains covering the sheets beneath her. That part wasn't voicing itself very effectively, however.

1,946 km east of Jakarta, INDONESIA
18 years, 155 days after Mutation 4

He wasn't jealous, or was it envious, he could never quite tell the difference between these two. As he watched the children across the Pit clamouring from one end of the football field to the next, Mica wished he could join them. Alas, his mother had recently been through a phase of sorts.

"You are not to leave the house, Mica! Not for the next two weeks, or until I say so. I mean it. No exceptions. You are staying put. This isn't a discussion, Mica!"

This was only day three. He swears his mother couldn't even pronounce his name now without shouting it. Thankfully, she was currently out running errands. Not so thankfully, his eldest sister was manning the shop and monitoring his every move from near the front door. He had made it all the way to a small gap between his home and the neighbours' from where he had his present view, and yet still, his sister could see him.

The wind carried the children's sounds across the Pit, along with the stench, but the latter he could easily ignore now. As Mica stood effectively doing just that, the noise of two items hitting the floor, one after another, each with a hollow thud were followed by the faint utterance of a curse. This wasn't carried by the wind, this came from his left. The neighbours' home.

Gasoline cans. He'd forgotten about the gasoline cans. Again.

"Sienne! I forgot the gas cans. Mum told me to take them out, I'm gonna do it now. I'll be right back!"

Not waiting for an acknowledgement, though Mica did see his sister step forward just before he turned towards the other house and ran up the handful of stairs. Technically, his mother had asked him four days ago, which meant he wasn't doing anything wrong.

Acting on his usual habit of simply walking in to pick up the cans by the door, he didn't consider it important to knock. Talking generally to whomever was inside, he pushed open the door while announcing himself, happy to be out of his sister's sight.

"Sorry, that's my fault. I'll pick them up now. How—"

Two steps in, Mica froze as the door hit the back wall in momentum and swung itself shut behind him. In front, there on the ground, was Kivran with gasoline spilled around her, trailing down towards the courtyard, the cans had tipped over nearby. This was the worst he had ever seen her, she looked pretty sick and her clothes were filthy. What was that other stuff on the floor? Eyeing the trail, he saw it spread in one line from Kivran to her room.

"Is that—is that... blood?" Pointing with his index finger, he gestured up and down the visible mark.

But Kivran wasn't paying attention. Her hands were folded around her stomach, and she moved her neck from left to right. Inching closer, unable to wipe the disgusted look on his face, he spoke again.

"Are you okay?"

Holding her head still now, she looked up at him. "Mica?"

"Uh-huh." He knelt down, wanting to see what was wrong with her.

"Mica. What day is it?"

"I don't know." The trail was clearly coming from whatever was going on under her hands. "Thursday, I think."

"I need you to go to the clinic and bring Innaya here. Right now, Mica." She was out of breath, the smell of sweat hovered near her. She started curling up on her side, gasoline spreading further with her movement.

"What?"

"Christ, Mica!" Again, everyone shouting his name. "Go to the clinic. Find Innaya. And bring her here. Tell her I need her; don't tell anyone else about this. Got that?"

Her eyes were closed, but she was definitely crying.

"Uh-huh." He stood up, inhaling deeply to allow the gasoline smell to cover up Kivran's. He couldn't stop looking at the mess.

"Mica!"

"Got it!"

Turning back, he was at the door again having not realized he'd been inching away while inhaling, unsure of what was going on, when she spoke again. "Mica?"

"What?" He could hear is sister shouting from outside now, too.

"Take your bloody cans with you!"

He was running on adrenaline alone now. And from the looks of it, Marek was running on anger alone. That man's fury was palpable at this point, and as he had eyed the worker who had come strolling into the cremation room, whom they "escorted" back to base, and as he sat across the two strange men on the transport back, and now as his unit was holed up in a singular room on base. The adjoining room held the other two men. Little oversight had its shortfalls from time to time, this was one of those times.

"Who the hell would we send this up to if we could? I mean, who did the orders come from?" Walcott asked. Out of the group, he seemed to be the most composed. Likely since he hadn't been on the ground to witness the overbearing presence of those men.

The others looked towards Marek, awaiting the answer.

Garrett watched as Marek rubbed hair against the grain, a physical habit he had for attempting to gather his thoughts, and looked back to the other room. As though on cue, the remaining unit looked over as well. There, seated on the same side of the table on plastic chairs, sat the two men facing away from the window. Their expressions were entirely out of view. They could've been conducting a conversation without Marek's knowledge from this vantage point.

Their sight seemed to upset Marek more. "They came from The Akureyri Base."

"Shit."

Grey mountains. It's funny, the things you remember at the weirdest of times. This time, it wasn't a specific memory flooding through Garrett's senses, it was a general experience: his father's constant trips to and from Akureyri and the rare moments he was dragged along himself. He was never taken past the base of the fjord. His father would leave him whilst he would venture up towards campus. What his father did up there was always a mystery Garrett never cared to solve. By happenstance, it was revealed in a conversation approximately five months into his unit stationing by a drunken Odeli that The Akureyri Base was the mothership for all units. Faceless superiors doling out unit orders left and right. Allegedly, all satellite labs sent every one of their reports up there to a primary lab as well, but Keuhl would never corroborate. Odeli couldn't say how long ago the mothership had landed there, and Garrett didn't have the courage to tell him how far ago he believed it had.

"And what exactly did they say the men would be doing?" Odeli chimed in.

"They didn't. Not really. Just that we were to take them to that hospital, at that exact time. The men would know what to do, we were just their security. That's it." Marek stared off at nothing in particular. The anger seemed to be subsiding, only to be replaced with regret. "I should've asked further."

"What am I missing here?" Keuhl pushed his chair aside and stood facing Marek. "What the hell are we upset about? That they killed something? That some dude's organs were stolen? What?!"

Moving his own chair to look around Keuhl at Marek, Garrett impatiently awaited the reply. Garrett knew why he felt off about the whole thing, but he wanted to hear someone else say it. He needed this feeling validated.

Looking directly at Keuhl, Marek stepped forward, mirroring Keuhl's stance. "We're upset because we don't kill people, we're supposed to help them. If we don't do that, we don't have a purpose. We let these men attack civilians without just cause." An accusatory arm was now pointed at the adjacent room.

"You think we don't kill people?" Keuhl let out a sarcastic laugh, to the surprise of the others. "We quarantine thousands of people in a heartbeat, over nothing, and what do you think happens to them? Do you think we just lift the quarantine after we make sure they're all okay? Jesus, Marek, don't bullshit yourself. Those people end up deprived of anything that could sustain their life, and we let them die there in the glimmer of hope that maybe, just maybe, we'll end up with a real Mutation case, and we'll get to see how it would affect the general population in an enclosed space. We're experimenting on these people and killing them as a direct result." Keuhl moved around the table to place a hand on Marek's shoulder. His tone had been gentle all the while, making his words heavier in a sense.

Garrett couldn't stand to look any longer; his head was pounding. Experimenting.

"So don't be upset, Marek, this is just a regular Thursday. Except this time, a gun was used."

"Enough, Keuhl," Walcott said, lacking conviction.

Garrett looked up to see him with his head down, he couldn't swallow it either.

"If you ask me—"

"We aren't," Odeli interrupted.

"Chances are, those two men, they were conducting another experiment. That bag they have, it's used to transport organs."

The question burned in his mind, and yet, Garrett stayed quiet, allowing Odeli to state what was on his mind. "It could have been a legal transplant being conducted at the hospital, which explains the location and exact time requirement."

Astonishingly, Marek replied, "No, that hospital isn't authorized to conduct allografts."

Garrett finally looked in that direction. A smug smile was spread across Keuhl's face, and Marek seemed weighted down by the hand on his shoulder.

Killing them as a direct result.

In that moment, seated close to the corner of the room, facing away from the accused, Garrett thought two things:

1. This, sadly enough, explains why the units that conducted quarantines were entirely separate from the units that conduct the initial visits; and

2. There was no sense of shock or surprise on Marek's face—he had known all this already.

1,946 km east of Jakarta, INDONESIA
Same day

Barely keeping herself upright against the wall, Kivran found it difficult to cease her crying. It was partially brought about by the pain searing through her abdomen and partially brought about by her having yelled at Mica. She had regretted it the moment he stepped out that door. He was doing her a favour. Said crying in turn was making her clench the abdomen muscles, increasing the pain, and thus increasing the crying. What a wonderful circle.

She couldn't see the clock from her position, but it felt as though Mica had been gone for quite some time. He should've returned by now; the clinic wasn't that far away. If it really was Thursday, he would've found Innaya with ease. So what was taking him so long?

Slowing her breathing, she tried to gain composure. She couldn't wait any longer, she had to get up herself.

As she wiped the tears off with bare hands, she flinched at the gasoline odour now stinging her eyes. Finally having vision enough to see her surroundings, Kivran noticed she had thankfully dragged along a blanket, which now lay within arm's length. Tipping over in a way to again keep the stitch stretching to a minimum, she pulled it over. Not having the strength to pull herself upright again, she stayed on the floor while haphazardly tying the blanket around the centre of her torso where the pain was most intense. She already knew the makeshift tourniquet wouldn't stay there for long.

Heavily leaning against the wall, Kivran gradually began to get to her feet. Once there, the nausea settled in. Tightening the blanket, wiping some tears that had escaped, she began to trudge along the wall towards the door.

Eventually, and with great difficulty, she made her way to the street and began dragging her body against the buildings to the right of the road. Inching along. She couldn't tell you if there were people curiously watching her. She couldn't tell you if the sun was still out. She couldn't tell you how painful it was without shoes. She couldn't tell you when in her journey the blood had started seeping through the blanket and down her legs. Kivran couldn't tell you a thing about how she got from her home to the clinic.

It was only when her destination was in plain view that she finally began to hope she could be okay. As though on cue, Innaya and Mica came rushing out.

"Oh my God, Kivran!" Innaya caught her as Kivran stumbled to her knees.

She tried to catch her breath; she was failing. Guiding Kivran's weight onto her own, Innaya lifted her up and motioned for Mica to take the other side. Together, Kivran was brought in, head lolling about.

She tried desperately to get the words now swimming around on her tongue out. They were vital, but she just couldn't string them together. She needed to say something before they reached the clinic's threshold, it might be too late by then. Frantically grasping at the other woman's sleeve, Kivran tried to get her attention. By the time Innaya finally looked over, Kivran had lost her words. Thus, in her delirious state, the only thing she could mutter out as she tightened her grip on Innaya, was:

"Tell no one."

Jakarta, INDONESIA
Same day

Their first visit would be to the hospital worker at the opposite end of the wing, held within a room guarded by a single police officer. Having no boundaries between each other, all five men opted to join the interrogation. Correction: you couldn't really call it an "interrogation," we simply lack a better word for this, whatever this was about to be.

Odeli and Marek led the group through the halls of the local police station not so graciously offering up their facilities to WHO, the former member held confidence in each stride while the latter looked defeated. Right behind them was Walcott, head still angled down, hands in pockets. That man's composure was going to fray any moment now. Garrett followed behind him with Keuhl at his rear. Unfortunately, not for long.

Garrett heard the other man jog up to him against the bustle of the front lobby they were currently traversing before registering him in his peripherals. He quickly tried to suppress the involuntary disdain.

"You get it, don't you? I mean, I know you see it." There was a slight hint of excitement in Keuhl's voice.

Garrett shook his head, picking up pace now to close the distance between himself and Walcott. "I don't know what you're talking about."

"Come on! Sure, you do." Keuhl went in to nudge the shoulder just as Garrett side stepped in time, avoiding him. But the man continued without a hitch.

"You see that quarantine is necessary. The lesser of two evils, if you will. Why take the chance that a case could be false when it would be safer, and in the long run, beneficial to us all, to simply cut off the party altogether. Treat it like a microcosm and just observe. I mean, sooner or later, we're bound to get a proper case. Can you imagine the plethora of data we'd get from something like that?!"

Walcott came to a standstill, rendering the two behind him the same. "You have absolutely no problem with sending these people to their death?"

Odeli had turned around as well. "Not here." Tilting his head, he motioned to an occupied room just to their left with open doors a few feet away, an officer had stopped what he was doing to pay attention.

Walcott lowered his voice to a hush but continued. "We've quarantined what, six locations, how many people is that? Thousands? Hundreds of thousands?"

Garrett watched as the smirk widened across Keuhl's face. "Technically, all those people aren't dead. Yet. They're still under observational quarantine. Their outcome is certain, though." The man looked directly at Garrett now, evidently searching for a missing link in their trains of thought. Keuhl wasn't going to find one. "Besides, we're combating the ever-looming problem of overpopulation on the side."

Garrett felt a shiver down his spine.

"Keep moving," Marek ordered, not bothering to look back.

Without another word, they continued to their destination. In silence, Garrett tried to subdue the reason behind the shiver: he had always believed the

Mutation, and in turn, the quarantines were designed to combat over population. And he hadn't had a problem with that notion.

Following the others inside, he found the hospital worker seated at a small desk against the wall. Upon seeing them, she smiled, pushing the chair back and situating her body to face the door.

"Gentlemen."

Odeli let out a short-lived chuckle.

The moment she spoke, Garrett regret his decision to come along. This woman oozed insincerity. She reminded him of a juvenile version of… himself.

Odeli took the reins upon Marek's momentary hesitation. "Afternoon, Miss. We didn't catch your name earlier."

She sat up straighter before proceeding, smile still plastered. "Eshaal Ghorbe. Pleasure."

"Sure. Care to tell us what was going on in that hospital? From the top, please." Odeli stepped forward, leaving the others by the door.

"Absolutely. I'm always happy to help those in authority."

Garrett noticed the new puzzled look across Walcott's face.

Uncrossing her legs, she continued. "Well, a few days ago, my aunt came to me looking for an illegal kidney. She probably figured I'd have access to that sort of thing seeing where I work, that is."

"Did she say precisely what purpose it was for?"

Eshaal shook her head.

"Did you ever say anything to make her think you would have access? To that sort of thing, as you put it," Marek asked the question, not looking at her.

Her smile faltered in the instant she looked from Odeli to Marek. "She's told me before her son has a problem with his kidneys, and the wait line is just too long. And then I may have said something to the effect that I could easily get one. I mean bodies come through my office all day and all night."

This time Marek looked up. "So you did say something to make her think that."

"Well, I mean, if you want to look at it that way, sure. I mean, I didn't exactly say I can get you an illegal kidney, but yeah, I made her think that so I could hand her over to the proper authorities. We all know that sort of thing is frowned upon."

Walcott shot a glance at Garrett who mirrored the motion. They both knew who she sounded like.

"So you baited her?" Walcott broke his silence.

"Absolutely. I mean, I was doing the right thing."

To Garrett, it seemed as though she was acting how she was supposed to be, expected to be.

Odeli took another step forward. "So what happened after that? After you made it clear you could get what she needed."

The smile was back again. "Well, I obviously got in touch with the illegal organs department at WHO and told them the situation. They, in turn, told me they would provide me with a kidney that I was to give to the aunt, no strings or paperwork."

Curious, she didn't say "my aunt."

"Hold on," Marek interrupted again, hand held up. "They *gave* you a kidney?"

"Yes, that's correct. I obviously told them we weren't doing the operation, because, you know, we can't, but yes. I was told it would be dropped off today, which I'm guessing were the other men in my office, but they were so late that I had to improvise, so to speak."

Marek went forth and knelt beside her. "You're going to have to elaborate that whole part there."

Rather than addressing the man by her, she continued looking at Odeli. "The men were late so I just took some body's kidney to hand off. He was dead, of course."

How was it possible for that smile to get wider?

Marek continued, carefree as to whether she addressed him directly or not. "And that first thing."

She paused a moment, taking the time to glance at the other three standing men. "As you know, my hospital isn't authorized to do those sorts of operations."

He heard Walcott beside him mutter under his breath, "Those sorts."

"So I was told by the aunt to just have a kidney ready, and someone would come pick it up. I did what I had to in light of those men failing to arrive. She went on about some mutation I was supposed to check for in the kidney before handing it over, I had no idea what she was talking about so I just said, "Yeah, I check—""

"Mutation?" She had caught Keuhl's complete attention. "How would she get you to check that?"

She returned the man's gaze. "I may have led her to believe I knew how with nothing to support it. I mean, she mentioned some guy she knew who could check, and it clearly seemed important to her, I wasn't going to make her think I was incompetent. Besides, I know a guy who can do that as well."

Odeli let out another chuckle, and within an instance, the woman's smile vanished. Marek got up to back away just as Walcott whispered, "Don't we all."

Evidently, Keuhl was the only one who didn't feel the tension encompassing the room now. "Did you mention this to the people who said they'd give you a kidney? Did you say you needed one with no defects?"

"Not specifically. I told them what I needed it for, and they said to not worry." Even her tone had drastically altered.

"Thank you so much!" Keuhl practically leaped the remaining length of the room to shake the woman's hand, who surprisingly was taken aback by the gesture. "You have been incredibly helpful, Eshaal was it? Thanks, Eshaal."

Turning back, Keuhl made his way out, not waiting. "Let's talk to the others, shall we?"

"Wait!" Keuhl had already left but the others were in earshot of her. "The guys I know who can check for what that thing is you'd check for, they're the ones who came to get the kidney."

Most in confusion, with the exception of Odeli who seemed more entertained when he added, "We aren't done with you just yet," they filed out. Garrett being the last had the misfortune of witnessing the woman shift herself back to her original position facing the table. As he shut the door behind himself, he could've sworn he saw her plaster that smile back on.

The rest of the unit was almost at their destination by the time Garrett had jogged back. Upon hearing him, Odeli turned around in a mockingly wide smile and dead, unblinking eyes. Garrett couldn't help but laugh. He was glad her terrifying behaviour hadn't gone unnoticed by the others.

Just before opening the designated door, Keuhl turned around, speaking to no one in particular. "I'll take the lead, if that's okay? Thank you."

Stepping through, Keuhl kept up the cheerful persona. With not a moment to lose, he was off before Garrett even had time to close the door behind him. "When did the program get implemented? Last I heard, it was still on the drawing board."

The men, unfazed by anyone's presence, looked at each other before the one on the right answered. "Which program, sir?"

"I'm not your superior. The program to deliberately place mutated organs into circulation in a given, isolated region."

Walcott let out a whispered, "What?" just as the two men looked from Marek to Garrett and back.

The right one spoke once more. "You said you were cleared for illegal organ extraction. What is your clearance to have knowledge of such a program?"

"The girl said enough, so I'll ask again: when did this program get implemented?" It was still with excitement that Keuhl spoke.

They looked at each other again before the right spoke and only after first receiving a single nod by the left. "One week ago, when it was deemed an opportune time to initialize with the situation brought to our attention in Indonesia."

"Keuhl." Marek got his attention before he could reply, gesturing towards the door.

Putting up an index finger to Marek, Keuhl asked his final question. "You're out of The AB, yeah?"

The two men nodded once in unison.

"Keuhl, now." Marek, with more authority in his tone.

The others began to turn towards the exit.

"Why open fire at them?" Unable to remain silent any longer, Garrett forced the question out. If it hadn't been for the other members of the unit standing alongside him, he never would have mustered the courage to ask them alone. The two men had an air of authority about them, similar to his father.

The men under question remained silent, blankly staring at him, perhaps waiting for Garrett to elaborate. He let them down.

As the other unit members turned back with raised brows, burdening the two men into a verbal reply. It didn't escape Garrett that Keuhl was the last one to turn around and only then did the men speak.

"Such an opportune time may not have arisen soon enough again for our liking. We could not risk abandoning this test subject."

"Hardly a test subject if you know nothing about them." Walcott spoke, just loud enough that only Garrett would've heard.

"The firing was for what, then?" Marek took the reins once again. "Making sure the... the test subject, as you put it, didn't receive alternative care?"

"Precisely." Their expressions remained cold, disconnected, unable to recognize the weight in their actions.

Garrett could have sworn he saw the corners of Keuhl's mouth rise.

"Now." Marek was without a doubt definitive this time.

Convening in the hallway again, they all looked at Keuhl, awaiting an explanation.

It's funny, the things you remember at the weirdest of times. Almost two weeks before Garrett's mother left his father, not divorced, just physically left, the two had gotten into a heated argument. If he hadn't been sitting in the backseat of the car they'd chosen to have the argument in, Garrett knew there was no chance of him finding out about the event. He was fifteen and well over the idea that his parents were constantly on the brink of jumping down each other's throats, which is why, there in the backseat parked at a gas station, Garrett didn't care to do anything but look out at the mountains. Having said that, the reason this particular memory surfaced in his mind at this particular moment was because it was the only time his mother had accused his father of being unethical. She had found out something he was doing, and though his father was severely reprimanding her for having looked through his stuff, she had stated it twice: it was unethical, what he was doing. As though he had never recalled this memory before, and he most likely hadn't, that argument came back to Garrett. His father had found a way to study the potential mutation whilst battling the ever-looming disaster of over population—that was the unethical bit.

Garrett looked at Keuhl, processing what was being said, and yet, it felt like a memory speaking.

"When I was still based in the research division, there was a program that reared its head every now and then. Some team was chosen to mock up what the implementation of such a program would entail, its results, its variables, the works. The idea was to introduce the Mutation into a controlled environment and observe the rate of multiplication, identify who was infected and how, and find out how it would potentially skip people. Basically it was a last resort; if we couldn't find the Mutation by non-invasive ways, we would have to force the study. The team reports were always the same: population control highly effective; global resources became conservable to sustain the population at that rate; however, no common variable could be isolated in the afflicted individuals themselves."

"Hang on." Still in a daze, Garrett began to actively participate. "You're saying these men were going to… deliberately place an infected organ into the populous and… and watch it multiply. And they were just going to watch, just watch how it did its business?"

Keuhl nodded, wonderment in his eyes. "I guess they just got tired of waiting to effectively isolate the mutation gene. They were just going to take the whole kidney and infect a large enough sample to work with, hoping they could find it from one of them."

"How would they even know *that* kidney was infected?" Garrett inquired.

Keuhl shrugged, looking Garrett dead-on. "I haven't been to the research division in so long, I can't even say. But jeez, that woman said she knew a guy who could find the Mutation. How did he do it?" During the last sentence, Keuhl trailed off as though only addressing himself.

"That's absurd." Marek was rubbing his head against the grain again. "Surely WHO isn't that desperate and that bush-league that they'd have to resort to such measures. Deliberately infecting the populous. Surely."

He didn't sound so confident towards the end.

1,946 km east of Jakarta, INDONESIA
18 years, 158 days after Mutation 4

Still no sign of Aydin, or even Salar, for that matter. They had never been gone this long before. She had sent Innaya nearly every day to check if either one of them had come home, and every time she had returned sporting a defeated expression. Even if she could go out looking for herself, Kivran wouldn't even know where to begin.

And thus, here she sat on the second floor of the clinic, in a room shared with one other patient, an elderly woman whose pneumonia had deemed her serious enough to admit. The woman's presence was soothing: she prevented Kivran from feeling alone and though she rarely spoke now in her weak state, the woman would smile every time their eyes met.

Don't get attached, Kivran.

Innaya had done what she could to keep most of the nurses and doctors away from Kivran, or at least their questions to a minimum. Regrettably, today, Innaya was visiting her son in the capital, which meant there was a pretty good chance someone was going to come inquiring about her condition. It was one thing convincing her friend to trust her and say nothing, it was something else entirely to ask this of someone she herself didn't trust. Surprisingly enough, Ines had paid a visit the day before, so much for Mica keeping quiet. Though that wasn't the surprising part. Ines had been interested in finding Aydin, and fast. She only seemed to vaguely care for Kivran's health, she was distracted following the moment Kivran had said she hadn't seen him. At this point in the conversation, Kivran didn't have the strength to dwell on the meaning behind this. However, since then, it hadn't left the back of her mind.

Feeling up to it, she figured she could venture a visit home herself, only to check if anyone had come back. She was in no state to be spending long periods of time unmonitored.

In the wee hours, she dressed herself, repositioned the blanket over her room companion, and slowly began to walk down towards the clinic's entrance. Barely making it halfway down the stairs before running out of breath, Kivran stopped on the landing just above eye level to the people standing in view by the primary op room. Hoping they would disperse momentarily, she put a hand to her abdomen to inflict a sense of safety— so her insides wouldn't fall out—and knelt in the corner, out of sight.

The people in question happen to be Dr. Thi and a nurse Kivran wasn't quite acquainted with as the man had only been here the last few days. Most probably to cover work in both Aydin and Salar's absences. A question shot to the surface of Kivran's mind, yet didn't remain afloat for long, so she didn't rest on it: why hadn't most of the staff questioned where they both were, at least not with any genuine interest?

The following, I'd like to preface with the fact that Kivran wasn't eavesdropping, she's not the type to do so. However, it could be easily construed as such with her slouching in a corner, away from view but within earshot.

"Don't sweat it, there isn't much you could have done for either of them. She came in too late, and that beating, that beating was her end before she even got here." It sounded like the doctor. "That relationship was a mess, you could tell off the bat."

His voice began to move farther away, Kivran could've sworn there was a giggle in it, shortly followed by the sound of a door closing. Moving again, Kivran went slower this time, unaware of how far they had gone exactly. As she gently walked, with shoes in hand, down the remaining steps and on to the small stretch of hallway separating her from the exit, she noticed the only doors wide open. The primary op room.

A sheet with dark red blotches had been partially dragged out, the strong smell of fresh antiseptics and iron was lingering as she continued. Instinctively turning at the sound of a metal object hitting the floor, Kivran turned her head into the room. She wished she hadn't. There, about to pick up an object stood a nurse facing away. Lying on the bed with one leg dangling off the frame, arms staged on either side of her torso, and head tilted unnaturally to the left, beneath a thick curtain of bruised flesh, lay the woman Kivran had met towards the beginning of her career. The woman, who at the time, was one-month pregnant. Now, here she lay with a still swollen stomach and patches of red littering her body, dead.

She could already feel the warm tears building up, if she didn't move now, she would become entirely immobile in a few seconds. Kivran had quite a vivid memory of the day she'd met the patient, how she had hoped the woman was happy.

Kivran stumbled back up to her room and closed the door, awakening the other patient with the hollow thud. She wasn't ready to face the rest just yet.

Undisclosed location, Asian WHO base, EASTERN CHINA
18 years, 159 days after Mutation 4

The inaction was frustrating Garrett. It had been nearly five days since Eshaal had identified the single survivor from the boat as one of the two men who was to pick up the illegal organ and stated, without a doubt, his residence. It was assumed they were to find this residence and turn it upside down, yet no one had stated anything explicitly to that effect.

Across from him, on the opposite opening of the helicopter, Walcott stopped scrubbing and looked up. "She said she didn't really know the men who would pick up the kidney, how does she know where they live?"

Garrett shrugged, it was a valid query.

"Her aunt." Odeli spoke from the co-pilot seat, twisting to face the two. "She asked for a call, and we figured we could tap in and find info indirectly. She called her aunt and somewhere in there, it came to light that they were neighbours."

Garrett dropped his own wash-cloth and joined. "And the aunt wasn't worried? Wasn't it her who was looking for the kidney in the first place? She didn't ask why she hadn't yet gotten it?"

This time, Odeli shrugged.

"Are we heading out there?"

Hopping up onto the bed of the transport, Walcott spoke in a lower tone. "Since we found it, Marek's thinking we should be the ones to see it through.

Whatever 'it' is, a full-blown illegal organ storage facility, a Frankenstein lab, what have you. I think Keuhl's convinced him the men didn't pick this situation at random. 'An opportune time,' come on! There's something else not being said, and Keuhl's thinking he can go out and find it on his own. Marek's trying to convince The AB as we speak. If they green light him now, that is."

"Something else like what?" Odeli climbed to the back. "What if this is all for attention? That woman doesn't seem nearly bright enough to be wrapped up in all this. And more likely, Keuhl just wants to find the guy who can actually identify the Mutation and swap brains with the dude."

"You've seen the place they dug Keuhl out of, those WHO labs are massive," Walcott replied, staring downwards. Garrett briefly wondered under what circumstances Odeli would've gotten this opportunity and how could he place himself at that cross-road. His father was always going back and forth between a lab and home, Garrett was curious.

Walcott continued, "I wouldn't put it passed them to have orchestrated every single nuance and minute detail of this fiasco."

Nodding, Odeli had clearly considered this. "I just find it hard to believe that WHO got so desperate that they had to pull something like this. They've got a butt-load of any and all types of research facilities, but they still can't find any info on this Mutation Four?"

"Maybe that's why they chose this situation," Walcott thought out loud. "It's an island, it's geographically quarantined already, small, away from any Western attention. WHO could've just been impatient and thought 'why not?' It sounds to me like the two guys were the conductors here, she just happened to be a convenient door."

"Speaking of convenient door!" Odeli was looking just past Walcott. A transport had just landed, its doors hadn't even opened all the way yet. The man looked down at his wrist in a mocking fashion. "Hello DWBs, and a day early at that!"

Leaning forward to peek out the other opening, Garrett witnessed a group exiting the transport, each one dressed in military uniforms, each one looking worse for wear than the one preceding them. "DWBs?"

Walcott answered while getting out of Odeli's way, who was eagerly hopping out their helo and strutting towards the group in question. "Doctors Without Borders. Or also known as Odeli's female."

"Ah!" Nodding in understanding, he recalled the day he had joined the unit. That was when this had been vaguely alluded to, the woman Odeli got information from.

"What do you know?" Walcott's voice changed drastically, he was rarely this serious.

Garrett turned to look at him. "What do you mean?"

"You went pale the second Keuhl finished with those men. You knew what he was gonna say before he said it."

"No." He had to break eye contact. He didn't want to lie to the unit, but he also didn't want to state the truth. The last thing he wanted was for anyone to believe he was the echo of his depraved father. "It's just terrifying, and yet logical, simultaneously."

"Sure." Walcott didn't sound satisfied with the response but his tone completed the conversation.

For simply a moment, he felt a clenching in his gut.

He screamed. A sheep died.

Jakarta, INDONESIA
18 years, 161 days after Mutation 4

"You're going to take him and not me!" He'd be cringing at his own whiny voice if he hadn't been so consumed with arguing his point.

Odeli was jogging along side Marek's vehicle, one hand hanging on to the window keeping pace.

"I need you here to run point with the locals, sorry mate," Marek replied in a hushed tone, turning away from the other two men in the vehicle, who just happened to be said locals. Municipal police officers.

"Come on, Marek! Keuhl's useless out there, and I'm useless here." He was starting to lose breath, albeit desperately trying not to show it. Not in front of the locals. After having flown to and from their closest base and this place half a dozen times in the past few days, it was beginning to wear Odeli down.

Other vehicles were parked on the brown grass running parallel to the gravel road leading up to the municipal police quarters. From his peripherals, Odeli observed at least a handful of officers scattered amongst the cars, each one looking more idle than the one before. Perhaps Keuhl wasn't the only one who shouldn't be going on this expedition.

Marek shifted in his seat, pushing his shoulders outside of the vehicle. "We don't know what we're walking into down there."

He had never heard Marek shaken like this. What exactly had The AB said to him during the last communication?

"I trust *you* to have our backs up here no matter what happens there. I need you to bring us back."

Odeli halted just in time as the gate in front of him opened, the vehicle rested in wait. "What the hell is that supposed to mean? What're you anticipating down there?"

The man's body slid entirely back into the confines of the vehicle, the tinted windows began to draw up. Odeli wanted to shout after him in frustration, but thought better of it. Not in front of the locals.

1,946 km east of Jakarta, INDONESIA
18 years, 162 days after Mutation 4

Crouching behind a waist-high graffitied wall, Garrett checked his watch, it was almost midnight. Looking over the wall, he had a clear view of a seemingly endless row of shacks approximately one quarter of a klick north of their position. From appearance alone, the homes were part of low-cost housing units commissioned in the early 2020s to house all those emigrating from continental Australia. It was also, according to a conniving woman named Eshaal, the home of the men obtaining the infected kidney. It was also the intended target for a raid.

Lowering himself back down, he faced south, with his eyes fully adjusted to the dark, he was able to make out the figures of eight men positioned just as he was. It seemed a bit excessive to Garrett, having such a big unit for a tiny residence like this. But Marek had been quite clear when stating this order came from those who couldn't be touched—there would be no questioning it. Orders from them seemed to be coming in quite a lot lately. Even with all its red tape, the plan seemed simple enough: repossess all organs located inside the dwelling, if any, whether they be in useable condition or not; confiscate any valuable documents; determine from the evidence in said dwelling whether anyone else knew of its purpose; and arrest anyone who questions or interferes with any of these duties. The final one is primarily why half of these eight men were on the local police payroll. The WHO unit had no authority, or even means, to arrest anyone.

Other than his original four-member crew, Garrett didn't know any of the other men. Once Marek had received his orders, a small unit was sent from the Indonesian secret police to their hotel room. Though curious in his own right, Garrett hadn't emotionally invested enough in this mission, or any mission for that matter, to be concerned about whether or not he could trust these men to watch his back. Nonetheless, he felt an unease towards them.

Squinting out over the heads of the men, he tried to determine what they were currently standing in. Shaped similar to a trench, the dugout of sorts was emitting a rancid stench, a mixture of various indeterminable odours. It was awful.

Hearing the faint noise of a match being ignited, one of the men positioned far away from him lit a cigarette. He could somewhat make out one of the men beside him grab the cigarette and put it out immediately.

"You ass-hat, we'll be spotted!"

The Scottish accent rung out against the relative silence. Garrett knew Walcott well enough to know that was the man's irritated attempt at whispering.

"I've been waiting all bloody day! No one's gonna notice a tiny flicker, especially when it's beside this shit show," one of the local officers retorted as Walcott shook his head and averted his gaze.

The shit show in question was the thing in the trench. Shifting himself to secure footing, Garrett looked down. Funnily enough, a glowing green substance was seeping up from the soil in the exact place his foot had just been.

He felt Marek shift closer to him, Garrett looked for the glowing substance beneath his footing as well. It was there, droplets rising to the surface. Marek had been looking at his watch for a while now, punctuality and precision were the cornerstones of that man's life.

"Okay, it's exactly midnight, let's go."

One by one, the men stood and followed Marek over the wall and through backyards towards the intended residence. Garrett noticed all the grass in their path was dead. It couldn't have been the heat, there was something else different about this spot.

Marek lifted his fist, signalling them to halt and move into position. Four men split off to the entrance, the tail looking around the corner of the shack awaiting Marek's signal. Standard comms had been authorized on this mission, however, they were to remain off until the target building was cleared. Garrett remained part of Marek's team, taking position on each side of the back door.

Marek's arm came swiftly down, and the team burst in through each door. Quickly sweeping his designated room with a weapon at the ready, Garrett heard the others shout in turns. After one final check in his area, a small bedroom on the south side of the home, he chimed in.

"Clear!"

The group armed the safety locks on their weapons and shone their flashlights in different areas to determine the complete layout of the house. Just left of the bedroom's doorway, Garrett could make out the outline of a deep freezer. Finding his way there, he lifted the lid. Inside, clearly visible from the freezer's internal light, were organs. All neatly stacked accordingly and labelled with names and descriptions.

Liver - Origin: goat 2 - Mutation 4

Spleen - Origin: goat 1 - Mutation N/A

Kidney - Origin: goat 4 - Mutation 4

Clearly labelled organs with Mutations, Keuhl's living dreams were about to come true. Garrett shut the lid and turned back towards the main room to get Marek. On his way there, he pulled the front of his shirt up to cover his nose and mouth. That garbage dump was revolting. He'd never been this far east in the world, and all his days here had exposed him to the constant smell of pollution and dirt. There was something else mixed up in those very smells, it seemed familiar, but he couldn't put his finger on what it was.

The main room appeared to be some sort of surgery room. Littered with pages of notes and diagrams on the walls, clear plastic liners on the floor. Marek was gathered with Walcott and a few of the other men beneath the metal-sheet roof of a courtyard from the looks of it. Walcott spoke first.

"There aren't any computers. That seems odd, no?"

Looking down at the dirt floor, with puzzlement, Marek replied with his own questions. "Do you smell that?"

Letting out a chuckle, Walcott replied, "Yeah, shit show."

Garrett didn't find himself immediately agreeing. Behind him, he heard the noise of a match catching fire, accompanied by a man's arrogant voice.

"Finally!"

As he squinted in the glow of flashlights and watched the match head towards the floor, Garrett figured out what was off about the smell. Although it was diluted with dust, manure, and mud, there was no denying it. Gasoline.

1,946 km east of Jakarta, INDONESIA
18 years, 163 days after Mutation 4

She couldn't go home just yet, not even to recover in peace. There was a reason neither Aydin nor Salar had come looking for her, logically the hospital would be the first place they'd look other than at home. Something was wrong. What if something had happened to them? What if they were caught? Did Ines know something, why had she been looking for them?

Gazing out the window from her recovery room on the second floor of the clinic, Kivran waited for Innaya to finish writing her notes before speaking.

"Firstly, I checked with everyone who worked the front desk the past few days, no one's heard from Aydin or Salar still." Innaya placed the clipboard on the table by the door before swinging the door shut. "Secondly, everything seems to be better. Although I'm not quite sure what sort of symptoms I should be looking for." She took one last peek behind the divider at the other patient before coming to sit beside her friend.

Kivran's anxiety was escalating every day her brother didn't come to look for her. Logically, she figured she should get herself healthy before going out to find him but was having trouble uttering precisely why she had stitches up and down her without raising an indeterminable number of flags.

"Any more thoughts on what the sharp pain was?"

"Oh I don't know, Kivran, maybe it was the giant gash in your abdomen! Why don't you just tell me what it is?"

"It's better for your own good to not know Innaya."

Innaya gave Kivran a blank stare, it was only a matter of time before she figured it out. Although they had been talking the past few days when Kivran was strong enough, there was always someone within earshot hindering the anticipated topic. This was the first time they had been alone since Kivran fell in the doorway almost two weeks ago. Innaya came closer to sit on the edge of the bed, took another look across the confined room at the other patient, and changed her tone to a whisper.

"The antibiotics are only supposed to take four days, Kiv, and you've been here nearly eight. Don't get me wrong, I love having you here, you're way better company than…"

Innaya nodded towards the partition over her left shoulder.

Every time she did this, Kivran felt a pain in her chest. She had grown attached. What was she supposed to do, feel nothing for that fragile woman? Such an illness at such an age had made her recovery longer than average. So long in fact, that Kivran was beginning to worry. Though she'd never voice that, present company included.

Innaya continued, "Promise me you won't let it get so bad that we can't help you with whatever it is you've gotten yourself into. Please."

Before Kivran could respond, an explosive sound filled the room, strong enough to slam the window shutters in the opposite direction. Looking at one another before proceeding, the two women leapt from the bed, Innaya helping Kivran, and craned their necks out as the other patient jolted up, knocking something off the side table with a metallic noise.

Above the shacks, six streets from the clinic in the direction of the Pit, hovered a massive mushroom cloud, fire billowing beneath it, emanating a blinding light probably visible for kilometres.

As the cloud slowly dispersed, Innaya voiced an inquiry Kivran already knew the answer to.

"Isn't that where you live?"

1,946 km east of Jakarta, INDONESIA
Same day

Ringing. That's all he heard, ringing.

Gingerly opening his eyes one at time, Garrett lay stationary beneath rubble consisting of metal sheets, clay bricks, and burning paper. The last of which was clustered near his right hip, billowing in his body's direction. With his right arm pinned underneath an unseeable item above his head, Garrett lifted his neck enough to get a clear view to his lower half.

The fire wasn't visible, just the bricks lying on his bulletproof vest in such a way as to lift the stiff material up, obstructing his intended view. He also felt a trickle of something wet along his neck but chalked it up to sweat. Turning left, he was able to see Walcott bent backwards unnaturally over something he couldn't make out. Walcott's wide eyes reflected another fire nearby. He was already dead.

With the fire getting dangerously uncomfortable now, Garrett closed his eyes and tried to feel each limb. They were thankfully all still responsive, relatively. Using his ankles to start shifting himself out of the rubble, he rolled onto his side trying to avoid the flame and to unpin his arm simultaneously. Looking up, he found Marek on his arm face down, unconscious and covered in flames.

Genuinely perplexed at why he hadn't felt the heat, Garrett sped up the process of trying to get to his feet. Tugging harder than what felt comfortable on his right ankle, he finally crawled out enough to stand.

Looking out over the blast radius, it was difficult to determine just how far the rubble fell due to the smoke around him. Coughing while undoing the vest, Garrett observed multiple fires, the homes on each side of their target contributing to the mess, the south-facing walls of homes across the street knocked down, a few civilians hopping above obstacles heading away from his position. To his south the dump of unidentifiable items looked to be in the worst condition, no doubt forcing the citizens on the opposite side into evacuating as well.

Coming to, Garrett limped his way through a path in the rubble towards a house across the narrow street, bumping into a resident on their way out. Scanning the three-walled room, he found a bed to his right. Grabbing the blanket thrown on the floor next to it, Garrett limped back towards the fires from where he had he had just crawled out of, trying to at least save his friend.

1,946 km east of Jakarta, INDONESIA
Same day

Waiting impatiently by the wedged-open double doors, Kivran limped in and out of the clinic. It had been nearly twenty minutes since the blast. The doctors had decided the ambulance wouldn't be able to clear much of the visible debris, even if there was enough fuel in it, it would just be easier to bring any patients back on foot. The one doctor and two nurses all on duty had grabbed stretchers and medical kits without a moment's hesitation and beelined for the area. They would wake up—if they weren't already awake—the other two nurses on the way. And Kivran had volunteered in her state despite refusals from Innaya. Her state, when we think of her, we're thinking the surgery, but in her mind, her state is that of running on next to no sleep for the past two weeks.

She was terrified of what would occur within her body involuntarily in the night. She would rather lie awake in a puddle of anxious sweat and apocalyptic-level dread than face that test.

Shifting past the pile of clean sheets, gauze, and spare IV drips, she hoped today wasn't the day her brother and cousin decided to come back. Unintentionally flinching upon feeling a pang in her abdomen, Kivran tightened her hair elastic. Best give her body something else to focus its pain on, and subconsciously inhaled deeply. She was expecting crisp air but began coughing as smoke fumes and dust rushed in.

Someone came into view, down the narrow street less than two blocks away. Holding a stretcher behind him, Dr. Thi led the group, followed by Innaya holding the tail of the same stretcher, and then followed quite closely by the two other nurses. One of whom was pacing alongside the second stretcher wrapping something around the patient's arm, the other nurse was dividing the weight of this stretcher with a man Kivran didn't recognize, at least not in the dark. Bringing up the tail end of the party were two other men she didn't know, one holding the weight of the other as they shuffled along in the dark. The fire was behind them, casting a shadow in front of the oddly formed group.

At least one of the patients was shouting as they passed Kivran in the doorway. Standing to one side, she saw the man on the first stretcher had much of the sleeves of his shirt and clumps of his pants burned into the flesh beneath. He was holding one of his hands up to his left eye. Kivran could see multiple streams of blood seeping through the fingers as he passed underneath the fluorescent lobby lights heading towards the operating room. On the second stretcher, the man didn't appear to be in worse condition than the first, however, the flesh on his entire right arm was asunder, someone had cut the tattered sleeve up towards the shoulders, stopping just at the unfastened bulletproof vest. It was evident he had trouble breathing. Gasping and frantically thrashing on the stretcher, Kivran came to in time to hold his left side down and allow the other nurse, Dian, some room to work with.

"Kivran, can you please sedate him?"

Nodding, Kivran kept one hand on the man's shoulder and used her other hand to grab a syringe in the medical kit lying atop the clean sheets.

"Wait, hang on!"

Thi returned, taking over Kivran's station and signalling for her to look after the remaining two men. The second stretcher disappeared behind the same doors as the first, patient still thrashing.

Turning back to the other men, they seemed in better condition than their comrades. One man helped the other settle into a chair before taking one himself, each breathing heavy and reeking of what can only be described as, unfortunately, burning meat.

Grabbing the still-open medical kit and a set of gloves, she knelt beside the one clutching his left leg. All along the dark material sat glistening embedded pieces of metal. She began to pull out the larger ones with her hands, the man winced but didn't budge.

As she switched to a set of tweezers to pull out the smaller pieces, she noticed the other man sitting two seats down. Slouching low in the chair, he had his hand firmly clasped on the right hip. Still unsure of what happened, not wanting to raise alarms and not having heard any of these strangers speak, she thought it best to maintain the silence. Taking a moment though, she took note of their garb. Dressed in black from head to toe, bulletproof vests, heavy military-style shoes. What had they been doing at her home?

Finishing with the shrapnel, Kivran made a vertical cut in the pant leg allowing her unobstructed access to the lacerations. Dousing a piece of gauze in rubbing alcohol, she clinched it in the tweezers, making her way up the leg whilst cleaning each cut. This patient was now leaning with his head rested against the wall, eyes closed, he seemed to be asleep. Following the cleaning, she proceeded to wrap gauze around the entirety of the leg; there were too many lacerations for individual bandages. Once done, she looked up to see whether the man knew his current state—he was still stationary.

Shifting, she took the seat between the immobile man and the one clenching his hip, she moved her attention to the latter. Hovering her hands over his, seeing the mixture of soot and blood caked on them, she attempted to indicate she could now take a look. Releasing his grip, he tilted his upper body away from Kivran, giving her free rein. She lifted his shirt expecting a similar shrapnel injury, taking note of no bulletproof vest on him. An area approximately six inches in width and four inches in visible length was burned, flesh peeling off in clumps. Taking a look back at the inside of the shirt, she had sure enough inadvertently peeled some flesh off. Feeling his eyes on her the entire time, Kivran met his gaze. An amused face greeted her. Amber eyes, blackened face with streaks of sweat streaming down, leaving clear lines in its wake, filthy hair pushed up and away from the face. She was questioning how he hadn't expressed pain. Even she had involuntarily felt a stitch in her abdomen near her own incision at the sight.

He held her gaze with heavy eyes for a moment as she sat still, taking in the sight before her and the gentle wheezing of the man behind her. He could feel the sorrow in her eyes—at least that's what she sensed because he broke the silence in a deep voice. In clear English and a slight American Southern accent, he spoke.

"Don't worry, miss."

Dropping her eyes back on the injury, Kivran's mind began to race. Seated there in the clinic lobby amongst military-looking personnel clearly not from around here, with no visible signs of affiliation, and only now registering the gun strapped to the upper thigh of the man beside her telling her not to worry, Kivran began, albeit to her own dismay, to nurse the very logical notion that her brother wasn't coming back.

1,946 km east of Jakarta, INDONESIA
18 years, 166 days after Mutation 4

At exactly 4:06 p.m., a post was uploaded. The post was made on an independent site focusing on staging protests in Berlin, Germany. The reason for these protests were primarily government policies. This particular post addressed the secretive meetings happening all over Europe with World Health Organization briefings at the helm.

Post Title: Why Governments Discuss Their Citizens' Health Behind Closed Doors

Author: Albano Silnor

Posts such as these had been popping up recently on various regional sites, all posted by one user, all aimed at one idea: there is an epidemic of sorts, building up, readying itself to wipe out a third of the world's population and change the very face of modern medicine for the worse—and the government was the one guarding its gate. The infection in question could be released by the government whenever it so pleased. Which government you ask? Can't say—the author never specifies. What the author primarily rambles on and on about, however, is why the democratic government—again the proverbial government—hasn't addressed the fact that, and I'll paraphrase here: they make dangerous deals, putting the lives of innocent constituents on the line, communions in secret alleys; cult-like behaviour from people who were to be accountable to the very people they were preparing to wipe off the face of the Earth.

The author's got a flare for the dramatic, evidently.

No sources were ever cited, no real-life experience was ever mentioned in any post, just the guarded gate and the looming health crises behind it. The comments section was everything you'd expect: a medley of conspiracy theorists and practical, logical skeptics, with just a healthy dosage of trolls.

In hindsight, it became glaringly obvious that something was, in fact, a stir in the medical community. At the time, however, a call to protest by a semi-lunatic on the Internet wasn't quite enough to rile up the masses. It's a shame really, if only the author's gratification had been satisfied with a measly protest, he wouldn't have escalated his behaviour. If only.

Albano—remember him.

1,946 km east of Jakarta, INDONESIA
18 years, 168 days after Mutation 4

"Do you think they blew up another farm?"

Kivran continued tracing Innaya's laid-out bandages, trying to smooth them out as much as possible, but paying more attention to her friend.

"What?"

"You know, a farm. Like the one a while back."

Being the only ones on duty during this particular night shift, they were on their last round for the night, redressing the severely burned patient in room three. Correction: only Innaya was on duty, Kivran happened to still be in the intermediate state of being a patient herself and being discharged. In a sense, at least. And besides, she didn't mind the graveyard shift in the least—it's not as though she was going to sleep anyway. Inadvertently, she thought of Aydin and how he'd be upset if he ever found out she was behaving this way again.

Innaya continued at her friend's silence. "There used to be a farm just down by the abandoned pit, the Pit. It blew up like twenty years ago, complete mess. My mom tells me that's the reason the abandoned pit is just an abandoned pit—the military owns that land. I'm telling you, that's why they're here."

The woman, with her hands tangled in gauze, nodded in the general direction of the rest of the small room. Along with their current patient, there was one other stationed in here, the one with a burned hip.

"That's no farm, that place is a dumping ground for anything and everything under the sun."

"What if it's hidden, though?" The excitement in the other woman's voice was escalating.

"Don't be ridiculous, Innaya." Smoothing out the last bit of gauze, Kivran pinned down the ends and tucked the arm underneath a sheet covering the patient. The night was warm on its own, but laying eyes on the man had become unsettling, and thus the nurses had silently agreed to always cover him up.

Removing her own gloves and waiting for the other nurse to remove hers, Kivran continued, "Besides, if that was true, maybe you should be a little more careful when it comes to who you throw such theories around."

Kivran kept her head down, believing she had seen the man at the opposite end of the room stir in his bed from her peripherals. Following a moment, she looked up to find two of Innaya's fingers resting on the newly re-bandaged soldier's bare left upper arm, sheet thrown slightly aside. From her position, Kivran could see about two inches above those fingers was a perfectly circular piece of flesh missing.

Why did this man have this particular scar?

"Oh, you mean like this slab here?" Innaya pushed her fingers deeper into the man's flesh. Kivran felt a wince inside herself. "Yeah, I'm sure my theories cause me a real threat here, Kiv."

Fortunately enough, it was Kivran herself who had given him painkillers a couple of hours ago, enough to last him through the night. Hopefully. Though he hadn't woken since being admitted, she didn't want him to be in pain in the event that he did come to.

Handing her gloves inside out to Kivran, Innaya left the room, ready to settle in and do nothing for the remainder of this shift. Following her departure, Kivran shifted closer to the man's upper arm, tossing the gloves in a garbage can close by. Taking a glance towards the open door before proceeding, she lifted a portion of the patient's makeshift gown's sleeve to get a clear view.

There, in plain sight underneath the artificial lights: a polio vaccine scar. It had been eradicated decades ago, and possibly before this man was born. Regardless of its eradication, this method of vaccination delivery had died out eons ago. Why would he have such a thing?

Running a bare singular finger over the circle, she felt the smooth, hairless patch. Confirming to herself that this was no newly enacted scar but rather done years ago. Perhaps childhood, judging by the way the surrounding skin healed and stretched, merging with the unsullied skin in its vicinity.

"He usually likes to be awake for that sort of touching."

Jumping slightly and retreated her hand in one simultaneous motion, Kivran was startled at a voice just above a whisper. Turning around, she saw the other patient perched up on his forearms smirking at her, clearly amused.

Mentally straightening herself, she tucked her hands into the pockets of her uniform, gently holding the stitches on her abdomen as though her very insides might begin to leak out. She was ready for any further dialogue coming her way.

It never came. The man just lay there, unable to wipe the smirk off his face and holding in a chuckle, evidently waiting for her to speak.

She never did. Waiting a moment longer than she should have, Kivran made her way out of the room with the man's eyes still on her and his heavy drawl still resonating within.

1,946 km east of Jakarta, **INDONESIA**
18 years, 170 days after Mutation 4

Garrett had never been in love, and he wasn't now. But there was something about the woman preparing to redress his burns that infatuated him. He couldn't quite put his finger on it though, like an itch on the roof of your mouth. She had thick, shiny, light brown hair that fell just past her shoulders. Always had it up, though it seemed to weigh too much for her elastic. Her skin was tanned and smooth to the touch. Then again, anything would feel smooth in comparison to his coarse, burned palms. The injury was solely from his, thankfully successful, attempt at getting Marek out of the rubble. The woman had been stingy when it came to showing any emotions towards him. He could hear her with others in the hospital holding an expressive conversation but never with him. Her eyes always seemed to give her away, though, because every time she came near him, they softened as if she felt his pain. He imagined this was likely how people saw him from the outside, people he deemed insignificant enough to iterate emotion towards. It felt lonesome on the receiving end.

She also happened to be the only one on staff who could understand him completely and vice versa. Though he knew not a lick of Indonesian, she ended up being fluent in English. An underlying accent would surface every few syllables or so, he hadn't been able to pin it down yet. The only other person who had come close to potentially sustaining a conversation with Garrett wasn't someone he wanted to sustain one with:

that imbecile doctor. Throwing in big words into an English sentence doesn't automatically convey brilliance, though it'd be a challenge to explain this to that man.

Having lost track of time for quite a few days, Garrett had eventually calculated and gathered enough information to be strategically aware of his surroundings. His hip was severely burned, his hands slightly less so, and he had inhaled a significant amount of black smoke before the nurses arrived at the target building to find him trying to put out the flames consuming Marek. In his imagination, he had a heroic image of him saving his friend with grace and efficiency, but he knew it was more along the lines of him shouting for the fire to be put itself out than him doing so.

Just a few days ago, he had been able to walk through the small hallways and determine the following, as well:

1. Marek was alive, though he had burns all along his limbs, as well as a burst blood vessel close to his left eye; he had spiralled into a coma shortly after arriving at the hospital;

2. Keuhl had some manner of shrapnel embedded, allegedly, in his leg and suffered a severe hit to the head during the explosion;

3. Walcott had died at the scene before anyone had arrived; and

4. There were two other men from the co-operating team within the hospital, but Garrett knew little about them and made no exhaustive effort to find out. For all he

knew, those men had already been released. This was their home, after all.

The final item on his mind couldn't have been clarified in any manner from walking around the small hospital, however: how they were getting out of here.

He knew it'd be best for Marek to make the first communication, in whichever manner, since it was him who corresponded with the local officials and the base on the unit's behalf, but he also knew Marek wasn't currently in any state to be communicating the circumstances effectively. Besides, the man hadn't regained consciousness since that night.

Cautious in terms of what was discussed within these walls, Garrett deliberately avoided conversing with anyone regarding what was observed in the building prior to its explosion. If they had seen anything in the vein of what he himself saw, someone needed to be notified immediately. There was no way of knowing for sure now if this was the only such facility in the region, or who else may have been involved in the endeavour. The source didn't seem all too reliable or exhaustive. He involuntarily thought of that woman's plastered smile before drifting his thoughts to Odeli. Luckily, he was near certain that if he himself couldn't find a way to get word out, Odeli would find them— hell or high water.

Currently, however, with this woman in his vicinity, he didn't dwell on his handsome-in-his-own-right companion. He needed to focus on this particular interaction, get as much information on the circumstances as she'd allow.

Garrett watched as she held an elastic between her teeth, hands occupied with gathering her hair, and eyes downward at the notes his doctor had taken last night. He found himself eager to hold her gaze once more.

1,946 km east of Jakarta, INDONESIA
Same day

Similar to her cautious footing around Marek's cot, Kivran moved from the right side of Garrett's bed towards the left while tying her hair. She was scheduled to redress his abdominal burn wounds and minor neck lacerations today. She maintained the same demeanour for the other foreign men currently occupying the facility, she desired nothing more than to complete the job as efficiently as possible.

She couldn't shake the image of blood on these men's hands. They had been scrubbed countless times since that night, but the red tinge persisted. Right? She wasn't imagining that. Hopefully. She didn't dare speculate to whom each drop of blood belonged to.

Settling on tending to the neck wound first, Kivran took a set of clean gloves out of the box by the main door and snapped them on. Feeling the patient's eyes on her, she gestured to his neck without a word.

Garrett slightly tilted his head to the right, giving her clearer access to his afflicted area. She wondered just how long he had been out here, tan lines ran along his collar bones and upper arms, separating the olive-stained skin perfectly. Upon the neck, the skin illustrated signs of healing for the most part, around the multiple small puncture wounds. She had been mentally kicking herself since the day of the blast; she should have seen these wounds in time.

Always following this mental kick, however was a ricocheting thought: should she feel for someone who may be responsible for tearing her home asunder?

There was also that looming question of the blood.

"How is it?" he asked, breaking the silence. She watched the punctures move as he spoke.

Hesitating for an instance, Kivran knew it would be best to tell him the truth on the chance that this was perhaps a manner in which to test her. For what? She couldn't determine, but empathetic bedside manners didn't seem the route. His tone made that clear enough.

"These lacerations have been healing at an expected rate. The few stitches present do appear strained, so a rest in movement would be recommended. However, there are no visible signs of infections, thus the recommendation to limit movements is a conversation that should best be had with your doctor."

Kivran once read in a psychology book, stolen by Salar from his parents' clinic, and, in turn, stolen by her, that barring any extenuating circumstances that alter the muscular makeup of the visage, an involuntary smile cannot be formed on just one side of the face. An involuntary smile will instinctively pull the muscles surrounding the mouth and cheekbones at an even rate, causing a smile to spread on both sides of the face at virtually the same rate. A smile forming on one side of the face can only be the result of a voluntary movement of muscle. This information was somewhere within the chapter detailing the physical indications of psychopathic and sociopathic individuals. It was quite an outdated text and a largely disproven theory.

Finishing her statement, Kivran looked from the neck to the soldier's face and found a smile spread evenly on both sides. She watched his eyes as he looked from her right eye to her left and back. To her surprise, she didn't feel scrutinized but rather comfortable.

"Well, I can't fault you for your honesty," he stated through the smile.

Knowing she had done everything by textbook standards, with the exception of the aforementioned oversight of the neck, Kivran had no idea what he could, in fact, fault her on. What was she doing wrong?

Unable to contain herself, she stopped mid-redressing and matched the man's gaze. "What would you fault me on?"

Moving his neck back to indicate he was taken aback by the question and immediately wincing at the pain, he instinctively reflexed a hand towards the bandages. Kivran moved hers in the nick of time as they grazed each other on their directed paths.

"Sorry." Hand hovering over his neck, he apologized.

Kivran shook her head, cautiously moving her hands back to finish the work. "Don't worry, miss."

She regretted the words as soon as the string ended. She'd forgotten where she was and who she was interacting with for an instant. Familiarity was the last thing she needed to evoke in herself.

Innaya's voice rang out in her mind, *Don't get attached.*

She could see the man with his mouth open in mock shock out of her peripherals, didn't acknowledge it, though. Kivran finished the neck bandages and took her materials with her to the other side of the bed, all the while refusing to look at his face.

As she unwound fresh gauze, he lifted his shirt just enough to expose the previous dressing. Although his smile remained, he held up his side of the silence and allowed Kivran to go about the remainder of her business. For the first time in quite a while, she was grateful.

1,946 km east of Jakarta, INDONESIA
18 years, 171 days after Mutation 4

He waited for the dead of night on this day for two reasons:

1.   Fewer witnesses, especially the nurse at the front desk, the disconnected one who needed sirens accompanied by flashing red lights to go off before she'd pay attention to anything; and

2.   The ringing emanating in his ears the night he arrived hindered his ability to map out where he'd come from and where he was going. If he went by night rather than broad daylight, the chances of him recalling something would hopefully increase. Hopefully.

Stepping out the hospital's threshold, Garrett observed the alleys to his left and right looking for something that would jog a memory. He remembered seeing the dark-haired nurse standing in a doorway to his left that night. He couldn't have misremembered this of all things.

Garrett went right.

Having borrowed Keuhl's crutch for this outing, he was going to have it back in Keuhl's room before he noticed, no sweat. The clinic wasn't equipped with a sufficient amount, go figure. Garrett hoped to accomplish this mission at a reasonable rate. The last thing he needed was to shuffle along at a snail's pace, exposing himself for a longer period of time to an unknown number of eyes.

Exotic scents overpowered his senses as he proceeded along. Having spent next to no time in this region of the world, Garrett took each scent in deeply. Spending a handful of nights at a military base in mainland China wasn't really being counted here. That, and the only thing he'd been able to smell the past few days were disinfectants and burned nose hair.

It was oddly comforting to believe these people existed around him, going about their lives but not interacting with him. It really was his favourite type of human interaction: at arm's length and indirect.

Having come south two blocks, Garrett determined he had to turn. While a handful of lights sprinkled the alley directly in front of him, there was darkness to his left. And a burning scent.

Turning left, he slowed his pace now, attempting to observe as much of the scene as permitted. Other than the smell, the first item catching his attention was the coarse dirt beneath his feet. Unable to see the details on the ground, he continued farther down this alley. The next item he came across were scattered bricks, some still intact, most in pieces. They littered his path as he squinted whilst stepping forth.

He felt as though he'd walked farther than should have been necessary. This walk felt much longer than the one from a few nights ago. Deciding to stop and get his bearings by the next alleyway, which was emanating a heavy glow, Garrett made the decision to take his time now. He may not get the opportunity to return here for a round two.

Bending down on his good side while keeping the other hip straight, he bent at each step trying to make out any items scattered among the bricks. This was much more difficult than he initially anticipated. He needed light.

Tilting his head back out of frustration and pain, he was somewhat regretting his decision to venture out in the dark. Noticing the stars, he felt soothed slightly. As far as he could see in any direction, stars shone. He felt comforted.

Looking back down at the alley, he figured he might as well start close to a light source and hope for the best. Once again taking off around and over debris, he ventured over to the glow.

Why hadn't he done this earlier?

What he took for a bend in the street was actually a blast radius carrying through the light from the still-burning garbage pile to its south. Shit show indeed.

Mounds of rubble now occupied the space where homes once sat, the scene was unrecognizable from a few nights ago when all they came to do was detain anyone in a particular home. Deducing where the target home was most likely located, Garrett walked closer to the courtyard clearing.

The bodies were gone. Every single one of them. Though traces of torn uniforms remained, no physical bodies did.

Looking over both his shoulders, he had to make sure no one was watching him. Who had come for the dead soldiers? There were no clearly illuminated signs of dragged cadavers. None of the men in the hospital had come out here yet to order an extraction. Nor communicated with the closest base in any way, only Keuhl had a comms device but it had no remaining battery. Even after all this time, that boy was far from prepared for field dispatch. Someone needed to get word out though, it had been almost a week now. That's what he was here for.

Stepping around a brick partition somehow still erect, Garrett moved towards a familiar looking metal sheet beneath which he had stored his bulletproof vest. A part of him didn't anticipate it still being there. He did anticipate the bodies, however.

Balancing on his good hip, he used the crutch to shove the sheet out of the way to reveal a small pocket of space. This is where he'd woken up after the blast, and where his vest now sat. He wasn't anticipating gunfire at this point, but he kept his satellite phone clipped to the vest and that's precisely what he needed.

Lowering himself do to sit on the brick partition, he unclipped the comms device and tossed the vest at his feet. Making one last sweep over the area for any prying eyes, Garrett switched the device on from sleep mode.

A blue light instantly started flickering at the top while the screen indicated it was searching for a signal source to pick up. Coughing into his sleeve to muffle the noise, he had exhausted himself. If the device didn't get a signal soon, he'd have to make his way back. He didn't like the idea of having to communicate with the base back at the hospital where eyes and ears could be around every corner, but if it came to that, so be it.

Feeling the vibration before the screen switched, he knew he'd gotten what he needed. There was only one source available to which the comms automatically connected: JM16. The base coalitioned by Japanese and

Chinese military forces near the southeast coast of China and manned almost exclusively by WHO personnel. Where he'd been deployed from but unfortunately not where Odeli currently sat.

Opening up the messages, Garrett set about communicating with JM16 as he regretted Marek's decision to not leave a comms device exclusively with Odeli.

Garrett: Major Asher OF-3 requesting evac. estimated 1,900 klicks east of CGK. 3 men, Colonel incapacitated. Mission CGK-Allo, unsuccessful.

He didn't know who would be on the other end of the line, he needed to relay titles for them to understand the gravity of the situation.

Leaning over to rest his forearm on the wall and perhaps release some stress on this hip, he waited for the reply. Moments passed with nothing, Garrett began drifting his attention towards the fire. The hue was off, not your regular run-of-the-mill fire. A light blue tinge hung in the air around the flames, ebbing with the light breeze.

He felt his hand vibrate.

> JM16: No record of mission. Confirm and state again.

> Garrett: CGK-Allo

Another few moments passed with nothing. Pushing himself up and off the wall, making his way towards the flame. A familiar odour became stronger as he came closer. Sulphur. Growing up in Iceland, if he couldn't recognize sulphur, he couldn't recognize the back of his own hand. Cautiously stepping nearer until he reached the edge of the elevated ground with just the garbage below, he was met with a glow covering the base of the trench. Not the fire. This was a liquid-like substance covering much of the floor, inflammable from the looks of it. The same substance that had been seeping below his feet the night of the blast, yet the hue differed.

His hand vibrated again.

> JM16: Confirmed. Tracking position now. Evac ETA 52.5 hours. Confirm men will be ready.

> Garrett: Confirmed. Base know local members cannot be found. 4 men.

> JM16: Local members critical to mission?

> Garrett: Negative. All 3 unit men alive but injured, 1 deceased but unable to be located.

> JM16: Cannot be located in 52.5 hours?

> Garrett: Will attempt.

> JM16: Confirmed. Preliminary quarantine measures to be implemented upon arrival.

> Garrett: No issue present to warrant quarantine.

> JM16: Mission unsuccessful - you cannot have enough information to confirm this. Evac arriving in 52.5 hours.

> <conversation terminated 0103>

He looked down at the comms device, thumb still poised to continue typing. He'd never cared enough to defy orders.

Slipping the device into a pocket, Garrett turned his back on the flame and headed back towards the wall. Lifting his vest, he slipped the upper part of the crutch through one of the arm holes and tucked it between his arm and torso. Looking down to watch his step, he headed back towards the hospital. Under the faint light behind him, he saw dark patches covering his clothes and crutch. He figured it was safe to say he was once more covered in blood and soot.

**1,946 km east of Jakarta, INDONESIA
18 years, 172 days after Mutation 4**

Manning the front desk of the clinic was by far the best rotational position in all the nurses' opinions, since it was probably the easiest, but chiefly because it was directly by the fan. It was Kivran's rotation at the desk today. She sat there with her face more or less buried in the fan, staring through the grate towards one of the wedged-open front doors of the clinic.

It had been raining since late evening, a pattern her brother once described as "the most beautiful sound there is." She'd never found similar comfort in it, and more so now, the noise irritated her.

Earlier that day, Kivran felt strong enough to venture out two blocks away from the hospital. Venture home. Or what remained, which wasn't much.

Late afternoon, she expected the neighbourhood to sustain a healthy buzz of activity, but was greeted with an eerie silence. The dust remained visibly unsettled even before she saw the debris. No residents in sight. Just disheveled homes. Disheveled lives.

Taking a moment to soak in the view, Kivran stood across the street from her home, mesmerized by the scattered bricks every which way. Black soot lined any wall still standing, the Pit still sustained a healthy flame to add ambiance to the post-apocalyptic-like scene before her, in the dulled colours of her broken home were sprinkled bright points. Vegetables flung from the market next door.

Those young children, those poor young children.

Cautiously meandering through the rubble, Kivran walked towards the centre of her home. She didn't possess enough specific knowledge to determine where the blast had occurred, but judging from the lack of clutter and displaced oxygen tanks in Aydin's lab, it was safe to make a guess.

Moving farther towards the said lab, she noticed a trail of thick blood running between crevices. It wasn't dried, which meant it couldn't have been from the soldiers. Someone was alive. Not bothering with the tears or the pain in her side, Kivran manoeuvred over bricks and lifted a metal sheet to follow the trail.

It was just the upturned freezer.

Having tipped over at some point, the metal sheet's removal exposed Kivran to the stench of rotting animal organs within. Her chest tightened. It wasn't until just now that she truly felt alone. She shouldn't've taken Aydin's ambition for granted. How many people have family who loves them to such an extent? Had she truly ever told him she loved him? Or thanked him? Did it come across as genuine? Did he believe her *if* she had said these things?

It's funny, the things you remember at the weirdest of times. One of the few memories she still recalled from her childhood was one in which Aydin saved her. Although he'd said it was the same day their mother had passed, Kivran couldn't remember feeling the sadness that would've accompanied such an event. What she did remember, however, was waking up pinned underneath something. Having tried to wiggle herself free and failed, Kivran couldn't think of anything to do except cry. Unfortunately for her, there were others around her crying as well. Mass amounts of people crying in every direction she looked, drowning her out. So she wailed louder.

Finally, she caught the attention of her brother kneeling not too far from her. He was also crying, though not as aggressively. Kivran stretched her arm out towards him, wanting him to pick her up and the very instant she did so, he rushed to her side. Without hesitation and without a second's thought, Aydin had come to save Kivran.

That's how she remembered it. Her brother never told his side of the story, but how could it be much different? Though never voicing it, Kivran was always thankful Aydin had heard her in that swarm of people. That he'd found her.

She couldn't figure out if she was thankful or not for his not being here now in this mess. Regardless, she wanted him here.

Paying no mind to the decaying odour now mingling with the burning smell, Kivran sat down beside the trail and watched the Pit burn. She sat here as the sun began to set to her right, illuminating the mountain of rubble upon which she sat.

Allowing her eyes to become hazy from the tears, her sight fell upon a thin piece of paper pinned under an unrecognizable object. Stretching forward from her position, Kivran gently slid the paper out. Though little light remained, her memory filled in any blanks as to what she was looking at to reveal the picture of a skyline her mother had adored. Thinking nothing of it, she placed the paper onto her knees and smoothed out the creases before she tenderly folded the picture.

Kivran clasped it in her fist the entire way back to the hospital. Genuinely no longer caring as to who witnessed her in this state of tears and filthy attire. Then again, there was no one to actually witness her.

Upon crossing the threshold of the hospital, she'd become absentminded in her actions. Without thought, she had washed her face, changed into a clean uniform, and sat herself in front of the desk as if it were a regular shift for her. She vaguely recalled a fellow nurse speaking to her but found no retained memories of the encounter.

Now that her lower body was becoming numb, abdomen throbbing intolerably after having remained stationary and hunched over the desk for an indeterminable amount of time, Kivran was becoming aware of her state.

Turning to the staircase at a dragging noise, Kivran saw one of the foreign men coming down. He was always wandering about the clinic whenever he got a chance; it made the entire staff uneasy. As no one had offered their names, and their comrades deliberately evaded calling each other, the staff resorted to nicknames as markers for each. This one was Limp. He was the one Kivran removed shrapnel from, following which he had acquired a limp. Clearly these nicknames were only used between staff.

Dragging his right side along the wall while utilizing the crutch on his left, he slowly made his way down. Each step letting out a wince. It didn't sound authentic. Kivran turned back to the fan before he knew she was watching.

She could hear his shuffle towards the front door. Soon enough, he entered Kivran's line of vision, leaning himself against the door frame looking out.

"If only it had rained like this that day, we may not be here."

He was baiting her. He wanted her to ask "which day" and "what happened." It took an ineffable amount of power for Kivran to not encourage this conversation. As desperately as she wanted to know what happened, she didn't want to be the one to ask the questions. It'd be a test she felt she'd fail.

Looking back at her, Limp raised his eyebrows evidently waiting for her to say something. She let him down.

Turning back around, he continued without encouragement. "It was utterly incredible, feeling the air get sucked out of the room, yet feeling everything almost imploding around me at the same time. You speak English, right? I'm surprised I made it out."

Kivran felt nauseous.

"Have you ever been in a dangerous situation like that? I mean, it really makes you think. I could have died in that God-awful place. Yet here I stand. Isn't it a bit humorous as well?"

She didn't think she could keep still or silent any longer. The incessant rain, the high-pitched voice of this disgusting human, the pulsing within her, the image of blood now riddled around her home. It was going to spill over.

Limp began to turn his neck, Kivran prepared herself to stand, but he never looked at her. Instead, he glanced over towards the stairway.

"Easy on the self-pity there."

Barring much thought, Kivran knew it was the man with the disfigured hip who spoke. He sounded quite close to her.

"Just reliving the glory days." Limp had turned around entirely, making eye contact with the man standing to the right of Kivran from the feel of it.

Weak footsteps moved closer. "That's not how that cliché works. I'm not your superior, but I suggest you stop reliving and get back to your room."

With a nod, and surprisingly without a retort, the first man hobbled out of view following which were a few moments when the remaining two individuals listened patiently until the man reached the second floor.

Attempting to alleviate some of that nausea, Kivran stretched her legs out underneath the table. The other man walked farther into view, not looking at her though.

"I'd apologize for him but I've already got a full-time job."

Kivran let out a small chuckle that vibrated against the fan's wings, distorting the sound and ruffling the paper bag of candy left by the other nurses sitting next to her. Leaning back from the noise, she began to brace herself to turn in attention but was stopped short.

"Don't get up for me, you can remain as you are. I'm just here to try out some new material. All you'd have to do is laugh."

"Sorry." Wiggling her toes to regain feeling, she tried to push the image of her home imploding towards the back of her mind. "I may not be the best person to do that just now."

"Don't apologize."

Another few minutes passed with them remaining as they were accompanied by the rain's patter and the fan's buzzing filling the silence.

As the throbbing in her side ceased, Kivran slouched a tad, relaxing despite her circumstances.

Hearing the intake of a deep breath, she instinctively glanced at its direction. The man stood still staring out the open door, arms crossed over chest, hair weighed down from sweat, ill-fitting sweatpants and T-shirt ruffling in the slight breeze. The other nurses had taken to calling him Two Hip—with one hip being burned and the other perfectly intact. Kivran hadn't caught on to it; she didn't really call him anything.

"You lived there, didn't you?"

Kivran's breath hitched in her throat. He turned his head towards her.

"I saw you come back, clothing riddled with blood and soot. There's not many places around here you could exit looking like that. Or so I gather. So I'm guessing you lived in one of those homes. One of the ones that were destroyed."

She felt like she hadn't blinked in minutes. What could he do knowing this information for certain? She'd rather not take this test than fail it.

So she blinked and left the question unanswered.

The man turned back towards the door. "It's okay, silence is a sufficient answer. My other question would be what happened to the man who died? What did you do with his body?"

She remained silent, anger searing through her veins.

"Why steal the body, what good could come of it? It's heinous."

Kivran stood up, allowing the impulse to consume her. His nonchalant tone aggravated her without reason just now. "Heinous?! You have the audacity to speak about heinous acts to us? Yeah, I did live in one of those homes. The ones you thought it'd be a brilliant idea to raze to the ground, paying no mind to who was inside. One of those."

He turned back, this time limping towards her. "It wasn't deliberate, and I'm sorry it happened. We paid for it, same as you."

"Not same as me! Because from what I gather, you all agreed to come here and potentially die in a firefight of sorts but we didn't. We lived here in peace; we don't live our lives expecting to be blown asunder every other day of week. And if the body you're looking for is gone, don't you think ours are too? We're not morally deranged, we buried them for their own dignity. We haven't hidden your man away in our back pocket to pull out when we so desire—he's at the cemetery, where he belongs. That's where they all end up!" The final sentence carried a different weight within her, the "they" she was referring to was Aydin and Salar. She didn't even know they were deceased for certain, and the idea that she was already assuming they were ate away at her.

Though her legs remained faintly numb, and she had to brace against the desk to keep upright, Kivran hadn't felt her blood course this fast in weeks. She was furious at the foreigners in her hospital, every single one of them.

The man nodded, looking down he seemed to collect his thoughts before replying. "And how do you gather that? That we all agreed to come here and potentially die?"

He looked back up at her. This had to be rhetorical question, anyone in their right mind could come to this conclusion.

She answered to humour him. "Because I saw you come in, all black clothing not riddled with identifiable labels but with bulletproof vests and various weapons. There's not many kinds of people who would enter a place looking like that."

Without realizing, her tone had become hushed yet urgent as if this was a secret. However, she knew full well the rest of the staff had deduced this as well.

Surprisingly, the crease between the man's eyebrows that had been there moments ago faded and a smirk spread on him.

"You're mocking me."

Kivran crossed her arms now, not open to humouring him any longer.

"But I'll allow it, I can at least hold up a conversation with you easily." Unfolding his arms, he outstretched one, looking to shake her hand. "The name's Garrett."

Her arms remained as before; she didn't quite feel like being touched just now. "Kivran."

Retracting his hand, the man nodded while turning to leave. "That's quite an enchanting name, Kivran."

She watched him reach the stairs and begin to take them one at a time at a sluggish pace. Both feet resting on one step before continuing on to the next.

"Don't worry, I'm not trying to flatter you."

Kivran's limbs were finally tingling back to consciousness.

"I can see that'd get us nowhere. Hell, it might even set you and I back, Kivran."

When she could no longer see him, Kivran turned back to the open door. The rain continued, however, she didn't feel irritated by its pattering any longer. In fact, she could have sworn it was rhythmic.

1,946 km east of Jakarta, INDONESIA
18 years, 173 days after Mutation 4

She tried to distract herself, focusing on the woman in front of her. They were making their way to the transport, and Tamsin was desperately trying to keep her heart rate down.

Odeli as supposed to have returned by now, surely. They didn't know a thing about each other's schedules but he'd mentioned this in passing, Odeli had said they would return in a few days. It had been ten.

There was no point in getting herself wound up over this, he'd return when he returned and they'd cross paths when they crossed paths. *It wasn't that serious* she kept reciting to herself.

"What's the matter?" The woman in front of her spoke. She had already situated herself in the transport, now looking down at Tamsin who hadn't even stepped aboard yet.

She made a split-second decision, her heartbeat catching in her throat. "How long until wheels up?"

"About two minutes, just waiting on the rookie to pack up. Why?"

"I'll be right back, don't leave without me." Her feet were already set in motion before she finished speaking, no attention was given to the response from behind her.

Breaking into a run, she rushed to the main communications room. It was three in the morning, she encountered no one on the way and only one man stationed within, who bolted upright in his chair as Tamsin came storming in. The man had clearly dozed off, the motion sensors didn't kick in the lights until she entered. He immediately stumbled against the new ambiance.

She tried to control her voice, stop herself from stuttering, something she had a habit of doing when nervous. "Have you had any recent communication from a deployed WHO unit?"

The man scrolled through his screen, puzzled look on his young face. "I don't know, maybe. I only just got here no—"

"Move!" Pivoting to the opposite side of the table, she nudged the man out of the way to have a clear view of the screen.

"I don't think DWBs are privy to this information."

"You'd think right." Her eyes skimmed frantically through the log.

"You're gonna get me in trouble for this one, yeah?"

There. Incoming message two days ago. *Extraction requested. Cleared. ETA at base 1520.*

She hadn't even realized she had been clenching all her muscles until now as she let her shoulders fall down, relieved. At least to an extent. Extraction, that meant something had gone wrong, and their original evacuation plan would no longer suffice.

Letting the man tilt back into his previous position, Tamsin left him, now with a worried stare. Stepping back into the dark of dusk, she hurried back to transport. There was a refugee camp with a potential Ebola outbreak they needed to assist with—on the south eastern border of Turkey.

1,946 km east of Jakarta, INDONESIA
Same day

She had passed some time between the last nurse checking on her and now, when Kivran had walked to her bedside upon not hearing the woman's usual wheezing during the night.

The woman lay there, the breeze from the ajar window lightly ruffling her nightgown, a thin layer of sweat glistening on her face in the moonlight. Kivran turned over one of the woman's hands so that the palm was facing up, she then placed her hand on top, loosely holding it. With her free hand, Kivran took a tissue from the bedside and began to pat away the sweat. Once done, she used the same tissue to move strands of hair off the woman's face so she may clearly look upon her.

What a thing: to die alone.

Kivran felt that tightening in her chest once more, her breath began to quicken. She was panicking, what if she died like this? Alone?

Allowing herself to quietly sob, she lost her footing as her legs could no longer bear the weight of her heart, and knelt beside the woman, still holding the woman's hand. A part of her cried for her own inevitable death, while another part finally began to grieve over her brother. There's no proof, her logical reasoning kept reminding her, but for now, the notion that had been festering in the back of her mind came forth: Aydin wasn't coming back.

Tired of the tests, not giving a damn as to who saw or heard her. She wept for a life that would never be and for a life that was likely already gone.

1,946 km east of Jakarta, INDONESIA
Same day

Thank God she was passed out, he wasn't the most stealthy of people, and as his hand shakily progressed into the nurse's vicinity, Keuhl held his breath.

He hadn't smoked in months, it wasn't an attractive quality as he saw it, hence why he had abandoned the habit. The abandonment happened precisely two days after meeting Garrett—Keuhl couldn't connect any dots there. Nope, none at all.

Carefully sliding the pack and lighter away from her wrist, he exhaled out of the corner of his mouth as he stood upright. With the familiar weight in his hand, he already felt relief.

Turning towards the door, he took shallow breaths now, he didn't dare take large doses of whatever that rancid smelling thing in the air was and put it inside his lungs. Despite his overall revulsion to this place, he found himself becoming borderline giddy with anticipation at this miniature silver lining. Keuhl limped out of the clinic and took a left.

Five. Five painful steps, that's exactly how many steps away from the door he felt was a comfortable distance for the intent of his safety. Resting his crutch against the side of the hospital before leaning himself next to it. Without thought, his hands completed their movements on instinct, and before he could even pay attention, Keuhl found a lit cigarette between his lips.

He no longer pondered over the incessant itch in his leg, that feeling as though there were still small pieces of shrapnel lodged in there beneath the gauze. That girl had done a half-ass job, but he was honestly too terrified of what he might encounter beneath the bandages, which is why he hadn't unwrapped them himself. In fact, he turned away every time it was being redressed. That itch also happened to be the reason he couldn't fall asleep.

Lost in thought, it wasn't until there was a stomped-out bud next to his foot and a fresh flame between his lips that Keuhl came to, remembering why he came out into the night to begin with. He pulled a comms device out of his pants—it was held against his hip between the precipitating flesh and semi-taught elastic waistband of his shoddy hospital clothing.

He was going to have it back in Garrett's room before he noticed, no sweat.

For the time being, however, Keuhl needed to know exactly what the secretive communication had consisted of. What? Was he really not supposed to have witnessed Garrett the other night from his bedroom window standing out in the centre of the blast zone clutching the only other light in sight and not be curious?

Curiosity: he held a strange relationship with the concept. If Keuhl hadn't blocked out the majority of his childhood memories and experiences, now is where he would recall the time curiosity had left him in a handicapped stall in an elementary school with soiled khakis and a scratch across his left cornea. Fortunately, or unfortunately, depending on your depravity tolerance, Keuhl blocked things out with great ease.

Thumbing through the call log, he found zero recents. Thumbing through the messages, he found zero stored.

Temporarily satisfying his urge, Keuhl shut off the screen but remained clutching the device. His eyes adjusted to the dark once more.

He didn't feel alone.

At a snail's pace, he turned his neck towards the hospital doors, the only origins of glow nearby. There in the faint shadows stood Garrett in profile. He looked peaceful, for a change. That man was always so caught up in trying to keep up an air of ambivalence, or disconnect, that any moment his mask was off was like laying eyes on a shooting star. It would be fleeting yet beautiful to behold.

For a split second, Keuhl entertained the idea of not approaching him at all. Not simply because he enjoyed the view in peace, but also because he felt he was doing something he shouldn't be by even stepping a foot outside of that hospital door. Once that moment passed, however, Keuhl remembered he didn't give a shit what the others thought he "should" be doing as a soldier.

"Keuhl."

His deep voice didn't sound husky from sleep, he hadn't simply woken up in the middle of the night. Garrett hadn't fallen asleep.

Dropping that second cigarette, he picked up his crutch, placing it beneath his forearm is such a way as to completely put out the flickering bud.

"Asher." Lingering in the shadows a tad longer, Keuhl intently watched the other man's face as he tried to wedge the comms device back into his pants without drawing much attention.

"What brings you out here on such a depressing night?"

Depressing? Any night Keuhl had the pleasure of having a decent conversation with Garrett was anything but. Honestly, he couldn't remember the last time this had even occurred. He tried to count, and came up with a zero.

"Just needed some fresh air," he lied. "And yourself?"

Garrett's profile nodded as he shifted his weight, one arm snug against his afflicted hip.

"Same as you, Keuhl. Same as you."

Keuhl felt him pulling in again, bringing the conversation to a narrow halt. He wasn't ready to let go just yet.

One step. One step is how much closer he was able to get before Garrett turned to face left, his gaze finding Keuhl's in the pitch-black night.

He had to catch his breath in his flickering amber eyes. Keuhl smiled.

Garrett didn't.

"You've got the subtlety of an RPG, Keuhl."

"What exac—"

"You're lucky Odeli isn't here, you've be neck deep in bulge jokes galore. Sadly, I can only come up with: is that a comms device in your pocket, or are you just happy to see me?"

On cue, he felt the device slipping beneath his waistband.

Garrett held up a hand. "Actually, don't answer that. A part of it might just be the latter."

Why did he always have to belittle him in such a manner? Keuhl had done nothing but been civil for the past two months to this man. This perfect man, as long as he didn't speak. Well actually, that voice was pretty something, though.

He blinked, clearing his mind.

Something was worthy of Garrett's attention inside.

Keuhl stood still, curiosity kicking in. How would Garrett interact with someone he actually seemed to care for rather than... rather than with Keuhl, really. No words were exchanged inside but judging by Garrett's movements, someone had come down the stairs and made their way toward the desk.

Two steps. Two steps closer is what he dared to move.

Garrett had shuffled from the doorway now, this allowed Keuhl to crane his neck into the foyer. He had a clear view of a nurse, head down on the table, shoulders heaving. He knew exactly which nurse this was, not because he knew her appearance well enough, but because he knew the manner in which Garrett looked upon one of them: as though he had never seen anything more captivating than this person.

An anger was emerging within him, one he could not specifically justify nor acknowledge without hesitation. Keuhl hated this woman.

What bothered her the most was the silence. No wheezing, no shuffling from the bed in her room, the silence had chipped away at Kivran all night. She felt a dread, her chest tightened as though preparing for something awful.

She hadn't had a seizure in precisely twenty-six days and yet still, she couldn't bring herself to slumber. No longer able to withstand the confines of the room, Kivran made her way out. Judging by the darkness, it was approximately an hour until sunrise.

The hallway was illuminated by a singular light at the farthest outlet, bright enough to set the stairs aglow. Stepping down, finding comfort in the cold floor beneath her socks, she already felt her chest loosening upon seeing Innaya at the desk.

Without looking up, the woman addressed Kivran from her position, her face practically against the fan's grate. "Come on down."

Despite herself, she laughed at the noise ricocheting off the blades before gradually pulling up a chair beside Innaya and mirroring her posture.

"How are you feeling?" Innaya looked at her this time, whispering away from the fan.

Kivran shrugged. "I'm doing okay."

"You haven't asked about Aydin in a while." Both their heads lay flat on the table, enthralled in an exclusive conversation of hushed tones.

"For some reason, I don't think I ever will again." The answer spilled from her as though it had been lying in wait without her ever registering so. She felt her shoulders sink not from exhaustion but from relief. Minutely dreading the idea, she discerned a numb acceptance was about to spark within her.

Innaya placed a hand between Kivran's shoulder blades, gently rubbing her back. "I'm here if you need anything, even just an ear."

She felt a tear trickle its way down the small distance between her eye and the desk as she nodded. "How are you, though?" Kivran needed a distraction. If she wanted to cry, she could have done so in that confining room.

"I'm well, heading out to see my son tomorrow for a few days." Innaya smiled in her response.

The tightening within her chest elevated - another thing she lost in life. Kivran wasn't one for self-pity, but there were nights during which she couldn't contain her indignation, though she never had the courage to act upon the feeling. Like all other things, she kept it bottled within herself, dreading the day it would become too much to hold captive.

"Two Hip was looking for you not too long ago."

Kivran remained silent, unsure of what to do with this knowledge.

"Insisted you needed to take him to the cemetery. I gave him directions and told him to take a hike on his own."

She nodded, afraid the lump in her throat would catch any words mid-motion were she to speak.

Closing her eyes, shedding the tears sitting on the brim, Kivran listened to her friend carry on speaking and took none of it in. As the hand on her back continued to rub, she felt for a moment she had drifted off, for when she awoke, the beams of sunlight were cutting across Innaya's face. That couldn't have happened, Kivran couldn't have fallen asleep because that's exactly what she had been trying her damnedest not to do. She couldn't have fallen asleep.

1,946 km east of Jakarta, INDONESIA
Same day

"Kivran, what's a farm?"

She stopped moving, hands halted mid-motion in clipping his gauze closed. He could see her chest rise and fall at a faster pace as her pupils shrank.

Down the hall, just a few feet away from them in the first examination room, voices echoed. Paper-thin walls. The hospital was evidently carrying about its business as usual, and why shouldn't it? Garrett noticed Kivran's eyes shift towards the room—the voices—before she herself spoke.

"It's typically a place where livestock is kept and raised. Sometimes families live on the same property as the livestock. I'd like to say the most popularly utilized form of modern farming originated from the French back in th—"

"Kivran."

She finally looked up at him, sternness painted across her face. She knew exactly what she was doing. After sitting with her last night as she coped with whatever it was she was going through in complete silence, save for the awkward shuffling of Keuhl going back to his business, he had believed they'd be passed this, possibly naively.

"You know what I mean. What is it?"

Focusing back on her task, she shrugged. "Actually, I don't know what you mean."

Once she leaned away to attain something from the tray sitting behind her, he lifted himself up into a better position upon the uncomfortable chair. He had deliberately come looking for her in the lobby, he wasn't about to turn back now. Thus, he continued as she redressed his burn in the foyer. "You already know I heard you that night, so you might as well tell me."

The conversation from his adventure was still bouncing around his mind: this region was about to be placed under quarantine. He already knew preliminary quarantine didn't mean much of a difference.

Standing tall next to him, she looked him dead in the eyes while removing her gloves. Garrett tried not to smile, her eyes were a mesmerizing hue of grey.

"I'm not sure what notion you have of me, but I don't have to tell you a thing." At the last "you," she rolled her eyes to indicate a greater meaning than just him.

"You're still angry over your home."

"Perceptive, you are." Hands on her hips now, unsanitary gloves still clasped firmly. "Tell you what, I'll tell you what a farm is if you tell me why you're here."

Garrett stopped staring into the grey. "I can't tell you."

Nodding, she went to throw out the gloves. "Bully for that." She was about to sit back at her post behind the desk.

"Wait." Shifting his weight on to the good hip, he tilted sideways, waiting for her to come back. She did, hands back on her hips.

Quieting a moment to confirm the occupants of the nearby room were still preoccupied, he continued, albeit in a quieter voice. "We're leaving tomorrow, the other men and I. An evacuation team will be here by morning."

She smirked, nodding. "So now that we'll never see each other ever again, I'm supposed to be spilling everything to you? Is that why you're telling me your itinerary?"

"Well, you're definitely colder than usual today. I'm telling you because…" Garrett trailed off as something he'd only briefly pondered previously now crossed his thoughts. Why hadn't he paid it proper attention earlier?

He didn't know which house this woman lived in. Sure, there were multiple homes affected by the blast. but it had never been established as to which house hers was. For all he knew, she could have occupied the target dwelling.

Leaning back, he let his head bang against the wall.

He'd unintentionally been shedding his callous skin in her presence. Time to bring that to a screeching halt.

"Garrett?"

Looking back at her, he noticed her eyes had become softer and her hands hovering just above her hips, ready to move, as though she was about to comfort him.

"I'm telling you so you'll know precisely when to jump for joy." His tone oozed sarcasm but didn't have the affect he was aiming for.

Rather than her parting in frustration or content, she remained standing before him for a few seconds longer than should have been necessary. The corners of her mouth went down slightly just prior to losing all expression. Nodding one last time, she exited his vicinity.

1,946 km east of Jakarta, INDONESIA
18 years, 175 days after Mutation 4

She didn't like being watched in this manner. She felt it was a test she was about to fail. Seeing him out of peripherals, he was dressed in the same manner as those military men the night they'd come to the island. Except where those men hadn't openly brandished weapons in her presence, these men did.

Feet shoulder width apart, stern expression, some model of gun cradled against the chest, one of these men stood at the foot of the comatose burn victim's cot as Kivran and Thi got him ready for transportation. Innaya was, thankfully, visiting her son in Jakarta, thus sitting this memorable morning out.

She'd never seen Thi so quiet, it made the situation seem more dreadful.

No more than ten minutes ago, everyone in the clinic was awoken to the sound of a helicopter that had set itself down in the vicinity of the blast. This must be the evacuation Garrett had mentioned. Not even changed into a uniform yet, one of the nurses, Dian, had burst into Kivran's room and found her staring out the window at the spectacle.

"More of them?" Dian had asked. Kivran just shrugged in response, she genuinely had no idea whether these men were only here to take their injured team members, or occupy themselves here in exchange.

The two nurses had watched as a handful of soldiers appeared one by one out of the alley towards the clinic. The dawning sun illuminated two of the items these men held: stretchers and weapons.

Hearing shuffling in the hall, they peeled themselves from the window to witness the scene inside. In the hall was Keuhl pacing between the entrance to two rooms, each of which held his fellow comrades.

The nurses had looked at each other in that moment as they both evidently realized the same thing: whatever this was, was big enough to unnerve Limp, which wasn't a comforting notion.

"You're coming with us."

His hand was over hers, grasping the stretcher as he stood close, keeping pace with her as she carried a patient towards the clinic entrance. The patient's head was gently bobbing from side to side with each step. Kivran looked over at the man holding the stretcher opposite her, thankfully he hadn't heard anything, and if he had, he was doing a pretty good job of pretending otherwise.

"Excuse me?" Keeping her eyes down, trying not to miss a step in the now cramped stairwell, her tone became accusatory.

"Don't argue with me just now, Kivran." Reaching the main door, he let go of her hand just as other men came into view.

Not risking a retort back in present company, she stayed quiet, letting the comment fester within her as it held back the wave of... something she felt when that coarse, burned palm had been placed upon her. The texture, the imperfection of it—it felt real in a moment of daze. Following the seemingly lengthy walk to the transport, she concentrated on lifting the stretcher up and onto the helicopter's bed. The door of said large helicopter directly opposite her was slid wide open. From over the left shoulder of the crouching man in front of her, she caught a glimpse of two children standing on the former football field opposite the Pit. She found herself silently wishing for them to have not been witnessed by any other living soul in this moment. Thoughts of what might happen to these children if one of these men lay eyes on them were forcefully held back.

Once her task was done, Kivran turned with the face of unadulterated anger to Garrett who in turn looked at the other conscious soldier. "We'll take it from here, Lieutenant, you should get the others."

Nodding without a word, the man turned on his heels to set about his orders.

She now had Garrett's attention, she hoped the stern look she sported was enough to make him explain his behaviour.

"This place is about to be quarantined." He lifted himself onto the transport and stretched a hand out to help Kivran in. She kept her arms as is, crossed over her chest.

"What is that supposed to mean?" Her heart began to race; what was happening to this place that she needed to leave now? She knew what quarantine was, that wasn't in question. What was, however, was why here? The same thing she'd asked the day of the blast: why were these men here?

Putting his hand down with a frustrated look, he came back out to stand opposite her. "It means WHO is going to descend on this place any second. No one goes in or out. If you're stuck here when they come, you're here forever."

She shook her head. "You mean I'm stuck here until the quarantine gets lifted, yes?"

It was his turn to shake his head. "No. We've never lifted a quarantine order, regardless of what level it's categorized at."

"Well, good thing I never leave this place then. But why the hell are we being quarantined?" She untied her arms and began to talk animatedly, succumbing to her frustration. "What were you doing that night?"

"I can't tell you." Departing from her gaze, he looked down. His cheekbones began to turn red. Kivran couldn't decide whether this was due to embarrassment or frustration. She liked to believe the former.

Pouting her lips as if she was even giving this some thought, Kivran stepped back from him. His eyes shot back up at her. "Bullshit. I'm not going anywhere if you can't even tell me why I'd be going."

Turning on him, she began to walk back towards the clinic, though admittedly slower than her average pace. A part of her hoped he'd say something to get her to turn back.

He didn't.

1,946 km east of Jakarta, INDONESIA
Same day

Witnessing her walk away, hair reflecting the dawning sun, Garrett felt immobile. He hadn't felt like this since the night he was left on that bloody island.

The notion of being confined to that small mass of land amidst a world of indescribable wonder pained him. He resented his father for initially taking him there, passing on his own irrational fears to his one and only son. Angry at his circumstances, sixteen-year-old Garrett ran the length of the island screaming at the top of his lungs the moment his ride was out of sight, over the horizon. Ignoring the sheep's own terrified sounds, he didn't cease until an unusual thud sounded out separate from his own shouting, the sheep's shrieks, and the waves lapping around them.

Holding his breath, Garrett had walked over to a flock, each sheep frantically turning in various directions, unsure of what to do with themselves. He related. As he made his way through them towards the cliff, he noticed a part of the border fence had been trampled. And there, over the cliff, fallen on the rocks, red streaks flowing in and out with the tide, lay a dead sheep. For a moment, hearing the remaining sheep behind him, a thought grazed his mind: he could just let them all plunge, they weren't his responsibility. Yet turning back towards the remaining flock, still hysterical, a sense of fear in their eyes and movements, Garrett knew he couldn't go about terrifying them.

He hadn't screamed for the remainder of his time on that mass, nor had one other sheep fallen to its death. He went quite far out of his way to make sure of the latter.

As Kivran disappeared into the hospital, Garrett realized he couldn't let her live out her life under a quarantine when he could prevent such a thing. He would have to go out of his way make sure of this.

He began to move, at first slow, then into a jog towards the hospital. Stepping in, he saw her waiting for another stretcher to clear the narrow staircase, it was carried by two members of the evac team with a Keuhl lounging upon it, eyes shut and groaning. Milking it for all its worth, he was.

"Kivran." He lightly touched her on the shoulder.

Arms crossed, she turned to face him, stern expression still present.

"I don't work for the research unit... obviously, so I don't have the details to hand you." Lightly grasping her upper arm, he guided her towards the side of the stairwell upon eyeing another evac member coming down. "What I can tell you from the grapevine, though, is quarantine is not going to make this place safer. It will destroy this island. Everyone will be tagged for genetic variables, everyone will eventually die of malnutrition, and no one in the outside world will know a thing. It's just an excuse to find something they've been looking for all along. I'm sorry. If that blast hadn't happened, there may not have been a quarantine. I'm sorry, I can't change that, but I can get you out of here, Kivran. Please, let me at least do that, let me do the right thing."

She kept with him throughout that, nothing for him to read, though. "Excuse for what?"

Guiding her again, he led her behind the front desk, at the opposite end of the staircase's prying ears.

"An excuse to find the next plague. It's not plea—"

"You're talking about Mutation Four, yes?" She became anxious.

Taken aback, Garrett was a touch relieved. "How do you know about that?"

"Never mind that. Is that what they're looking for?"

"Yes."

"Why? To find a cure?"

"Not exactly."

"Elaborate, Garrett."

He needed to pause and gather his thoughts. The information she was looking for didn't exactly go out in a mass memo, much of it was classified, most even just preliminarily conclusive.

"Most of the world's current diseases have evolved, fuelled by overpopulation. This Mutation spreads with similar characteristics to a plague but thankfully not at that rate just yet. With different physical markers appearing on different individuals, it's difficult to find those infected, let alone track it. Their blood, their organs, there's almost infinite possibilities as to who could be infected." He paused as a set of soldiers re-entered to hospital and made their way up. "A quarantine is just an excuse for them to experiment on this population, maybe find what they've been missing." He could almost hear his father's voice coaxing him along the back of his mind.

She shook her head, evidently having difficulty swallowing this. "You wouldn't experiment inhumanely though, right?"

"I can't say for sure, depends on the people assigned." An image of Keuhl danced behind his eyes. "But if the Mutation took hold, it wouldn't matter how brutal the experiments are, because the symptoms would supposedly be bad enough. And they wouldn't intervene."

She shook her head again. "From the sounds of it, you don't even know the symptoms. Besides, this is ridiculous! No one's blatantly doing that to other people, other humans."

"Like I said, no quarantine's ever been lifted."

"But also like you said, it's just the grapevine. You don't know the accuracy of your statements."

Kivran looked towards the entrance, Garrett followed her gaze, wondering how he could explain anything further without compromising something else in turn. He found her looking where the doctor was conversing with the other team between the thresholds. Turning back, he recognized that look. Naively, he had assumed she saved this expression solely for the moments that she was in his presence, a way of illustrating her trust in him, but he could see now clearly—she was saddened.

The lump in his throat swelled. She was going to break the fence and fall on the rocks, and he'd have to watch.

"Don't ask why I'm asking, but that house you were in the night of the blast, was there anyone else in it?"

Surprised at the turn of discussion and now holding back the urge to ask, Garrett simply shook his head. This he could remember with clarity: every soldier in that house had stated "clear" before the explosion occurred.

"What's out there? Where would I go?" He watched her eyes lift from the people up towards the partially clouded sky visible just outside the door.

He swallowed the lump before answering, feeling easier now. "Well, the first one, I hope you find that out for yourself, Kivran. And the second, there's an ad hoc refugee camp not too far from where we're headed, you can claim status there."

The anxious expression was creeping on to her face again, he was about to lose her. "I don't know. From there wh—"

"Don't stay here, go wherever you want but please, don't stay here." Garrett couldn't explain why he allowed the desperation to seep through his voice. Perhaps he was shaken by the idea that he might have to fly away from that beautiful grey. Again.

57 km northwest of **HONG KONG**
Same day

You can never go home again.

The notion rung out between her ears. She had never left the handful of islands surrounding her home, and now, a mere few hours ago, she had watched them minimize in the horizon. Sitting on her hands the whole ride, unnerved at the experience of a first flight but terrified of leaving behind… whatever it was that remained. Kivran did her best to bottle any and all emotions.

Deliberately crouching to keep her physical existence to a minimum, she had tucked herself between the side of the helicopter and an occupied stretcher. This was the farthest she could get from any conscious being in the flight. Yet their gaze, she couldn't escape.

Kivran had focused all her energy into counting the amount of threads on the patient's gauze, attempting to keep herself alert but zoned out from any communication within the confines. It was only once she could no longer hear the background humming of the helicopter blades did she realize they were on solid ground once more. Blended in with the bustle of the exiting patients, she found herself exactly where we ourselves now find her: beneath the sweltering sun on some sort of military compound by a body of water.

Unable to actually move her feet, she stood in place whilst turning her neck to observe her whereabouts. She could hear waves crashing against a shore somewhere behind her, a metal fence enclosed the area, a long portable office unit lay a few metres ahead while the surrounding land was occupied by dark green tents. This wasn't quite what she expected, though she also would have a difficult time describing what it is she was expecting.

"Kivran?"

Garrett stood beside her, carrying one half of the burn victim's stretcher, the opposite side held by a man who was neither in the clinic nor on the helicopter. This man watched her intently, however, not in an accusatory nor inquisitorial manner. Even still, Kivran instinctively hunched deeper.

57 km west-northwest of **HONG KONG**
Same day

The stern expression Garrett shot him upon opening the doors immediately halted any questions Odeli would have had in the proceeding few seconds. For in those proceeding few seconds, he witnessed two stretchers lowered from the transport, followed closely by a woman caught in headlights.

She sported some form of light blue uniform spotted with blood stains, a torn cardigan with sleeves stretched down to her fingers—in this heat—and a petrified demeanour. At least that's what he could observe from her rooted position behind Garrett.

Curiously, he carried the opposite end of the stretcher currently in Garrett's possession, occupying an unconscious Marek, and smirked at his conscious friend. Said friend, in turn, shook his head but maintained the stern face. It wasn't every day that that man brought back a companion. It was actually never.

Turning around to properly hold the stretcher, Odeli glanced back every few steps. The woman was coming along just behind Garrett but lost in her surroundings. Her eyes didn't stand still as she took in everything. The gaze resting longest on a group of toddlers mucking about outside a nearby refugee tent. He noticed Garrett whispering to her as they went along, but she didn't seem to concentrate much on him.

Talk about a fish out of water, even for a refugee holding facility.

Reaching the infirmary tent, they carried Marek to the nearest empty cot. Garrett went off to fetch a medic, granting Odeli enough time to watch the woman. Habitually reverting to an at-ease stance, feet shoulder width apart and hands clasped behind his back, he observed as she slowly walked among the cots.

He had seen Tamsin do this countless times: at home among the blood and guts, determined to cure anything and everything in her path, to the max. This woman, however, lacked that final element. She wasn't cringing, she wasn't holding her nose, she looked almost mournful.

Great, looks like Garrett's picked up a real Mother Theresa.

Smirking again as Garrett returned, Odeli pointed his chin at the wandering figure. "That's your type, huh? Could've fooled me. Is this perhaps the 'apocalyptic level failure' we've all been patiently waiting for?"

"It's not like that. She was the Doc down there."

"Sure. That explains precisely why she's *here* then?"

Turning his back on the woman, Garrett focused on Odeli before proceeding in a hushed tone. "She *had* to come with us, O. Marek wasn't stable enough for the journey, and our medics weren't familiar enough with his current condition to properly handle the transport. Correct?"

He looked, with exaggerated bewilderment from Marek's figure on the cot up to Garrett's face and back again. A few times.

"I'm not quie—"

Garrett stepped an inch closer as a medic passed behind him. "It was necessary. She will claim refugee status shortly. She will not be transported back."

Odeli had never witnessed Garrett in a serious state, and that included such an authoritarian tone. The kid was always somber, or indifferent, unbiased in his words and his emotions. Everyone clearly had a grand ole time on that island, sad he had to sit that one out.

The woman had meandered back to them now and was standing facing away by Marek's feet.

Putting on a smile, Odeli thumped a hand on both of Garrett's shoulders, making the other man smile as well. "Correct. But honestly, I think you could've done better. Just saying."

As Garrett's smiled widened, Odeli stepped over to the woman and directly into her eye line.

Wait, did she have an eye line? She looked blind. But he had just seen her perfectly navigate the floor… was she looking at him?

Curiously inching his neck closer, he saw a slight difference between the whites of her eyeballs, her pupils, and her… crap what's it called? He could've sworn Tamsin was mentioning this just the other day. Bugger it, she was right, he wasn't paying attention. That was a long day, okay!

The woman warily smiled for a moment. So she could see him. Odeli's neck craned back.

"Thank you for your necessary work, and for bringing the loves of my life back." He could see Garrett holding his head in his hand in the distance. "Odeli, by the way." He stretched out a hand.

With her own covered hand, she shook it. "Ki-vran." The voice was raspy but not shaken. He had so effortlessly judged her in all the wrong ways.

"Pleasure." He broke eye… yes, eye contact with her before waving over her head to Garrett, delight and sarcasm blended in his tone. "Congratulations, mate!"

Odeli then took his leave to see what the holdup was with that damned medic.

57 km west-northwest of **HONG KONG**
18 years, 176 days after Mutation 4

Walking past the nurse hunched over in the dim lighting, who lightly grunted at his passing at least acknowledging his presence, Garrett gently walked towards Marek's cot. It had been decided the patients couldn't stay here long, the temporary base wasn't equipped to handle severe burn victims such as him. Marek, along with the rest of the unit, voluntarily would be migrated to the primary Asian base in two days' time. For now though, Marek resided in a shoddy excuse for a medical tent pitched up beside the base trailers.

Upon his approach, he noticed a figure seated cross-legged on the floor next to Marek's cot, his head lulling about in slumber. Angling one of the lamps strung above the aisle, he shone light on the figure. Odeli shot awake with a wince.

"Shut it!" hissed the hunched nurse.

Both chuckling in the dark, Garrett joined Odeli on the floor, which evidently turned out to be damp from the soil beneath the tarp doubling as the floor.

"What're you doing here?" Garrett inquired.

Rubbing the back of his neck, looking upon the resting figure of Marek, Odeli replied. "Same as you, mate."

Garrett nodded, finding himself glad to not be alone.

"Besides," Odeli continued, shifting to sit upright, "and I don't much listen when she rambles on, if I'm honest, but Tamsin always says the worst thing a patient can go through is waking up alone."

He felt like an idiot still nodding but he knew what the man beside him meant—that feeling.

"I'm sorry about Walcott." The words spilled out, he hadn't even realized they were on the tip of his tongue. And yet, there they were, lingering in the air between them now.

Odeli's head sunk in a manner of defeat. "It's not your fault."

"I would've tried, if I could, but it was just…" Where was this coming from? He hadn't processed that death at all, let alone felt this guilt that was accumulating here, in this place with only Odeli's ears to fall on. A better question, that Garrett didn't dare entertain, though, was why emotions anywhere near this degree hadn't ever boiled within him at the other deaths he'd been privy to.

"I know, sometimes there's nothing you can do."

He would've preferred Odeli yelling at him, barraging him for letting their friend die. Anything but this—this complacency at the outcome.

"Don't carry that weight, man. That'll bury you, and it won't be quick. You'll wake up one day and come to the realization that you can't see the sky anymore, you're too far down."

Garrett watched him speak, watched as the playful wrinkles around the man's eyes flattened out, heard as his voice became heavier with each word. Odeli appeared to be speaking from experience.

With a burdened sigh, Odeli looked off into the depths of the dark tent before turning towards Garrett. Actually, he ended up looking past him altogether.

"Oh Captain, my Captain!"

"Shut. It."

Twisting around, Garrett surprised himself with the feeling of comfort that washed over him the moment Marek's eyes fluttered open one at a time. He felt like he had been holding his breath for days underwater until this very moment.

"Love you too, Odeli." Marek managed to hiss out in a rasp.

Both men on the floor slid closer as Marek coughed, slightly moving his neck then deciding against it and lying back as before. Even in the darkness, pieces of flesh flaked off the man's face, contrasting against the white sheets.

"What happened?" He looked at no one in particular, but there was no one who could've sufficiently answered that question other than Garrett.

"What's the last thing you remember?" Garrett tried to buy himself some time, he needed to wrap his own head around the past few days before he could effectively iterate anything.

"I remember clearing the target building." Marek's voice was getting clearer.

Where to begin? "I believe the oxygen tanks on the premises caught fire, it smelled like gasoline everywhere before-hand."

"I think I remember that. I think."

"It was pretty bad, I don't know how many tanks there were, but it must've been at least three. When I came to, there was… there wasn't much I could do."

He felt Odeli's knee gently, and momentarily, press against his.

"We lost Walcott, a few of the locals were gone too." He noticed Marek's face sink. "Before long, the neighbourhood descended. Some of them were from a hospital down the road, they took us all over. We were there for nearly two weeks before we got transport out."

"How?"

"One of the comms devices survived the blast, I requested an evac as soon as I was able to."

"They wouldn't tell me anything," Odeli chimed in. "Three days in, I was running around to every office that'd let me in the door, and they didn't say a thing. Kept saying they had no idea what op I was talking about. Then a few days ago, they shoved my ass on a transport to this place, no questions, no answers, nothing."

"Sounds right." Marek somehow managed to display defeat on his face even without access to much of the muscles.

Garrett had managed to summarize the events without any significant detail and still satisfy the inquirer.

A silence fell between them. Outside their triangle, unsynchronized breaths and groans littered the tent. Odeli and Garrett watched Marek drift his eyes shut once more, a tear slipped out.

"And me? What happened to me?"

He was glad he didn't need to meet Marek's gaze just now. "Severe burns. Everywhere. Blood vessel burst behind your eyes."

Marek nodded, or so it seemed. His right shoulder shrugged as though he was going to lift his arm and rub his hair against the grain. Instinctive behaviour. Marek's eyes momentarily flicked downwards before he most likely remembered he couldn't move. "That explains why I feel blind as a bat."

Odeli's belly laugh broke their hushed pattern. "We can finally play expert level Marco Polo!" The other two couldn't help but join in, Marek less so. "Let's be honest, you were the weakest link, you now have no excuses, soldier!"

The coughing stopped them all. Marek appeared to be refraining, trying not to jerk around in the cough, it sounded as though he were suffocating. The two on the floor shot up in unison, lost but trying to find something to do with themselves, to help somehow.

Garrett looked towards the entrance; the nurse was gone. His following thought was to summon *her*.

Marek shook his head, or so he thought.

"I'm fine." The rasp made a comeback.

"We'll let you rest either way, Marco." Odeli stretched, lifting the tent roof with the tips of his fingers. "They're moving us to the base day after tomorrow."

Marek muttered an acknowledgement, catching his breath.

"And, we've still got to introduce you to Garrett's female!"

"Jesus." Garrett shook his head, making for the exit.

"Jesus, really? Well done on finding him… her." Marek's humour evidently still intact.

Odeli continued through his chuckles, no longer holding a whisper as he followed Garrett. "Well, I wouldn't say she's that divine or ethereal, but I would say it's biblical."

He could just picture Odeli gyrating behind him at this point, he knew that man better than he knew himself. Garrett wasn't convinced that was a good thing.

"Oh yeah, it's gonna get so biblical, so fast!"
"Shut it!"

57 km west-northwest of **HONG KONG**
Same day

Her abdomen was in excruciating pain, and for once, it had nothing to do with the surgery. She had spent the better part of the night hunched over; she had wanted to cry but no tears had come. Her body shook in anticipation, and still nothing. Kivran couldn't bring herself to mourn the life she had flown away from, but it was there, that loss, that abyss within her. She gazed out the only window in the room, a small pane oddly placed like an afterthought. It didn't even face anything pleasant, just the wall of the adjoining trailer. An afterthought. Kivran found herself wishing it would rain, she wanted something familiar, a pattern she could find Aydin in.

Hearing the door click open, she gradually straightened herself on the medical table. She was about to go through the third and last of her immigration examinations.

The first one had been odd, it was the stepping-stone to determine whether she would even be eligible to claim refugee status, but no one had even spoken to her. Clearly there was an underlying theme in all this WHO behaviour. After having sat in line with the other refugees—an odd mosaic of terrified and hopeful expressions—Kivran had been waved along to the next examination without any direct communication. She felt tainted beneath the stares of those people, their hushed jeers still ringing between her ears.

The second test required next to no communication as well. An individual in military garb had come down the line, extracting blood samples from each applicant before leaving each person to fester impatiently in a long hallway with no chairs. Kivran had to lower herself to the ground as the low blood sugar set in. She had been too scared to find sustenance all day and too frustrated to seek out Garrett for help. Her head would begin slipping as she dozed in and out of consciousness, pinching herself harder with each waking moment. This was the last place she wanted to have a seizure.

Roughly three hours on, witnessing people up and down the hall be escorted off only to never return, Kivran was the last one to be taken into an examination room. No verbal communication, just gestures. Get up. Walk this way. In there. Sit. Somewhere in that in-between, she had traded in her frustration for fear and regret. Both of them constricting her heart, she felt nauseous to boot.

Now here she sat, upon the observation table in a room that suddenly felt claustrophobic, with the window behind her, an instinctual association with Aydin rattling around somewhere within her skull, and her hand flush against her abdomen scar holding everything in place. As her eyes drifted from the walls towards the opening door, her imagination filled the walls with hastily pinned-up diagrams and notes. He was gone.

Garrett stepped into the room wearing an expression of worry.

"There you are!" He looked down each end of the hall before shutting the door.

How was she supposed to respond to that? He brought her here. The frustration was making a speedy recovery to her surface, she felt the need to be entirely composed subside.

He approached with cautious footing, actually a bit of an imbalance still in his gait, his eyes taking her in from head to toe and back again. Teetering on borderline delirium, she could only imagine what state she appeared to be in. Her eyelids felt so heavy, she could barely lift her arms now, she felt as though she was slipping off the edge of the table. She just wanted to sleep, she was so tired, tired of staying awake all the time. When Garrett was within half an arm's length directly in front of her, Kivran found herself crashing her forehead into his chest. All stored energy to even remain upright now depleted.

Garrett didn't budge against her weight.

"I'm sorry to have to do this now." His tone sounded genuine. "I don't have much time."

She felt his chest rise and fall with each breath, Kivran concentrated on its flow, finding comfort in a constant.

"You're gonna have to clear this last exam, I'll do what I can to keep the inquisition to a minimum…"

She drifted in and out of his calming drawl as she heard him ruffling around in his… pocket? She wasn't sure, too much effort to open her eyes.

"If I lie, please go along with it. We're being transported to the base tomorrow… refugee wing… better chances of immigration from there… don't want you… left behind…"

Rise and fall. Rise and fall. In and out. In and out.

"Here."

Kivran opened one eye. Just beneath her eye line was a paper bag rolled open, a jumble of green gummy bears stared back at her. In hindsight, she would hate herself in this moment, but in it, she found herself smiling at the sight just before lazily craning her hand into the bag and shovelling a handful into her dry mouth.

"You all right?"

She shook her head, shifting his shirt with each movement, feeling better from the sugar already. She wanted to know exactly what had been happening to her all day. Pushing herself off him, she was about inquire this very thing when the door once again creaked open. This time, a doctor not much older than herself covering her military uniform with a white coat stepped through.

"Hello." The voice was monotone, Kivran already felt herself drifting off at the first word.

"Hello." She muttered back as she pinched her thigh. Stay awake.

It wasn't until the doctor had shut the door behind herself and toed the stool towards the table did she finally look up at Kivran. And taken aback at that.

"I wasn't informed you were visually impaired."

"I'm not," replied Kivran, eyes shooting back to the filthy floor, as though ashamed.

The doctor let out a grunt, Kivran still felt her eyes on her, though.

A moment passed, at least Kivran believed it was just that long, she may have unfortunately nodded off. When she focused her eyes again, the doctor was casually turning her head over towards the opposite end of the room.

"Anything I can help you with—" She craned her head and squinted towards his unbuttoned military jacket. "Asher?"

He stepped closer before replying, a pleasant grin on his face. "I was actually looking for you, ma'am. I'm a friend of Odeli's."

"Is that right?" Her tone changed, her interest had been sparked.

Kivran observed as the two individuals carried on a conversation; it wasn't an animated one, it didn't even seem like an interesting one. She found herself drifting her concentration towards Garrett's breathing once more.

She pinched her thigh again, this was the last place she wanted to have a seizure.

62 km northwest of **HONG KONG**
Same day

She was stubborn, just like him. If there was one thing Garrett had learned about the woman sitting beside him, it was that.

Knowing how refugees were treated through the system, if they went through the system at all, he expected Kivran to breakdown long ago. Yet here she sat, visibly thinner after her two days on foreign soil, with dark circles under both eyes, back straight, hands in lap, knees squeezed tightly together. He was almost afraid to ask again if she was doing all right, especially after the deadpan "I'm all right" he received last time. Even offering an extra meal to combat her weakened state, she stood stubborn.

Now, packed in with two dozen other refugees, he volunteered to act as military escort on this truck while the preceding one carried Marek and the others.

Turning his gaze away from the rear tarp and across the truck bed, he locked eyes with a young girl clutching her father's upper arm while the man was fast asleep, head bobbing against the vehicle's movement. The girl had striking chocolate eyes. The lack of any emotion on her face made their appearance nearly sickening.

Continuing to shift his gaze, he now looked at the woman he was hoping to lock eyes with. Instead he found a curtain of light brown hair catching light from the tarp's opening.

"Kivran, are you doing all right?" Remember, he was *almost* afraid to ask.

Only moving her head in the slightest, she nodded once.

There are at least three screening processes all refugees go through. One: brief interview to determine if you are in fact from a dangerous region and not one on the Quarantine Spectrum. Thankfully, Garrett knew the interviewer from previous introductions, this meant he was able to forego Kivran's interview without a hitch. This would limit the heavy questions, such as what is your country of origin; have you visited an infected region in the past six months; how you fallen ill recently? Two: security check. This was the WHO's broad term for running one's DNA through military records, criminal records, health records, and any other check they deemed vital enough for their own security or the security of the country said refugee could ultimately be taken to. There wasn't much he could help with here, but judging by the fact that she was sitting next to him meant everything turned up clear. Three: physical examination and general health checkup. No destination country wanted sick individuals who would leech services from the more deserving natural born citizens. No destination country wanted to house the plague. That would just be unacceptable. Once more, he had done what he could to sail Kivran through the examination, but then the doctor asked him to exit. Sitting in a pre-deployment meeting across the field when she had eventually come out of the final exam, he caught sight of her for just a moment. Puffy eyes, blood shot cheeks, shaky hands, and a hunched gait. This was when she had locked down.

He saw her gingerly exit the temporary wing with no shoes, tugging at the bottom of her shirt, stretching it down past her hips, never looking up as she made her way past noisy tents and out of view.

There was an odd frustration bordering on anger brewing within him. He didn't want to insult her by asking what had happened if she didn't want to willingly tell him.

Sitting now beside her in this truck, their knees forced to touch, he could feel her quiver as she nodded. Trying not to touch her more than necessary, he reached down towards a crate of his belongings tucked under the bench. Twisting his arm, Garrett eventually found what he wanted. What she probably needed.

Thankful for the gravel beneath their tires, he didn't need to worry about the crinkling of the paper bag now in his hand. Unraveling the top, he held it out for Kivran, who was already fixated on the object. He tried to smile but couldn't make the movement, it didn't seem appropriate somehow.

Taking the bag with a shaking left hand with the other clasped tightly around its wrist to keep such shaking to a minimum, she looked inside. Observing as she let her eyes wander over the gummy bears within, he waited for further movement.

It came. Kivran stretched out her arm with an involuntary audible inhale towards the little girl sitting across from them. With no hesitation, the girl took hold of the bag, opening it to have a wide smile spread across her thin face. Cautiously using two fingers to reach inside and pluck out a bear, she looked at it in awe before placing it in her mouth. Chewing with a smile still plastered on her face, she took another. Then another before leaning off the bench to look at the person seated on the opposite side of her father. A boy not much younger than her had been watching the scene. With her smile not phasing, the girl handed the paper bag off to the boy who took it with a whispered thank you.

Looking at the spectacle across from him, Garrett panned towards Kivran once more as a sudden yet subtle movement registered in his peripheral. She leaned her head back, allowing her hair to show her face clearly now. She looked back at him.

There they were. Somewhere during the few seconds this had all occurred, Kivran's eyes had gone from somber to hopeful. Just before closing her eyelids, she whispered something he could barely make out over the tires:

"Don't worry."

Undisclosed location, Asian WHO Base, EASTERN CHINA
18 years, 187 days after Mutation 4

Kivran's eyes shot open. She wasn't altogether convinced it hadn't been her groaning in her semi-unconscious state. The noise had cut through the silence of their wing at odd intervals, and though she hadn't been in slumber, she knew such guttural sounds of pain weren't out of character for her, but in the daze, she hadn't registered that it might just be her. Having now done so, her heart raced, preparing for something that was about to come. Sliding off the bed into a fetal position on the stone-cold floor, she took the front neck of her sweatshirt and bit down on the dirt-infused material, pulling the tongue flush against the roof of her mouth, hands shaky but gripping her ankles to prevent her flailing around too much.

She waited. And waited. Nothing.

And then the noise resonated through the confines, but it didn't originate from Kivran. Gently lifting herself up, she looked towards the cot farthest from the front entrance. And elder woman generally occupied it with her daughter on the right. The mother emitted the noise once more; she sounded like she was dying. Upon realizing she wasn't the one in trouble, Kivran squandered no time in jogging towards the woman. As she got closer in the dark, she noticed the daughter, not much younger than herself, seated on the cot by the woman, holding her hand but overall mentally thrashing like a fish out of water.

"What happened?" Kivran figured English would be the best way to approach this.

"I'm… I'm not sure," the daughter replied between sobs. "I think she's having a heart attack."

That may have been correct. The woman clutched a hand to her chest gasping for air as splatters of vomit trailed down the sides of her mouth and neck.

"Help me turn her over." Kivran began tugging at the woman's shoulder, trying to turn her enough to prevent her choking on her own vomit.

The daughter didn't move as she muttered in the dark. Kivran elbowed her.

"All this way. We came all this way, and she's going to leave me now."

The daughter wouldn't be much help.

Aggressively pulling apart their clasped hands, Kivran pulled the daughter towards the top of the cot whilst balancing the sputtering woman now awkwardly angled on the edge. "Hold her head up like this… no like this… there you go." It was already evident the daughter wouldn't remain like this for long. "Don't move, I'm going to get some help. Don't move from this position unless you are clearing vomit out of her airways, understood?"

The daughter didn't even look up in acknowledgement. Kivran would have to hurry.

Dashing into the windy night, she looked in both directions, hoping for some guidance. Some divine intervention perhaps.

She got it.

As she took a few steps to the left, she nearly bumped into a woman wearing a stethoscope of all things.

"Sorry there, I did—" the woman began but was cut short by another gut-wrenching sound.

"I need your help!" Not waiting to see if she would follow, Kivran went back to the wing, down the aisle to find the woman on her stomach half on the cot with the daughter covered from the waist down in regurgitated material… and blood.

The daughter was sobbing uncontrollably. Somehow, Kivran already knew that final scream had come from the daughter.

Behind her, the doctor—hopefully that's what the woman was—was jogging down the same path, now shifting the patient to obtain vitals as the daughter continued.

Kivran's chest tightened, turning from the distraught young woman towards the remaining cots. The audible emotion had been powerful enough to breach the walls of their compound, loud enough to echo within your ears. And yet, the other cots remained unstirred, unaffected, deliberately ignorant of the life lost around them.

Unknown location, EASTERN ASIA
18 years, 195 days after Mutation 4

Salar sat on the only seat in the room, a wooden ottoman pushed against one of the walls. Leaning just his left side against the room, his entire right side still sported an infected-appearing bruise from the angle at which he had made contact with the water and was subsequently hauled out. While all he got were bumps and bruises from the incident, Aydin wasn't so lucky.

Salar would be lying if he said he didn't take responsibility for his cousin's death. Responsibility, not guilt, let's make that clear. But he hadn't attempted to cry yet. He needed a captivating enough audience for that sort of show, if he could pull it off at all. Remember: producing actual tears wasn't something Salar could do on a whim like the other emotions.

Allowing the pain to control much of his physical and verbal expressions, he had gotten off quite easy so far. No one stayed with him long enough to warrant a full-scale production, which was just fine by him; he'd need time to rehearse this particular emotion.

Building up to it, Salar took in his surroundings. He'd been in this room for a few minutes already, but it was only just now the voices outside walked away. This got him on his toes enough to fully observe his surroundings. Four walls, hastily applied mint green wallpaper, surprisingly one window facing south. Salar walked over to it, well, more like shuffled over. Though the window was quite filthy, he could make out the view without a doubt. Rainforest. As far as he could see. He wasn't on his home island any longer, there was too much vegetation to evident that.

Hearing voices outside the door again, he quickly shuffled back to the ottoman and rested himself in the same position as before. Crease the forehead, squint the eyes slightly—a visual representation of a headache, allow the jaw to remain taught yet a few centimetres ajar—a visual representation of breathlessness, lastly, do not clear the throat. The raspier the voice, the greater the sympathy. Salar hadn't quite determined the reasoning behind the last one.

The only entrance to the room opened, bringing in two hefty men carrying an air of authority. Every garb, head to toe, a shade of black. No visual signs of affiliation or classifications. No expressions.

Salar couldn't play off of them.

The first man perched himself on the window ledge while the other leaned against the perpendicular wall.

Pushing himself off the wall to illustrate they had his attention, Salar hissed voluntarily and quite audibly, hoping to get these two on the sympathy train as soon as possible.

Neither of the men altered their visible state in any form.

Salar alternated his gaze from one man to the other holding his face in the planned position, now wondering if this was the audience he'd been waiting for. From the silence, there may not be another opportunity. He needed to produce tears quickly if he hoped to gain any ground.

Squinting his eyes more, Salar concentrated.

Both men, with arms crossed, waited for him to speak. Though the man leaning against the wall glanced at Salar up and down every few seconds, the one by the window honed in on his eyes. The sun began to set as the room gradually became darker. Salar was afraid if he raised his eyes to figure out whether or not a light fixture was present, he'd lose his momentum.

It wasn't until the standing man had become so numb that he needed to crouch down that Salar finally let a tear stream down his face. Hopefully it wasn't too dark for them to witness this rarity. He felt proud—necessity really was the mother of invention, then.

"Well, there it is."

The one by the window had spoken, pausing between each syllable. It wasn't too dark, but the desired effect was never portrayed. Judging by the man's tone, he was mocking Salar.

Tilting his head to one side, raising one eyebrow and pouting his lips slightly, he tried to portray quizzical. The physical portrayal of this was flawless, yet again, the desired effect was never gained.

"We're not too big on the empathy side of things, so you can drop it now." The same man spoke again. Thankfully it was articulated slow enough for Salar to follow every word—his English was broken at best.

"As you've probably gathered," the other man spoke now, pushing himself up and away from the wall, "we've found the… contraband… so to speak… boat. That's… stuff you're… in. What're… do with it? Throw a dinner party?"

This man spoke a tad quicker than the other, Salar had trouble keeping up with the statements' entirety, but why was he questioning dinner?

"Ripped… kidney, dead body… on hands, fleeing a scene. What… you doing, huh?"

It's funny, the things we remember at the weirdest of times. Almost four years ago, when Aydin had been so consumed with finding a cure for Kivran, Salar spent most of his own time assisting his cousin all the while his own mother was dying. The cancer had become too widespread, too much to effectively handle. The last time Salar had seen his mother alive, she was bedridden, occupying one of the cots on the main floor of the clinic. She had requested to see him. Although he worked in the very place, he avoided her vicinity. He hadn't mastered nor even attempted a grieving emotion, he wouldn't know what to do with himself around her. His father had died a few years earlier, his mother had thankfully displayed grief on behalf of them both. It was Kivran who finally convinced him that it didn't matter what emotion you expressed, or didn't express, his mother needed to see his face and that would be enough. Kivran said for his mother, it was more than enough.

So to act as he was now expected to, Salar stepped into his mother's room after a shift on an average day. He wouldn't be able to tell us anything significant about that day, because it wasn't significant for him. It was only the day his mother died. Nothing significant.

Upon walking into the room, he found his mother on a bed pushed against the window, sunlight streaming across her face. She smiled as widely as possible seeing him. Swinging the door shut behind him, Salar didn't step any farther, he was told this would be enough.

"Come here, Salar." She lifted an arm only an inch above the bed, unable to move further.

Walking over, he perched himself on the edge of the bed near her torso. She lightly touched his arm, she felt cold yet damp simultaneously.

In a raspy voice, his mother spoke. "Your father wasn't the best man. He had ups and downs, his mood changed like the breeze. I always thought he felt too much. He let small things get to him, aggravate him beyond anything that could be justified."

She paused, catching her breath. Salar continued to look at the floor, away from her.

"And then there was you. My boy, who didn't feel enough."

Salar's attention piqued but he still didn't look over.

"You don't have to pretend in front of me any-more, I'm sorry you had to for so long. It was refreshing to have you as the complete opposite of your father. It was nice to hold your hand and tell you what was right and what was wrong. I could be your mother for longer, in a sense. I did what I could, Salar, I hope you see that. I won't be here to tell you these things much longer, but you should know there are people who can. You just have to find kind people in life, Salar. Follow these people, and you'll be amazed at how compassionate you can become."

The next morning, after burying his mother, Salar moved into Aydin and Kivran's home. These would be the people he'd surround himself with, the people his mother believed would make him a better person. Though he knew it wasn't something he was ultimately capable of, a part of him wanted to follow his mother's wishes. After all, she hadn't let him stray too far from reality yet. And now ever.

Looking back at the man who had asked the last question, Salar wiped his face of all forced emotion. These weren't the kind of people his mother was referring to; Aydin and Kivran were.

Pushing himself off the wall and straightening his back, Salar replied, "I'm not saying."

The man by the window stepped forward to join his partner. "That's a damn shame."

Undisclosed location, Asian WHO Base, EASTERN CHINA
18 years, 197 days after Mutation 4

It was later than usual. Then again, who was she to judge what usual was in a place like this.

The machinery noise emanating on the base hadn't ceased all evening and now it persisted well into the night. From the sound of it, the moment a helicopter landed, another one took off. All she could do was track the sounds, as nothing was visible from within the physical confines of any of the wings the refugees had clearance for.

She found herself fighting the urge to sleep, which was now a norm, but something felt off tonight. And she smelled of urine. Ang, the delightful little girl who had sat across from her on the way here, had once again wet her bed with only Kivran left awake to take notice. It once again fell on her to help. There was no way everyone in that room was fast asleep, but no one wanted to get up. Like the other night.

Kivran had helped the girl change into clean clothes before tucking her into bed next to her younger brother. The soiled sheets were then taken off the thin mattress and placed outside the main door. They would have to wait for morning to redress the bed. After washing herself under the low-pressured water, Kivran had just gotten back into her own bed. She could still hear the little girl sobbing, while she herself still carried the stench of urine. She wanted to allow herself a moment of selfishness, but something felt off.

Giving up, she got up to kneel on her bed and angled herself up to look out the caged window. She was greeted with the customary clay of the neighbouring building. However, the flickering lights through the narrow alley in-between were not customary. Craning her neck in each direction to see why this was, she found strings of lights vibrating under a helicopter's current. Within a few moments, the flickering ceased, and surprisingly, so did the noise that had been there all evening. With the exception of Ang's whimpering, an eerie silence filled the room.

Two sets of boots. That's what shortly followed. They seemed to be coming down the perpendicular wing, slightly out of sync with one another. They both stopped not too far away. One had crescendoed and now retreated whence it came. The other set remained silent.

At once, the bar at their main door clicked, Kivran dropped down to a fetal position near her pillow, and Ang let out a stifled yelp. Someone entered the room but only briefly. A singular step had been taken in, a pause occurred, and then the person was gone, door shut behind them.

Raising her head slightly, Kivran looked towards Ang. There was no movement, nor was there from anyone else in the long room. This odd feeling she had had all day catalyzed her curiosity, because the next thing she knew, Kivran was slipping on her shoes and tip-toeing out.

Now that she didn't have the cover of helicopters, she took extra care to not make a sound—patrol didn't quite approve of refugees wandering about like free humans at night. Or ever really. Taking one last look towards Ang's bed near the centre right of the room, Kivran pulled open the main door just enough for her small frame to fit through. Using her foot, she shifted the dirty sheets she'd been handling minutes ago so they slightly held the door ajar, preventing it from clanging shut. There were a few metres between each wing that remained uncovered, and depending on your clearance, unlocked. Hence the accessibility of the women's wing.

Cautiously looking both ways, not sure what it was she was doing outside, she continued on the balls of her feet towards the helicopter pad, its spotlights cast shadows on alleys between each wing. This was a plus for Kivran. It seemed like a good idea to follow those lights.

A slight breeze swept through. Thankfully, this was a rare, yet welcome, occurrence since most refugees spent their days indoors. Becoming comfortable in her movements, Kivran cleared almost three wings and was halfway to the helicopter pad before she came to a halt.

There, about twenty steps away from her across the makeshift street, kneeling beside a water pump, was a man who saw her at the same instant she noticed him, whom she hadn't seen in days but felt like eons within this cage. The odd feeling now went away. Cautiousness disappeared. Standing up, Kivran saw he had removed much of his military gear, this now sat not too far from him on the ground, a safe distance from the water. Not realizing her hands had been clenched, she now eased them, tucked away in her sweatshirt's sleeves. Under the oddly illuminating lights, she found herself succumbing to the urge to smile. In response, the man, who also stood in half shadows, mirrored her joy. Kivran watched across the dusty alleyway as Garrett rubbed water off his face and smiled back at her.

250

As she walked over to him, arms flushed against her side, gait hesitant, Garrett found himself staring. It wasn't until she'd been stationary in front of him for a few moments now, that he came to.

Running the back of his hand over his forehead to wipe off any excess water, he picked up his gear off the floor and held it in one hand, the hand away from Kivran, as he walked beside her to where ever she was headed..

At a slow pace, they walked down the base's main alley, passing at least two wings. Garrett couldn't say for sure how many, as he honestly wasn't paying attention in their silence.

Their destination was a wing he vaguely recalled as a barracks for refugee women and children. This must've been where she was temporarily housed. Still side by side, they both came to a standstill a few steps away from the wing's main doors. Something crumpled up and white held one of the doors ajar.

Leaving his side, she stepped forth to pick up the object.

"Laundry," she whispered as she gripped the door, stopping it from slamming shut.

Garrett gestured farther down the alley towards what she needed. She was back at his side as they once again held a slow pace to their destination. This time, however, she spoke.

"What's out there?"

Knowing what she meant by "there," and also knowing she wouldn't like the answer, he withheld a reply.

Realizing this, he saw her face him, stern look spread across her features. Even in dim lighting, he could tell what her scolding looked like.

"Please. We have no way of knowing. We aren't granted access to anything; if we ask the soldiers, they tell us we can't be privy to anything. We don't overhear anything. Please, Garrett."

The rarity of witnessing her in such a desperate state wasn't something he could cope with quite yet. Reaching the maintenance wing, he held the door open for her. She stood there, arms crossed, until he finally looked back.

"Get inside and I'll tell you."

With one last glance at him, she stepped in. Garrett followed her down the aisle of washing machines, hearing the door click shut behind him. The room sat silent, no one else to occupy it.

Slamming his gear down on a machine to the left of Kivran, he prepared the machine to the right. Holding a hand out from his position knelt on the floor, she handed him the sheets.

Only once the familiar thud of the cycle and water rushing in echoing through the confined space did he stand to look over at Kivran perched against an empty machine. She was looking back, waiting with raised eyebrows.

Leaning himself on a washer across the aisle, it was only for a moment that he hesitated in disclosing anything. He despised the thought, and yet he couldn't bring himself to not feel guilty at the situation he'd put her in. It was his fault she was in these circumstances to begin with. The only thought that comforted him in the realm of this guilt was knowing she'd be worse off had she stayed on her bloody island. Or at least that's what he preferred to tell himself. For this reasoning alone, he felt it was admissible for her to know some things. Some.

"Well, as expected, the whole island is under quarantine. Public relations speak, it's under Pre-emptive Quarantine, but, come on." He waited a moment before proceeding, she had become paler than usual. "The silver lining is, the whole country is not yet under the same classification."

"Yet." Looking down, she couldn't see him nodding in response.

Her knees began to give way as she slowly slithered to the floor. Garrett watched the rhythmic motion of her heaving shoulders as she tucked her head down towards the chest. The silent motion decreased until finally, she looked up. Sleep-deprived, eye-lids heavy, skin discoloured, she looked defeated.

And then she asked: "Can I go back?"

He felt defeated.

She regretted the question as soon as it left her lips. He appeared as though she had let him down. Regardless, it had been her initial thought from the moment she had seen him return. If there was anyone she could sway in here, it was him. But Kivran also knew, despite the outcome, he was trying to help her. To save her from what he believed would be a worse life. And yet, he knew next to nothing about her life, who was he to judge what would be a worse life for her?

As he came down to her level and sat on the floor opposite, he stretched his foot out. The boot rested lightly against her tattered hand-me-down sneakers. Garrett shook his head, sullen.

"Is that where you've just come from?"

Again, he simply shook his head.

And so they sat there, with the hum of the machine churning to fill their silence.

It's funny, the things you remember at the weirdest of times. The first night Kivran's pneumonia patient was admitted to the clinic, the woman had the most energy, as though her soul was burning its brightest before extinguishing. She had told Kivran that night of her late husband as Kivran was changing her into a clean hospital gown. She had said, and I am paraphrasing from Kivran's memory here: *When my husband and I met online, we couldn't stop talking to each other, almost all day, all night. We just talked and talked. When we finally met in person, all we did was argue. Over big things, over little things, almost all day and all night. We couldn't stop fighting with each other.*

Kivran had smiled, expecting the woman to continue with a tale of divorce. Continue she did but not of divorce: *Two months this went on. My father told me to leave before it got worse, I obviously didn't listen. I didn't want to listen. One day, we were arguing over something silly, I don't remember over what anymore, but it didn't matter. And I realized, you don't stick with something for that long if you hate it. We both loved fighting with each other, there was no one else we could do this with. We seemed crazy, but the same kind of crazy. We got married a week after that realization hit.* Kivran's smile had remained throughout, she could understand such a sentiment. As she tucked the woman under the sheets, she gave Kivran parting advice, "Find someone who can keep up a conversation with you, even if it is an argument."

Kivran could never tell you why this memory surfaced at this precise moment. Nope, couldn't tell you at all.

"May I ask something?" He was surprised to hear her at all. Deducing by the somber look on her face moments ago, she didn't want to be anywhere near him or this place.

"Anything you like."

"How did you get that scar?" She nodded in his general direction across the aisle. He read her lips more than heard her. His brain had begun to hammer away at the back of his skull.

Without missing a beat, he knew exactly which scar she was questioning. Having dressed the wounds he received in her hometown, she had countless opportunities to question those particulars. However, there was one scar he bore prior to ever setting foot in her country: the one on his lower right hip about three inches in length, running diagonally just above the burns she herself had tended to.

Smirking, he asked anyway. It was difficult enough getting a few decent words out of her, if she was up to it, why not?

"Which scar?"

Lifting her right arm, hand buried within the sleeve, Kivran pointed at his torso. "The one on your abdomen. It looks as though it's been there for some time."

He watched her eyes shift from his mid-region up to his own, waiting for a reply. Not wanting to bare his skin in demonstration, he just told her the story.

"Appendectomy, actually just a few years ago." Some story.

Nodding, satisfied at his answer. Garrett didn't want her to retreat again. "You're not going to ask why?"

No longer matching his gaze, she replied, "There's really only one reason for an appendectomy."

"Really, sure, but not actually." He had her attention again. "WHO soldiers have a portion of their training in Antarctica. You have to have your wisdom teeth and appendix removed before you can travel there. It's difficult to evacuate a single individual for something as trivial as those things. Something about building us up to cope with extreme climates and isolation." Though we know isolation is something he was already familiar enough with by that point.

"I wouldn't call them trivial."

"They would, and that's all that matters."

"That explains the polio scar? WHO going out of their way to make sure you're protected against anything and everything?" She jabbed a finger into her left shoulder.

"That explains the polio scar."

"May I ask something else?" He couldn't read her expression. He was hoping something would change in her once he'd told her about the scar, but to no avail. This dejected version of her which had surfaced since he had whisked her away made it difficult to recall precisely why it was he wanted to whisk her away in the first place.

Momentarily shifting his left foot, he ever so slightly nudged her.

"You don't have to ask if you can ask me something, Kivran. You can go ahead whenever you like. Don't worry."

"You don't always answer."

"That's not true. I don't always give you the answer you want."

She gave him a rigid look once more but didn't retort.

"Why become a WHO soldier? Do you understand the lives you ruin?"

Expecting a more lighthearted question than the one he was confronted with, he tried to prevent the hammering from spreading. She had every right to ask this question in her state.

"There's nothing I want more than to be so far from any one's radar that I never register. But before I drop off, before I go off to become no one in particular, I wanted to see *it*. Everything I could see before the end. That's why I joined. And as for your other question, I'm hoping you'll get to a point where that question won't be important to you."

He hadn't realized he had been hoping for her to stick around long enough to get to that point. As he saw the disgust rise within her, they heard the entrance door click open. Kivran sank lower in her position as Garrett shot up.

Keuhl stood in the frame, baton at the ready. Garrett hoped she hadn't registered the object.

"Asher."

"Keuhl."

Stepping inside, Keuhl tried to observe as much as he could of the room, his eyes shifting hastily. Garrett stepped a little to his right, blocking as much of Kivran as he could. Inexplicably.

Simultaneously, Keuhl's eyes shot to Garrett's knees as he felt Kivran lightly grasp his calf.

With still eyes, Keuhl spoke. "Everything all right, Asher?"

"Just about. Doing rounds now, are you?"

"Merely for now. Making sure everyone stays… where they're supposed to."

Grasp increased.

"You should've been a warden, Keuhl."

"Care for an escort, miss?"

He felt Kivran let go and come to her feet behind him. Without so much as a parting glance, she stepped out and made her way towards the entrance.

"I think I'll be okay, sir. Besides"—she slipped past Keuhl—"I'm sure you two probably want to relive the glory days."

As the machine beside him chimed to completion and she left his sight, Garrett thought two things:

1. There was no way she didn't register that baton now; and

2. I don't think that's how that cliché works.

She hadn't even bothered to take her shoes off and lift her legs onto the bed. Exhaustion had hit her like a tidal wave the instant she stepped back into her wing. She had floated in an in-between stage of being zoned out but relatively aware of her surroundings, just too tired to interact with them. Still no seizures. Feeling someone playing with her hair, she tried to bring herself entirely to. The excited chatter around the room helped. Though not everyone in the wing spoke the same language, they were all whispering a variation of *Jerman*. Germany.

Finally opening her eyes, she found all pillows in her eyesight bearing no heads, women were bustling about, energetic.

Kivran stretched an arm behind her to stop whoever was fiddling with her hair, she caught a tiny wrist, looking back to find Ang smiling, cheeks blazing red, hair tangled.

"We're going to Germany!"

Unable to speak just yet, Kivran replied with an inquisitorial guttural noise.

"Mum says tomorrow. You're coming with us, right? Say you'll come!"

Kivran turned back. She had no idea how to respond.

During an introductory chat conducted just before any refugee were able to set foot on this base, she was informed that as countries were able to take refugees, they would do so. However, only a certain number would be accepted, and there was no guarantee of when any given country would open its borders, so to speak.

Lifting her upper body, she stretched her legs, attempting to get the nerves active again. She felt springs recoil beneath her as Ang hopped off and ran back to her family.

Trying her best to ignore the chatter for now, Kivran went to clean herself up first. The bathroom was thankfully deserted as everyone clearly had better and more important things to occupy their time with.

Back on her cot, running her hands through her hair, she inadvertently began focusing on a group of women standing on a bed at the opposite side of the wing. Through the small glimpses she was granted of the window, Kivran tried to determine what it was that so eagerly held their unbroken attention.

"How many do you think they'll let on?"

"Leave room for us! They just keep filling it with supplies!"

Knowing the area from which all air transportation vehicles departed was in the opposite direction from these women's stares, Kivran's curiosity brought her to her feet. And just in time, for the moment she turned into the aisle, ready to get the unadulterated view, the back door to the wing opened.

An unforeseen individual held the door open as a single soldier stepped through. On a crutch. Of course he was playing it up, Keuhl didn't need that crutch, he'd been on patrol last night without it. Seeing him slowly stepping through, already knowing he had the room's attention with the alleged pain induced groans, Kivran became sure of what Keuhl was doing: getting narcissistic supply.

Not a fan of psychoanalytical theories particularly, she'd still believed it best to be knowledgeable on all matters of the human body. I'll skip over the section during which a narcissist was generically described in the textbook that Kivran, once again, had snuck out of Salar's dad's collection. What she is currently thinking back to is the theory that a person requires constant praise or admiration from their external environment in order to feed their ever-starving ego. This room of fervent women and children were Keuhl's supply of narcissism, and he was milking it all.

Every eye in the room, sadly to say, even Kivran's, were on him as he struggled to stand up straight at the far centre of the aisle. If she didn't know him well enough already, she'd feel sympathetic.

Keuhl loudly cleared his throat. It obviously wasn't necessary. He knew.

"If I could please have everyone's attention."

Silence. Even Ang stood tentatively by her brother's side, looking up at the wounded soldier.

"We have recently been authorized to release fifty refugees to the German immigration department with transport to be conducted at oh six forty-five tomorrow."

What a poor choice of wording: release. Kivran's stomach churned.

"Who chooses the fifty?" someone shouted from the somewhere in the back of the room.

Keuhl took his time in answering, making sure to shift his weight around and run the back of his palm over the forehead to emphasize exhaustion. That explicit dramatic effect, Kivran couldn't take her eyes off him.

"Well, as I'm sure you all remember, you were interviewed prior to being placed here." His gaze somehow shot straight to Kivran. "That has already determined who is eligible to be transported and who is not. The names of all eligible refugees are with our HR wing already. However, as the destination country promotes an international equality agenda, it is possible for a refugee to not meet our standards of transport and yet still meet those of Germany. As they will be the destination country, their guidelines supersede our own."

Ang's mother spoke up, Kivran recognized her voice. "You're saying if my daughter didn't pass all your interviews, she can still come with us to Germany?"

Kivran looked down at Ang, who had now become curious towards the crutch. The little girl had been given amnesty from one test due to her age, according to her mother. However, no refugee in the camp had been able to determine which test.

"Potentially. She would have to be re-screened by different standards before anything like that could occur."

"But there's more than fifty of us." The same voice as the first question spoke again. "More than fifty people passed your tests. You haven't told us how you'll choose them."

Keuhl looked down, his motions once again appeared calculated now. His dramatic effect was about to reach a climax.

"The admin wing decides. It's on a first-come, first-qualify basis."

That's why the unseen soldier had been holding the door open this whole time. A few women closest to the exit raced out as the remaining people in the room stood paralyzed.

As Keuhl's silence persisted, women glanced at each other. Perhaps they were all thinking what buzzed in Kivran's mind: is it too primitive to rush and secure myself a spot when others could be so much more deserving?

Keuhl shuffled from the centre to the right side of the aisle, using the arm not occupied with a crutch to gesture towards the open door. Condescension was strong with this one.

It wasn't altogether unwarranted however, once seeing how women began to pace out of there and towards the admin wing's direction. Keuhl held a self-satisfied look on his face as he watched them leave. Within moments, Kivran found herself standing in a near-empty wing, personal items scattered about haphazardly. Looking behind at the sound of a cot scraping the concrete floor, she saw a woman she was more acquainted with than many of the others. But that wasn't saying much.

The woman sitting on the bed frame, hunched over, elbows digging into the knees, was the daughter. The one whose mother Kivran had failed to save.

She had every reason to not rush out the door. Where would she go? Her whole family was gone. Where would you rush to? And for what?

Kivran realized she was asking herself just as much as the sunken woman in front of her.

"See you around, Doc." Turning back, she found Keuhl shuffling out whence he came.

As he went from view, the person holding the door popped their head into view.

"Kivran?"

Stepping closer, hoping to get the light out of her eyes enough to make the person out, she recognized him as one of the men present in the team that had flown the wounded soldiers out of Indonesia. It felt a lifetime ago. Home.

"Yes?"

He shifted to come into full view prior to continuing. "Captain Marek would like to see you, if you have a moment."

Marek. She repeated the name to herself, aiming to recall why it sounded familiar.

"He's in the infirmary. I can take you through."

That's it: the soldier who had come in most critical of any of them, riddled with severe burns. She had only heard his name once before, the day they all left.

Curious as to what he needed with her, Kivran nodded. Leaving the daughter behind on her own, she followed the soldier.

They passed the back side of the air base where men carried black crates around a corner and out of sight. She caught a glimpse of Garrett appearing from around the same bend. He stood stationary, holding her gaze until out of view. They passed the administration wing, outside of which stood two men in heated conversation with a handful of women at the end of a line apparently stretching outside, the line held open the building door allowing passersby to witness the admin desk swarmed.

They reached the infirmary. Whereas all other wings had entrance walls painted a brownish green hue, this wing was painted white. At least originally, it was now covered in thick layers of dirt and grime. Using a key card to enter, the soldier held the door open for Kivran. She stepped inside and immediately felt a sense of familiarity.

The scent of antiseptics dominated the air, cots covered in white sheets lined each side of the aisle, translucent canopies encompassed each individual cot, steel trays were stationed at intervals throughout. Only three beds were occupied.

"The Captain is on the far left, miss." He motioned for her to go on alone.

Making her way down the aisle, she hesitated against her curiosity to view the other two patients. Not feeling the soldier's eyes on her, she still didn't feel comfortable enough in his presence to take a chance.

Reaching the last occupied cot in the room, she placed a hand on the canopy, unsure on how to initialize.

"Excuse me?"

Hearing a sharp intake of air before a voice. "Yes, you can come through."

She parted the canopy to find the well-known patient lying flat beneath a hyperbaric chamber, just his neck and head visible, a sheet had been strategically thrown over the chamber's glass shell. A bandage covered his left ear, temple, and head, but for the most part, the man's face appeared to be improving.

With a strained smile, he spoke. "You must be Kivran. Owen Marek, it's nice to finally meet you. Consciously, that is."

"Yes." That's all she could reply with.

"I wanted to personally thank you for what you did. You saved me and my men." His speech reminded him a bit of Aydin's, there was an accent there that slipped in and out.

"I honestly didn't do much. I'm just a nurse."

"According to Garrett, you single-handedly saved us all. Which is why he was warranted in bringing you back with us. You needed to look after us on the journey back to ensure none of us slipped back into critical condition, isn't that correct?"

The influx made it a question while the tone made it a statement. Kivran realized why she was here, by this man's bedside: she was to corroborate Garrett's story. It was necessary to export this woman out of an impending quarantine zone. Necessary.

Marek raised a strained eyebrow at her silence. She wasn't certain how to tackle this test. It wasn't essential for her to accompany the soldiers back. If she admitted that now, it would do little to change her circumstances. She wasn't allowed to return to a zone now deemed under quarantine. By admitting the truth, she would most likely only change Garrett's circumstances—for the worse.

"That is correct."

The man appeared relieved. "Good." He ran his eyes up and down her. "You seem like a bright person, Kivran; glad you're here."

She nodded, hands now in her pockets, minimizing her physical existence.

"I hear there's a transport headed to Germany in the morning, are you on it?"

Why did he care about this? "I don't believe so, no."

"Hmm." He genuinely seemed surprised at her reply. "Garrett was certain you'd take it."

"And why's—"

"You should take it, Kivran. There's only so much we can do before it's no longer in our hands."

Taking her hands out, she knelt to meet his eye line. "Am I missing something here?"

He focused on her gaze for the first time. Even his naturally sunken eyes embodied Aydin. "It's easy enough for us to justify your presence here as of now, but once others start to look into it, we can't guarantee a safe outcome."

His tone had changed, she found herself trusting him. Maybe it was the accent's familiarity. "Wouldn't I be looked into closely if I *did* get on that transport?"

Marek smiled again. "Bright. Yeah, you would, but the information wouldn't reach others in time to bring the transport to a halt. That's why we held off on announcing until less than twenty-four hours beforehand. You could be long gone before they find out."

"Now it's a 'they'?"

"Stubborn too."

"Don't call me that."

His expression softened. "It would be best if you left now. Please. Garrett's—"

"Garrett." She hissed while shooting up, ruffling the canopy behind her. "Maybe Garrett should've left me there like I wanted!"

Without waiting for a retort, Kivran left his side. Walking back towards the entrance, she saw the other soldier leaning against a side door, startled. Thankfully he let her walk back on her own.

Retracing her steps, she stopped in front of the administration building. The door was now closed, there was no way of knowing how many people waited inside. The two soldiers from before were now stationed on either side of the entrance. What kind of outbreak were they expecting from a group of malnourished women and children whom they outnumbered, that they needed to make their presence so prominent?

As she stepped up to open the building doors, her thoughts drifted back to the young woman sitting in the wing. Alone.

8 km southeast of Ankara, TURKEY
Same day

"You've got it all wrong, dude! This is the new evolution, next stage in our development cycle."

They all looked towards Keuhl for his ever-welcome remarks. There hadn't yet been a medical debate he could resist.

"It's the bloody plague, you imbecile! It's a mutated avian virus. By your logic, the bleeding Black Death was our evolution as well!" On the word "evolution," Keuhl made a grand gesture with rolling eyes and jazz hands.

Odeli let out a chuckle.

Leaning in to Garrett, he whispered as Keuhl and the resident continued, "Sometimes, and only sometimes, I'm glad our lab rat is *our* lab rat."

Garrett didn't have the will to reply in any manner. After trekking through the sweltering heat on foot from the drop-off some six klicks due west, he was just glad to be out of the sun.

They were out here tracking a potential Mutation 4 host. The first promising lead in months. A girl of five years sat in the hall with her father, waiting to be instructed further. His unit was yet to see her, however in accordance with the report, the girl had self-inflicted lacerations running up and down her limbs and overall skin discolouration, among other things.

The prominent qualm Keuhl had with the situation was, how were the doctors certain these wounds were self-inflicted? The resident had replied with confidence they were. The first afternoon the patient had been admitted for observation, they found her alone in a room, spots of blood all over the sheets, and the girl frantically clawing at herself. The motions were borderline consistent with that of a person going into epileptic shock. The way her limbs had jerked and stiffened, there was no better way of describing it. If the hospital staff hadn't witnessed it firsthand, chances are, no one would've come to that conclusion.

Garrett found it curious that this was, of all other things, the thing that caught Keuhl's attention the most.

Turning his back on the two medical geniuses, he looked out the small window panel he had just been leaning against. This must've been the door to the hallway, for when he looked out, he saw two people occupying three chairs. The remainder of the ward was closed off to other patients and nonessential personnel, they couldn't have been anyone else.

"If the marker was present at birth, or could consistently be found on the same cluster of genomes, we could rapidly identify each case. We just need funding."

"A virus of this nature isn't going to show up on a scan at birth, you moron! It mutates, that's why it's a mutation! All the funding in the bloody world isn't gonna find it."

"If you know what to look for, regular scans could easily identify it."

"Yeah, *if* you know what to look for. Jesus, and how the hell are you going to get eight billion people scanned on a regular basis? We've barely eradicated fucking polio!"

A child was lying across two seats, gauze covered what was visible of her arms and legs beneath an oversized hospital gown. Facing the ceiling, he could see her profile, mouth gaped, mouth guard visible, her chest rose and fell at a rapid pace as she twitched in the slightest. Beneath the hued lighting and his position, it was difficult to corroborate any visible signs of skin discolouration.

"I'm only saying—"

"Well, don't. Just tell us about the bleeding case already."

"Five-year-old girl, first came in three months ago complaining about skin irritation. Gave her the standard topical ointment, suggested light moisturizers in the event that this was an eczema symptom, though she had neither history nor visible signs of the condition."

"Brilliant."

Odeli chuckled again.

"She came back a couple of weeks later, worsened state. Scars now quite visible. Conducted extensive allergen tests, deliberately including the prescribed medication into the said test. Came back negative or inconclusive on all variables. Conducted tests to determine potential kidney failure the following week. Negative results. Since then, we've had her admitted, plethora of tests, and nothing is coming back. It's not malnutrition; it's not kidney or liver disease; it's not blood cell imbalance, in fact her white blood cell count is above average; it's not a dermal condition we can recognize. We can't find it on any test result."

The other individual on the seat appeared to be the child's father. The girl's head rested on his lap as he ran one hand through her dark brown hair, his other hand was occupied with confining the child's wrists together, held taught against her upper body.

"What was it exactly that made you flag it in our system then?"

"One of our colleagues in Prague volunteered to run her DNA through the WHO DNA Initiative so we could break down her genome, compare it to other samples in your system and maybe find a similar case."

"Which you didn't?"

"Which we didn't. We did, however, notice then the irregularity in her dermal cells. The irregularity wasn't there at birth, she was born after the Universal Initiative was implemented so we compared both sets of her recorded genomes."

"Oh, so it wasn't present at birth. Would you look at that!"

"Her parents were never input, so, just on a hunch, we ran both of them through. Nothing out of the ordinary showed up on the father's, but on the mother's, part of the baseline sequence of the girl's irregularity was there in the mother's sequence. On the dermal cells. Examined the mother; no symptoms, nothing. The mother's sequence wasn't completed to the point that it would create a prominent irregularity, but somehow, the girl inherited the base sequence and it became a mutation."

The dark bags visible under the man's shut eyes as he leaned back against the wall said more to Garrett than any conversation could have.

"Have you found any connection to the previous Mutations? Or do you believe this is an entirely new entity?"

"Her family ran a farm in Indonesia somewhere, a chicken farm. She moved here about two years ago, after the parents split. Don't ask how we found this out, but the farm they ran, they get their feed from the same source in Asia that supplied, many of the now-closed, farms over there."

"Thanks, Doc Sherlock, but I don't think it's the feed that's your problem."

"No, I know patient zero was a pig over in a breeding farm or what have you, but I'm just saying, there is a connection."

"Okay, sure. Back to the mother's sequence, did that, or a portion of it, get flagged in the system? I mean, does someone else have that abnormal sequence?"

"None that we could find."

The girl shifted on the chairs in a drowsy state. It was evident that her skin irritation didn't include the face, there weren't any visible scars in that region.

"Let's have a look then, shall we?"

"I'll bring her in. But note, she doesn't appear how she's described in the report any longer."

"How do you mean?"

"Well there's the anticipated increase in lacerations, unfortunately, the rate at which they occur is exponential, so a fair number of them have become infected. Her pigment has gone from pale white to gruesome yellow faster than we can keep track of it. Oh, and her eye colour has changed."

The girl slowly began to open her eyes, flinching against the bright lights.

"That's not unheard of, loads of people's eye colours change with age."

"This one's odd though. Overnight, her eyes went from brown to a thick, solid grey. And not just her irises, her corneas as well. Almost like she's blind, but not. It's genuinely breathtaking."

The girl looked directly through the window and locked eyes with Garrett. His pulse began to race as he tried to keep his composure. He knew those eyes all too well.

Undisclosed location, Asian WHO Base, EASTERN CHINA
18 years, 201 days after Mutation 4

It had been exactly fifty-three days since she had last seen her family.

The gnawing at the back of her mind kept telling her all hope should be abandoned. Though every now and then that idea's complacency would begin to increase, it hadn't quite reached her heart just yet. She felt alone, a sadness that couldn't quite be expressed. And yet still, she couldn't bring herself to properly grieve.

Her home was gone, all her relatives were gone, she had chosen to leave behind the only life she'd ever led, and now here she stood, in a refugee camp miles away.

To distract from the crippling anxiety, this afternoon she had decided to pay Marek another visit. Last conversation aside, he was the only person in the vicinity she would consider speaking to. No new refugees had been brought in as of yet, and only a dozen remained. Whatever had happened the day before the refugee transport had left for Germany left the remaining temporary residents resentful of each other. There was little to no interaction between the dozen women now, only enough to appear amicable in soldier company.

Finding her way to the infirmary wasn't difficult, what was difficult was avoiding the gazes of the military personnel. Grabbing the handle to find the door locked, she recalled the soldier had used a key card to gain entry the previous time. Kivran knocked.

Fortunately enough, she heard the inside door handle rattle. The same soldier as before opened up.

"Good afternoon, miss."

"Good afternoon. I was hoping to speak to Owen Marek, if possible."

A courteous smile remained on his face as he took a few seconds to reply. "Certainly, miss. Kindly give me a moment to confirm this with Captain Marek beforehand."

"Of course." She stood to the side as the soldier closed the door.

Less than a minute had passed before he returned. Holding the entrance open, he motioned her inside. "Captain Marek would be delighted to see you. He is at the last occupied cot on your left-hand side."

"Thank you."

Leaving the soldier at the threshold, Kivran walked down the aisle and turned to the cot Marek had been in the last time they spoke, when they had officially met. He was now the only patient in the wing.

"Sorry?" She was never sure how to initiate a conversation.

"Come on through, Kivran." He already sounded much healthier. The slight rattling in his voice had disappeared.

Stepping through the canopy opening, she found Marek surprisingly sitting up and sporting an eye patch.

Most likely having witnessed Kivran's instant shock, he let out a laugh. "I know! They said I'm recovering faster than anticipated, so they've moved up my schedule. No more hot box, but I've got this nifty thing!" He gestured towards the covered eye.

She instinctively found herself mirroring his smile. The hyperbaric chamber was no longer present, although sheets covered his body from the waist down, preventing thorough observation, he appeared to be better as well. The bandage was still present along the left side of his head, but his face had now regained its colour while his neck and left arm sported fresh white gauze, and the right arm showed scabbing beneath the oily healing ointment, his visible hazel eye remained bloodshot and heavy, though.

"Grab a chair." Gently, he moved his head to gesture towards the right. Parting the canopy, Kivran dragged over a chair beside the neighbouring cot. "I do have to warn you, I took my meds not too long ago, and they've yet to kick in. So if I begin to drift off, that's why."

She nodded in understanding.

"To what do I owe this pleasure, Kivran?"

"Nothing in particular, I guess I just wanted someone to talk to."

"Ah, that's right. Garrett hasn't come back yet."

Kivran shook her head, avoiding the insinuation in his tone. "I was hoping you could perhaps elaborate on our last conversation."

Marek smiled again. "You ask the questions, and I'll do my best. No guarantees, though. Sorry, love, but I draw the line where Garrett can't."

Again, she nodded in understanding, and again, she avoided the insinuation. How he spoke wasn't in a condescending or mocking manner, however, which is why she remained.

"Why do you need me to leave as soon as possible?"

The smile disappeared, he was going to take her questions seriously. "You came through the wrong refugee channels. From what I understand, the question of where you came from has either deliberately been withheld at every turn, or it's been falsified. I'm sure you can see why that would be potentially dangerous."

Kivran shifted the chair closer. "There were other men, men not part of your team, I believe, who were on that plane that brought us all out."

"Those men can all be trusted. For the most part."

Keuhl. That was the first face that flashed into her memory at these words.

"What would happen if someone were to find out?" She sat on her hands to prevent herself from fidgeting nervously.

Marek remained silent. It was deafening in the empty wing.

"I won't be sent back home, correct? Garrett says no one's allowed into a region once it's under quarantine. Right?"

"Sorry, Kivran." He broke their gaze. "It is possible for someone who has escaped a quarantine zone to be transported back. I know what you must be thinking, but no, it's worse to go back now. Even if it was home."

His voice had dropped to a barely audible whisper during the final sentence. He was speaking from experience.

"Best-case scenario, you get dropped back, this base goes into shut down mode until it can be conclusively determined you did not bring any contagions with you in any way, shape, or form."

"Why take me out at all?" Her frustration seeped through.

"You already know I'm the wrong person to ask that. I was, thankfully, unconscious at the time. I'm free to plead ignorance there." His smile returned.

They remained in silence for a few moments. Kivran was glad Marek didn't need to fill every moment with chatter. She saw his charm as the corners of his eyes softened in empathy. It was effortless for her to like him.

Which is precisely what brought the following question to her lips: "Why were you there?"

"I thought that would be your first question." Marek gently shifted to lie down. She saw the shedding, burned flesh on the sheets now as he moved. "There's my line, Kivran."

She had genuinely believed he'd tell her.

As his eyes began to close, she thought it best to leave him be. Moving the canopy to place the chair back, she spotted the soldier standing by the entrance, waiting.

"Kivran?"

She turned back at his drowsy voice, smile still plastered across his face.

"Yes?"

"Why didn't you get on the transport?"

She looked at her feet, recalling the anger and relief coursing through her that afternoon.

"I was too late; there were no spots left."

"Try not to sound so happy."

She chuckled. She was glad she had decided to visit him.

"Kivran?"

Her smile didn't falter. "Yes?"

"Thanks again."

"You're welcome, Owen."

Undisclosed location, Asian WHO Base, EASTERN CHINA
18 years, 203 days after Mutation 4

His nerves hadn't settled in five days.

They had potentially found the marker to determine whether or not someone was carrying the Mutation or a variation of it. They had found a case, a proper case.

And the case's physical state could've easily described Kivran. Almost precisely.

It wasn't the idea that she had exposed everyone at the base to this virus that shook him, and that was on the presumption that she was carrying the Mutation, it was the idea that she hadn't said anything.

And he had practically forced her onto that plane. How many people would she infect once she landed in Germany?

Garrett sunk his head deeper into his hands. He was going to have to weigh his options and find a way to keep this fiasco to a minimum.

Wait, she had already been screened. Sure, they never mentioned where exactly she came from but the physical examinations, the DNA screenings, there was no way she could have passed those with no red flags popping up. She would've been stopped at the first hurdle. Had she been carrying the Mutation, that is.

We can't find it on any test result. That's what the resident had said. If that girl was a proper case, and Keuhl certainly seemed convinced she was, she was proof that tests brought no conclusions.

Parting his fingers slightly, Garrett risked a peek at the man sitting on the cot diagonal from him in the infirmary.

Legs crossed, perched on the cot's frame, Keuhl was looking back. This was something Garrett had become used to, the infatuation hadn't faltered, yet this stare deviated from the others. Rather than a wide, picture-perfect smile Keuhl usually smothered across his face, a smirk sat in its place. He bit his lip, smirk widening, cheeks flushed.

He knew.

Garrett closed his fingers, breathing becoming heavy again. She was gone, last transport out. He hoped all paperwork on where she had gone was no longer on base, no longer located anywhere Keuhl could track it down.

Though the unit members were the only people currently present in the wing, Odeli's debrief to Marek happening to his right wasn't loud enough to drown out the metallic clang of the entrance opening. There, caught mid-step, with the eyes of the entire wing now most likely on her, stood Kivran.

He screamed. A sheep died.

The instant Garrett registered her figure against the glare emanating from behind, two thoughts simultaneously crossed his mind:

1. He was actually glad to see her still there; and

2. What the hell was she still doing here?

Undisclosed location, Asian WHO Base, EASTERN CHINA
Same day

"Why the hell are you still here?!" His tone was hushed and yet forceful as Garrett took hold of her upper arm and swung her back out the door.

"Excuse me?" Kivran could have sworn she saw a smile on him just a moment ago. Almost missing the last two inclines as he rushed her down the steps, his familiar calloused hands sweaty against the touch.

No reply. He kept walking but now slowed the pace as he looked around suspiciously. Skipping a stride, Kivran moved to stand in front of him, grabbing his wrist with reciprocal force. "Let go of me, Garrett."

He opened his palm, allowing her to take a step back. His eyes weren't focusing, shifting from over her right shoulder to the left. What was he looking for?

"What is it?"

He leaned in before replying. "Not in the open." Moving back, he lifted his chin towards the mess hall. It would be empty right now.

Stepping out of his way, she let him go ahead. Trailing, she watched him glance behind four times in the short distance to the wing. Once inside, he locked the dead bolt at the top of the door and jogged towards the back of the room, obviously still searching for something that wasn't there. Kivran sat herself down, watching him frantically jog about. Elbows on the table, head in her hands, she waited.

Eventually, he returned, leaning on the table opposite her, still standing. "You were supposed to be on that last transport."

"I didn't want to be."

His sweaty, light brown hair was matted down. He had just returned from a mission.

"Kivran." He clearly liked to say her name as a statement.

"Garrett."

He took a deep breath in, the following came out in one exhale, rushed as though he was afraid the words might get caught inside: "Do you have the Mutation, yes or no?"

Kivran became quite aware of her own breathing as she attempted to keep it under control, stop her movements from giving away anything. Dropping her hands down, she clasped them on the table, clammy. She didn't like this test.

"Why would you ask that?"

"Is that a yes?"

"That's nothing, Garrett. I passed all your inquisitions up until now, I was cleared by the health unit. I'm not unders—"

"You were supposed to be on that transport, Kivran. I needed you to leave."

"Why?"

Pushing hair off his forehead, he hunched lower, maintaining eye contact. "I wasn't supposed to take you off that island—"

"No, you weren't."

Her tone had risen to his, they were on the brink of shouting at each other.

"I'm afraid someone is going to find out and… I don't know, but I'd rather not find out."

"You should've thought of that before." She stopped herself from voicing the last thought: take me back.

"But now, if this is true, then we've got a bigger problem on our hands."

"Our hands? No 'our' hands in this situation, just your hands. I didn't ask to be in this position. You brought this on me."

"I saved you!"

"You tell yourself that, you won't ever hear me say it."

With an aggravated sigh, he pushed back, now marching the length of the table. Kivran watched; she found it calming as she no longer monitored her breathing. She observed the rise and fall of his chest instead, keeping pace with him.

Only hearing the odd set of boots passing by, they stayed this way for a few moments. Content in not filling the silence.

In time, he came back to her, now seating himself. She waited for him to speak as he looked at her, gathering his words.

"I saw a girl today; she was so young and so frail." The anger had disappeared. "And sick. She was putting on a brave face, but you can only keep that up so long until it starts to slip. I watched as she was treated like an experiment. She'll be poked and prodded at until the day she dies, which will be very soon. I saw her cry, I heard her say she didn't want to do this anymore. But it didn't matter, it won't ever matter."

He had a look about him. He was wishing he hadn't witnessed what he had. Aydin often had this look, it became more and more difficult to rest her eyes on her brother as his sorrow went deeper.

Garrett placed his hands, palms down, on the table near hers. "This girl had scars running up and down her body, some sort of physical outcome of her condition."

She couldn't keep time with his breathing any longer. Her breathing became shallow. Slowly moving his hands, he gently touched Kivran's right arm, turning it over. "And she carried a sadness you couldn't describe."

She wasn't going to pass this test. Unwavering in his eye contact, he moved her sleeve up with great care, exposing her skin up to the mid-forearm. He never looked down. "She didn't want to be what she was. You could see it in her eyes."

Kivran couldn't bring herself to pull back her arm. Any movement on her part would only cement the theory track he was currently on.

"She had these striking grey eyes. You couldn't look away." Pulling the sleeve back down, he let her go.

It's funny, the things you remember at the weirdest of times. Back when she was just four, Kivran used to spend her time staring up at a picture her mother had torn from a magazine. The picture, which was taped with great care beside her mother's dresser mirror, depicted a city skyline. No idea which city, no idea which country, Kivran would sit on her mother's bed for extensive periods gazing at the outlines of grand buildings that seemed to mesh into each other, becoming this one magnificent wall. Behind which,

Kivran imagined, was a collection of people and things far superior to her own world.

Upon staring at it long enough, the little girl would come to and find her mother somewhere in the home. She'd be picked up endearingly and now get the privilege of staring into her mother's eyes. The way she looked at her made Kivran forget about anything else in the vicinity. Though she couldn't label it at the time, Kivran felt in those very moments what it was like to be genuinely loved.

And it was now, away from what she'd known, that she realized she hadn't deliberately thought of that picture since her mother had passed. It was as if that imagined collection of people and things were no longer superior. She wished she had spent all that wasted time staring at a picture, staring at her mother instead. Spent that time feeling loved.

That picture was what she had plucked out of the rubble of her home that night, that picture to which she had inadvertently clung so tight.

She couldn't tell you just when the warm tears had started spilling over. But she could tell you the look in the eyes of the man across from her was familiar.

"Don't ask me to take you back to that place, Kivran. Please." It was almost a whisper as though Garrett were speaking to himself.

She mimicked his tone. "I wasn't going to." And lied.

Undisclosed location, Asian WHO Base, EASTERN CHINA
Same day

Bloodcurdling screams. That's all he heard in the back of his mind, bloodcurdling screams. The screams from that little girl as they pulled her away from her father.

He had watched her eyes for as long as he could. It wasn't long.

Garrett looked down at Kivran's hands, with sleeves pulled down to the wrist, no one would be the wiser as to what she bore beneath. From his view, he could see the tears falling down the front of her shirt. He thought it best to let her be.

After an eternity, she spoke slowly with a raspy voice. "Why did you come to that island?"

"We came looking for someone dealing illegal organs. The mission didn't exactly turn out as planned." He saw no reason in lying or concealing anything at this point.

She nodded but didn't continue speaking.

"Regardless of what's happened already and regardless of… what you may or may not have, we have to get you on the next transport out. No questions, Kiv." He kept his palms straight down, hoping to keep the shaking to a minimum. He aimed for authority in his voice, but felt it was failing as it became unstable towards the end.

That little girl's scream.

"Did you find them?"

"Find who?"

"The people you were looking for on the island, did you find them?"

This was the thing she chose to focus on? Not having the heart to deny any answer she needed, Garrett shook his head and replied. "Not exactly."

He saw her slouch down, a sense of relief in her expression, she pulled her arms away and tucked them in her lap. The change was drastic enough to pique his curiosity. He could understand the community on such an island would be close-knit, he knew her home was in the blast radius that night, but neither entirely explained why she was relieved at the notion that these criminals weren't caught.

Garrett couldn't tell you why he said the following, a momentary lapse in judgement, nay, in emotion, perhaps. Perchance it was the dark in him that also found pleasure in running around an island screaming. Maybe it was the manifestation of an emotion he rarely put on display, something Kivran, of all people, deserved to see.

Garrett finished his thought. "We believe they died."

Undisclosed location, Asian WHO Base, EASTERN CHINA
18 years, 204 days after Mutation 4

Garrett sat on the edge of his cot polishing his boots. He was scheduled to fly west at 1800 hours on yet another border reinforcement mission. This time on the northern-most Russian-Norwegian border. Famine-stricken refugees were beginning to flood west at an increasing rate, Norway lacked the personnel to effectively manage them. All other WHO units were already deployed on other assignments. Even after Keuhl's protests claiming their unit wasn't tasked to handle such "mundane" tasks, they were prepping to be deployed. It was opportune enough, though, as neither Odeli nor Garrett felt comfortable leaving behind Marek on anything other than a mundane mission.

There were no refugee transports scheduled for the next few days, Kivran would have to be left here. Again.

"Garrett!"

Looking up at the mention of his name, he saw Odeli enter the barracks via the north door. His pace was quickened upon finding the man. With a small pile of bent papers and a creaking noise, Odeli took a seat upon the cot opposite Garrett.

"The Turkey case details just came through the main line." He seemed excited at this discovery just as Garrett began to prepare for devastation. Gripping the boot, he tried to steady his thoughts enough to listen effectively.

"I don't know if your beloved Keuhl's told you yet." Marek leaned in closer, shifting his eyes around the vicinity to make sure no one was paying too much attention. They thankfully weren't. "But you remember how the DNA comparison stated that anomaly was present in that girl's mother too?" He continued without a reply. "The mother was a native of Indonesia. More specifically, of that island. Yes, *that* island. Do you see what that would mean?"

His brain was hammering at his skull again, looking for a way out of this madness. He pictured local men like those they had initially accompanied to the island, razing that entire island to the ground. What would they do if they found out people had left? He spoke out loud, more so for his own sake than a reply. "It would mean The AB is going to descend on that place. Pre-emptive Quarantine, my ass."

"Exactly! Think of the credit for finding an actual case, the origins of a case! All this time it was like we were chickens running around with our heads cut off, and now we fall on this by accident! Can you believe our luck? We're gonna be on the front lines of this thing, this thing called history."

Garrett dropped his boot to the ground, bringing his head into his hands, trying to stop the hammering.

"We are going to have to hang out here for a bit, though, until The AB gives us the go ahead.

"Why?"

"They've still listed the zone as Pre-emptive Quarantine in the records, but Keuhl's saying this'll just give them an excuse to vet the whole place top to bottom without drawing too many eyes."

"Vetting for what?"

"People who came in contact with that mom."

Garrett could feel the blood draining from his face.

"Don't worry, dude. We're good." Odeli shifted through the pages in his hands, looking for something. "Apparently the mom died before we even got there, and you have to come in direct contact with bodily fluid. So we don't need to be confined."

"How did she die?" The moment he said those words, Garrett couldn't tell you why they spilled out so easily. In hindsight, however, he knew the exact reason: he needed to know what might happen to Kivran, how she might die.

"Uh." Odeli kept up the noise while flipping back and forth through a few more pages. Garrett's fingers began to numb. "Ah! She died... in childbirth. At... What was the name of the clinic you guys were held at over there?"

He shook his head, surprisingly, he'd never bothered to look up at the sign. However, he did know one thing for sure. "I don't know, but there's only one hospital on that island. Why?" He knew the reason already, though.

"Masoom Clinic, that's where the mom died. Isn't the girl..." Odeli trailed off, noticing he didn't need to say the words, Garrett already knew where this was headed.

If he sat there and thought about it, he never would've gotten up, the courage would've left him. Slipping his feet into the semi-polished boots, not bothering to tie them, he made for the exit. Garrett stopped short, however, as he noticed the woman at the threshold.

Strawberry blonde hair, freckles covering the bridge of her nose, she looked awfully familiar. "Hey!" She quickly glanced at Garrett before roaming her eyes over the rest of the room, landing on the back of Odeli's figure. She repeated the greeting, this time louder in the other man's direction.

Odeli turned around, already a smile on his face, evidently having recognized the voice. "Ayo!"

Garrett's eyes shifted back and forth from the woman to the now-approaching man. His female, as Walcott referred to her.

"I didn't even realize the time. You all right?"

The two continued conversing, but Garrett didn't take in any more. What he did do, however, was stand awkwardly close to the two as they continued their reunion, staring dead on.

Eventually acknowledging Garrett, Odeli stepped back from the woman. "Apologies Tam, this is Garrett. Garrett, Tamsin."

She said something in response, but Garrett never caught it. His eyes began to shift between her, Odeli, and back again, this time his eyebrows raised. He was waiting for the man to catch his drift.

Taking longer than it should have, all the while Odeli looked on with a puzzled expression. When it finally clicked, Garrett smiled, putting as much charm as he could muster onto his face.

Undisclosed location, Asian WHO Base, EASTERN CHINA
Same day

"I don't know how it works in your unit, Devon, but it definitely doesn't work like that in ours." She was attempting to keep her voice down, but sometimes he just spat out some absurd things.

Put her on your rotation.

Was he kidding? The woman wasn't even a full-fledged doctor, let alone having passed the proper entrance exams to be a DWB. There was no way Tamsin could magically take her—Kivran, she believed the name was—under her wing.

Moving on to the next aisle, she grabbed a handful of antibiotic bottles and carelessly tossed them into the knapsack heavily dangling from her wrist. Her favourite part of being stranded here: raiding the WHO medical supply wing. Odeli followed her over, waiting at the opposite end of the aisle. The door to the wing perfectly poised wide open behind him when he was supposed to be keeping an eye out. She wouldn't say they were doing anything wrong, but she also wouldn't say what they were doing was A-okay. Fortunately, however, the infirmary was the only building opposite them, and that place wasn't currently busy enough to produce a significant amount of prying eyes.

He put on a pleading voice, the kind he reserved for special days. Days when he knew he was asking for something major. "Can't you make an exception, just this once?"

She spoke in a steady voice, the kind she reserved for special days. Days when she knew she couldn't give him anything major. "No."

"Fine!" His arms crossed in frustration. The fact that he still stood in front of her meant he wasn't done just yet.

They didn't get to see each other often, even crossing paths with him here was a pleasant surprise. She hated wasting their time in this state. Placing the bag on the floor, Tamsin tried to clean the slate in her mind. "Tell me again, from the top, why is this important to you and what exactly do you expect of me?"

A half-smile returned to his face. "Not really important to me, more so to them." He pointed over his left shoulder towards the infirmary. "We were hoping you could take her with you wherever you go next. She's a good enough nurse, she practically saved the others' lives—"

"You said they were just a few burns, Dev."

"She could help out, and then it's up to you: if you want to keep her with you, you can do that, or you can leave her where ever you land.

"Really thought this through, eh?"

"As long as you keep her off the log. That's it, that's all we're asking."

"We? I thought you said this was 'them.'"

"Oh you know, camaraderie and what not. I'm a compassionate guy, Tam, you know that!"

"And you can't tell me what or who you're clearly hiding her from?"

"No, love, sorry."

Taking the time to look over Odeli's shoulder now, she saw Asher and the woman seated on the said infirmary entrance steps. She hadn't realized when they had come outside. Both sat alike, elbows on knees, heads hunched over. The man's eyes met Tamsin's, he was watching them intently. Wow, this guy was not a master of subtlety.

Her, she recognized her as the woman who had helped the refugee a few weeks ago. She hadn't realized this was whom they had been talking about all along. She became open to the idea now. The young woman looked like she could use some protecting.

Tamsin continued watching them, knowing Odeli was waiting for some form of a reply. For the most part, that is the two times from afar she had seen this man, Tamsin had found him difficult to read. Then again, she hadn't put forth her best efforts. He seemed almost disappointed at the things around him, let down somehow. But as he now slightly extended his hand to touch the woman's, she was beginning to see him differently. He didn't look disappointed, but rather sad. And as the woman opened up her palm, letting him rest his hand on hers, Tamsin thought of the man standing in front of her in the aisle. When she announced her departures to him, he had the same look as that man on the stairs.

Turning back to Odeli, Tamsin sighed, unsure in the back of her mind but convinced in her gut. "Fine."

The surprise on his face was instant. "Really?! You'll do it?"

"Why are you surprised? It's what you wanted."

Really, sometimes he just spat out some absurd things.

Thick droplets immediately began to drench him the moment he stepping out. The musty odour only rain and wet sand could reproduce filled the air.

It's funny, the things you remember at the weirdest of times. Garrett had this very vivid memory from his childhood, back when his mother was still a prominent part of his life. His parents had been invited to a Christmas gala at the Reykjavik Music Hall, a classy sort of affair he was forced into as well.

The temperature hadn't dropped enough for snow just yet, even in late December, but heavy sleet hadn't been letting up for days now. Mesmerized by the sight of the ocean in such a stormy state, Garrett strayed from his parents' presence. Simply not satisfied with viewing this behind a glass window, the boy made his way outside towards the walkway hugging the shore, overlooking the grey mountains and unsettled waters. The mountains went in and out of view as the fog shifted, the rain was angled behind him drenching his clothes from the rear while the front remained relatively dry. Out of his peripherals, he could see two ducks bobbing against the current, attempting no escape at all. He wondered whether the birds felt the same way as him: content in a storm they had no control over, in awe and wonder of its dominion. Immobile.

He didn't comprehend the correct sense of time at that age for us to know just how long Garrett stood there, but it was long enough for him to now still remember as a man exactly what those mountains looked like. The particular hues, the jagged peaks.

His mother found him soaked, stationary by the rocks. Making no motion to cover him up, she stood beside the boy gazing out where her son was, and yet most likely not seeing what he was. "You'll catch your death, Garrett," she had said. "Ponder the irony in that, we come all this way to protect you and here you are: dying regardless."

Death, what a peculiar matter to discuss with a child.

Letting droplets slosh around in his untied boots, Garrett walked at a pace intended to draw as little attention as possible towards the refugee wing he had in mind. Along the way, he made note of the third-party transport being loaded. It brimmed with medical supplies and personnel.

Finding his destination, he hoped she was here and alone. Taking a second before, his hand resting on the door handle. He felt nauseous, unable to determine the origins of his hesitation.

He wouldn't scream. He wouldn't let this one die.

Opening one of the metal doors, Garrett stepped inside to find two women in the back left of the room seated near a window frozen amidst an animated conversation. While in the far centre, however, was Kivran characteristically continuing to go about her business as though nothing in her surroundings had stirred.

With squeaking boots, he made his way towards her across the floor but stopped a few rows short for two reasons:

1. The two unknown women were watching him intently to the point of unsettlement; and

2. He was dirtying the floor Kivran was currently busy cleaning.

Catching her attention, he bobbed his neck in such a way as to indicate he needed to speak to her outside, the woman leaned the broom against the nearest cot and tiptoed across to follow him out the door. She wasn't wearing shoes, just socks, even in this heat.

Only once the door had completely shut behind them did he begin speaking, standing under the slightly overhanging roof. "Why haven't you requested transport information from the admin office? They'll try to find you the next ride out, even if it's not from this base."

Arms crossed across her chest, whether out of cold or standoffishness, he couldn't tell. "Why do you ask?"

"I told you, Keuhl knows; and it's just a matter of time before he flags down somebody to pick you up."

She nodded, swaying to keep her balance on the toes. "I'll leave soon."

Stubborn, through and through. Shaking his head, he finally realized what she reminded him of: one of the birds in the water swaying against that storm, completely content.

"Soon is too far. The transports are probably all full now. We're trying to get a Doctors Without

Borders team to cover your transport somewhere safe now, off the record of course."

"Where?"

"I don't know yet."

"Alone?"

"Yes."

He allowed the silence to swell in between them before continuing.

"I'm headed out in a bit on an assignment, so I'll leave you here." He was waiting for the expression to change somehow. Sadness, perhaps, is what he found himself wanting. She didn't give any, or at least didn't show any. "If it works out, Odeli will likely come by to collect you—"

"Collect me?"

"Please just go with him, Kivran."

"Yes, sir."

He found himself slouching beneath her gaze and demeanour. A part of him was frustrated at his unintentional display of defeat. The other part was frustrated at her. Why did she always have to make it seem as though he wasn't trying to do the right thing?

"Kivran."

"Garrett."

This was the right thing, yes?

Allowing the former frustration to overwhelm him, he turned to head back to his barracks but stopped as soon as exiting the shelter of the roof.

We come all this way to protect you and here you are: dying regardless.

Turning around, he saw Kivran with one hand against the handle, straining to not let her heels down, she looked back with inquisitorial eyes. She stood in hesitation just as he had moments ago. With the rain hitting his back in a familiar way, Garrett realized this was a storm, his storm. The one he could be content in.

Undisclosed location, Asian WHO Base, EASTERN CHINA
Same day

She thought of the picture in her mother's bed-room for the second time that day. The first came when she instinctively folded the picture into her pocket early this morning, and the second time as she gazed upon Garrett as he stood against a backdrop of pouring rain, rhythmic pouring rain, and propeller hums from a few wings over.

Kivran understood what he was telling her, she could understand his intentions. What she couldn't comprehend was why he needed to dispose of her immediately? She hadn't told anyone about her condition; she hadn't even suffered from the symptoms in a very long time. If you could call it a long time. Since she had last seen Aydin and Salar, was that really a long time ago? It certainly felt so. She dug her free hand into the confines of the pant pockets and rested it against the picture. *That* felt like a long time ago.

If she left now, that skyline she had dreamed of, with the imaginary people with the imaginary lives could be realized. She could be out there, living lives she could only dream of behind her patients' eyes. And yet, she was having difficulty fighting the urge to weep. She had lost so much, and she couldn't go off looking for things she might just end up losing any longer. At least not if she did what she was told.

"Are you sure they're dead?" She needed to know there was nothing left for her in the old world. No one left.

"Who?" He stepped back under the shelter, shivering.

"The people you went looking for over there."

Garrett paused a moment, however it wasn't a result of hesitation. He appeared to be reading her expression closely. "Yes."

The urge was about to overwhelm her.

"I saw it happen. Why do you ask?"

"They could be alive still, right?"

"No, Kivran. Why do you ask?"

She touched her heels down just as she lost the fight.

Garrett held her gaze as he gently touched the wrist peeking out of her pocket. He felt warm to the touch.

Not thinking it possible, her chest constricted more as she silently endeavoured to steady her breathing. Logically, she knew this to be true, but time and time again she had systemically refused to acknowledge that logical rhetoric. Until this moment.

Gladly, the rain kept her spectacle to a minimal number of witnesses. Composing herself, Kivran stifled a yawn before pulling her head up.

Don't get attached.

Innaya's voice rang out between her ears. She didn't want to do that anymore, she had been alone so long, so hopelessly detached, she was beginning to lose herself. Kivran hoped Innaya was okay just as she let the acceptance of her circumstances finally wash the lingering doubt.

Concentrating on her left wrist, she could feel every pore rising beneath the touch. If he wanted this, him—the only person left who showed anything towards her—she would listen. But she needn't answer that particular question.

"I'll wait for Odeli to come collect me."

He didn't reply instantly, perhaps he was waiting for another retort. She let him down once more.

"I'm trying to do the right thing here."

She nodded; she had heard that before.

He pulled his hand away. "Good luck with everything." He tapered off towards the end, somehow not liking what he was stating.

Turning her face towards him, she swung open the door, stepping out of its projectile, ready to part ways. Still shivering, clothing only half done up and drenched from head to toe, Kivran emitted a somber smile as she took the sight of Garrett to memory. Surprisingly, she found it comforting to know he was beside her in that moment and not anywhere else.

Don't worry.

Budapest, HUNGARY
19 years, 178 days after Mutation 4

There are some deaths that weigh more than others. Some souls whose departures leave a greater sense of emptiness in their wake.

The man sprawled out on the operation table before her didn't represent such a death. She didn't even know this one's name, she had only met him a few breaths ago, the last one to be triaged and unfortunately last was the worst in this situation.

No, the soul in question was that of a young girl, child really, who had died kilometres away. The report may have stated "natural causes," but Tamsin knew better. After having sat with that girl, watching her tear away at her own flesh, and with her father helpless in every sense to stop her, Tamsin knew better. The father had given in, he had ended his daughter's suffering. No sane person could've stood by watching her day in, day out.

Tamsin had seen it in his eyes. He had known what needed to be done months ago. She wondered what took him so long. She hoped the girl had passed calmly into the night, without any more pain.

Pulling her knees up to her chest and resting her chin, Tamsin inhaled the stench of iron and must trapped in the room. She knew opening the operating room door wouldn't do any good, the smell was all over the place.

Nearly an hour ago, a significant chunk of the natural cave formations, which ran beneath the city's principal architecture, had collapsed. Some forty-five injured citizens had been transported to her hospital. There was no set figure on the number of casualties on site yet. Because of the accident, it wasn't until now that Tamsin had time to properly process the report she had been emailed regarding the girl. Having been one of the chief doctors to sign off on the patient's chart, she was required to receive a concluding report.

The report told her what the girl was initially admitted for, what she was taking before her passing, and what the preliminary autopsy had concluded. But the report didn't state she was one of the bravest people Tamsin had ever had the pleasure of meeting. That child did not deserve to go through the hell she was put through every moment of her existence. And yet still, she never revealed the true depth of how much that illness had eaten away at her insides.

For the first time in quite a while, Tamsin was mourning the loss of a patient.

Picking at caked blood with a glove-covered hand by her ankle, she thought of the young woman still alive in her care. The young woman with at least one significant similarity to the deceased girl.

She recalled the day this woman was thrust into her arms, shortly thereafter fusing into this world as though it was her first nature to be among those on the brink of death. Tamsin remembered that day quite vividly now than ever before. The day they had departed the WHO military base nearly eleven months ago.

That man from Odeli's team had found her in the mess hall early in the morning, Garrett, as she recalled.

The man looked as though he hadn't slept in days, there were dark bags under his eyes, he kept fidgeting with his hair and licking his chapped lips. His movements were agitated. If she hadn't known what he did for a living, she would have assumed he was on narcotics.

He had sat across from her in the near empty hall, initiating a conversation to her surprise. She had met him less than seventy-two hours ago, and that interaction didn't quite layout the patchwork for a solid communications-based relationship.

"I don't really know you, and you don't really know me, and I don't really have a right to ask this of you, but I need to." Though his words had come out clear and precise, the tone made it seem as though he was stumbling over them against the tip of his tongue.

She had told him to go on, curious more than anything.

"Please look after her, after Kivran."

"She looks like she can look after herself."

"I know, but please don't leave her on her own." He had stopped moving for the following part, his legs stopped bouncing under the table and his hands sat firmly grasped atop it. "You seem like a reasonable person, Tamsin. I don't doubt you'll eventually find out, find *it* out. You might be elated that day, but I might be devastated. On that day, you'll understand why I'm asking. Please, look after her."

The gravitas in his voice had reached her, made her forget these people were near strangers. She had looked him straight in the eyes and nodded. He had then proceeded to thank her before exiting the hall, no longer fidgeting.

Something had clicked the moment she read the girl's report, looking back at the symptoms again, she recognized them.

Today was the day she understood why Garrett was asking. However, she wasn't elated.

Undisclosed location, southeast of Akureyri, ICELAND
Same day

Mr. Mikael Keuhl,

In light of recent events, and your continuing temporary allocation with us, our research laboratories have revisited your application for a permanent internal transfer from Field Operations Units to the Research Division (The Akureyri Base) and we are delighted to inform you of your acceptance into the Research Division as a research assistant once more.

Kindly organize your own method of transportation to our facilities in order to commence work at 0800 on the 23rd day of March, 2038.

In the event that you are not present at the above location at the above indicated time, we will be of the assumption that you are no longer interested in the Research Division (The Akureyri Base) research assistant position and your file will be sent back to Field Operations Units at our earliest convenience.

Please do not relay further communication through this email channel as it will not be regularly monitored.

Thank you for your interest in the Research Division, we look forward to having you on our team.

Best Regards,

(undisclosed) Authorized Signing Officer, Research Division (The Akureyri Base)

Budapest, HUNGARY
19 years, 191 days after Mutation 4

The first door had to be shut before the second could open, like an animal enclosure.

He mustered all the patience he had in his bones waiting for the security doors to open before him. Behind said set of second doors, somewhere in that mess of people, in those dislocated, disoriented, possibly bloody and wounded people, was Kivran.

Garrett inadvertently thought of that chain-link fence he once guarded in the middle of the desert a lifetime ago. Funny, he was about to be on the opposite side of it now, and he wanted nothing more.

For the time being, however, stood Odeli in front of him, the usual giddy expression at the potential of seeing his fiancée was absent. Garrett lifted his chin in a questioning manner, knowing everyone else momentarily stranded between the two doors wasn't paying much mind.

"That little girl died."

He already knew who he spoke of. Feeling as though his body had been plunged into freezing water, pins and needles shot through him. He knew, and yet, Garrett slipped the question past his numb lips. "Which girl?"

"Blind-looking girl over in Turkey we saw a few months ago." Odeli's empathy was etched all over his face; he knew Garrett's secret. Garrett had foolishly thought he had hidden her away.

He screamed.

Garrett hadn't done this is in quite some time, the anger had simply been building up, but there was never enough for him to no longer contain it. He could do this no longer.

"How?" It didn't sound like his voice, nor did it feel as though it emanated from him.

The sliding doors Odeli had casually been leaning against, as though a serious conversation wasn't being conducted, began to slide upwards. The man, in turn, stepped closer to the petrified figure.

"One of her episodes was awful, she scratched away at open wounds, wounds brought about by the people studying her, scratched all night, tore herself apart."

He felt claustrophobic.

"She was strapped down but broke free. Her father left her there, afraid he might… catch it. Here's the kicker, Garrett—"

Garrett didn't want to know.

"Her cause of death wasn't blood loss. Her seizing became so extreme, her heart gave out in the night. How long do you think she lived with that? How much longer could she have?"

He hadn't even realized the confined space had been emptied out with the exception of these two. Behind Odeli, a setting sun became visible. And Tamsin.

The final of who stood pacing about a few feet from the opening. Garrett didn't know her well enough to know what kind of state she was in, but Odeli evidently did, for with only a simple nod exchanged between each other, Odeli walked out of sight, leaving the two acquaintances.

In a dreamlike state, he heard someone shout from somewhere up high that they needed to close the door, and so Garrett stepped out into the shore breeze.

Involuntarily, he found himself scanning the mess of people behind Tamsin in the distance, looking for something he already knew he wouldn't see. The last time he had been here, less than four months ago, the area had housed roughly three hundred displaced souls all hushed in their exchanges, terrified of one another, of the place. Beyond Tamsin's shoulders now wandered a swarm of no less than a thousand people loud enough to generate a constant static. How could anyone not find it deafening?

"Nice to see you again, Garrett."

Pleasantries he didn't feel like reciprocating.

"From your expression I can see Odeli spoke to you already. I asked him to, I thought it would be better coming from someone you knew well."

He was no longer searching, but he didn't have the courage to look at her just yet.

"That case isn't one that can be swept under the rug, it's only a matter of time before it leaves the WHO confines. Someone is bound to describe the patient's physical appearance, and before long, everyone is going to be looking for anything similar."

Garrett looked in her eyes finally.

"For what it's worth, I'm not elated. I'm sorry, Garrett, but I can't protect her anymore. It's out of my hands."

"Where—" His voice hitched. "Where was the girl when it happened?" The where was important, it would help him determine just how much time she—Kivran—had left in the dark.

Tamsin shook her head, the practiced stern expression fading at the unexpected question. "Last I saw of her was in Turkey, but the report said 'undisclosed.' The final sign-off was by Keuhl though. Wasn't he in your unit? Maybe he could confirm it for you."

The AB, that's where the girl had been. Right next to Keuhl.

A part of him, somewhere in the depths, was furious at himself. Furious for doing such a shitty job of this, for taking her out of quarantine in the first place. His utter shock at the situation numbed out the remainder of him, however. Which is why Garrett can't tell you how he and Tamsin parted ways, or how long he stood staring out at the herd of people. Eventually, when the sun no longer warmed him, and goose bumps rose along the back of his neck, Garrett moved forth.

Walking through the crowd, he felt the pit in his stomach expanding. Expressions on the faces of those who paid attention to his passing emitted a fear of sorts. They stopped in their tracks, waiting for him to pass before proceeding about their own business, they halted their conversations. He wasn't an imbecile, he knew the mere idea of his presence was a warning sign to crowds like these—crowds who had primarily been displaced by quarantine procedures. Whomever handled public relations on behalf of WHO was doing one hell of job, most of the world had no idea camps like this were trickled around major Eastern European cities. These people hated his presence, and for good reason.

Reaching the outskirts of the camp, Garrett inhaled deeply, there were no accusatory eyes on him now, and he could breathe, losing the static somewhere behind. Stepping farther away from those people's lives, he inched closer to the river. Zipping up his uniform jacket against the shore's breeze, he stood stationary, realizing if she was anywhere, it would be here.

And there she was: on the opposite side of a barrier intended to keep wanderers from unsteady footing, seated on the cliff's edge, feet swinging over, hair freely flicking about.

Quietly hopping the barrier, he took her in before speaking, deciding in that very moment he didn't wish to dwell on the conversation he'd been privy to on his way in. He just needed a moment with her, he may not get another after this.

"That looks quite familiar." He spoke against the crashing waves, a storm was on its way.

Garrett felt her smile before he saw it. Taking a seat next to her, he watched her expression. There was no fear, a stark contrast to what he had just walked through. Her eyes were closed, the cold reddening the tips of her nose and cheeks. Leaning over, he kissed her right temple before she met his gaze.

"Of all the places in all the lands, I had to end up here." Her voice sounded raspy, as though she had been crying recently. He didn't pry.

Looking out at the view once again, he watched the sun set against the skyline consisting of government buildings and financial institutions now half-shrouded in darkness, the other half in bright dusk. With the Danube before them, they stared down at the Budapest skyline. The same skyline Kivran kept a picture of for as long as he'd known her.

Getting more comfortable on the hard ground, he mirrored her by swinging his legs over the edge. She tucked her right leg behind his and stopped moving.

Somewhere beyond that skyline also lay his father six feet under. *Of all the places in all the lands, I had to end up here.*

Content in silence, he sat with her until the sun no longer touched the city before them, and until lights flickered on one by one, scattering about. He knew that small moment between was what she had been waiting for all day, like every day. She looked over when the moment had passed. As he watched her eyes glow, he tried to subdue the dreadful feeling sinking into him once again. She couldn't stay here any longer.

But he couldn't leave just this second, thus there was no point in wasting the second.

"Best thing that happened today?" He heard his voice shake at the beginning, he hoped she hadn't caught it.

Kivran looked down at herself before answering. "I got a few good kicks today, that's pretty 'best thing' material." She rubbed a palm over her swollen belly, resting it on the underside. "What was the best thing that happened to you today?"

He waited for her to look back at him before answering. When she did, Garrett saw the sincerity in her face, the storm he was content in.

"This, right now."

She laughed, shaking her head at his reply.

Garrett hadn't ever been in love before, but he was now. Though he didn't dwell on this much, either, instead, the remainder of the night, which was spent sitting exactly where we leave them, all he thought of while observing the stars looking for some comfort, was the following: I have to get her out of here.

Budapest, HUNGARY
19 years, 193 days after Mutation 4

She watched his chest rise and fall next to her, keeping pace with his breathing. It calmed her for the most part, hell, she had even begun to fall asleep in its presence, but with every distant noise shaking her concentration, she couldn't help thinking about what she had seen earlier today. What she thought she had seen.

It was normal for refugees to filter in and out of this place. Some stayed days, some stayed months, some forever, and some barely had enough time to take a breath before they were placed on another transport. Her daily round had brought her to a tent located close to the transport hub, where every bus arrived and every bus departed from.

The young boy she was checking up on had sprouted chicken pox just a few days ago. The nurse regularly assigned to him hadn't ever had the disease, and couldn't keep looking after the boy. That's how he had ended up in Kivran's care, and that's why she was near the transport hub that particular afternoon. And that's how she saw Salar.

At least she believed she had seen him.

They had inadvertently locked eyes as she came out of the tent, and he turned his head aboard a departing bus. His hair was grown out, a mangled beard covered much of his facial features. It was easy to mistake anyone for someone else in this appearance, but what had sunk deep in Kivran's mind were emotionless eyes.

318

Kivran couldn't explain it, she didn't have the exact educational expertise to explain it, but she knew in her bones those emotionless eyes belonged to one man and one man only. That appearance couldn't be faked by anyone. She had seen Salar struggle with emotions long enough to know his face when he didn't know what he needed to do, what emotions he needed to emit.

And that's what she had seen, that's who she had seen. At least that's what she believed. Convinced herself of.

Lifting her eyes, she watched shadows of droplets crashing and sliding down the small window cast around the small room. There was hardly enough space for the two of them on the cot, Garrett was still partially hanging off the edge after insisting she needed room to turn in her condition.

Her condition.

Removing a hand beneath her head, she slid it over her stomach, feeling the protrusion. She was petrified of what was to come two months from now. What would she be passing on to this poor soul? She would be lying if she said she hadn't considering losing it at the onset, but it was a feeling, *that* feeling, that prevented her. The feeling she somehow clearly associated with her mother, a feeling of being loved. She could picture that woman's eyes, and that feeling would wash over her. Kivran wanted to reciprocate that, she wanted to be a mother more than anything.

There was a point in her life where this would have been impossible, and yet here she lay. Who was she to throw away a miracle? Remember: bastardized divine intervention.

Her eyes wandered from her belly up to her fore-arms upon which she still sported scars. She hadn't seized since… the operation, and yet, she expected to every night. She prayed she didn't pass that part of her on; no one deserved that, let alone a child.

Her eyes wandered again to her left, to the only person she felt safe enough with to bare her scars openly. She watched the tiny specks of discoloured, scarred skin on his neck pulse above the circulating blood beneath.

Salar's face.

Kivran shut her eyes as she held back a whimper. Garrett had said they died. He said he'd seen them die. But she was so sure, so sure, it was him. She had seen Salar, she knew she had.

In the dark, and without realizing what she was doing, she slid her hand the short distance to rest on Garrett's hip, exactly where his scar was. Not altogether convinced this was good thing, but nonetheless: Kivran knew every inch of him by memory.

"What's the matter?"

His hushed drawl shot her eyes open. Garrett was looking upon her in a familiar way, she just couldn't place it in that instance. His hand came to rest atop hers as they moved with his breaths up and down in unison.

Kivran dug her head deeper against the already flattened pillow. Shutting her eyes, she concentrated on the rhythmic rain, hoping it would wash her to sleep.

She knew what she had seen. And he had said they were dead.

Her eyes shot open again, this time out of frustra-tion. He was still watching her. This time, however, she could place the look in his eyes: it's how her mother looked at her—with love.

A tear trickled down the distance between Kivran's eye and the pillow. She hoped it was too dark to see.

"Tell me again, why were you on that island?"

She expected him to refuse her an answer, or alternatively to get angry for asking him for the umpteenth time. Instead, he held her gaze, unfazed.

"We were looking for someone illegally conducting allografts."

"And did you find them?"

"We believe so."

"And you killed them?"

"No."

"But you saw them die?"

Their hands rose and fell quicker as his breathing quickened. "Only one."

She had asked this so many times, and he had never asked why. But now, of all times, his answer was different. Why now?

Kivran slid her hand back to rest beneath her head; she didn't feel like being touched just now.

He had always wanted to know what sort of people chose to live in the desolate world his father had warned him about time and time again. Were they people with no other option? Or people who didn't think the world was all that bad? Or something else he couldn't wrap his head around?

It was now, crouching across the hall of a torn-apart washroom, that Garrett felt his childhood question was finally graced with an answer: her. People like her, that's who chose to live in such a desolate world.

"I'm not going anywhere with you, Garrett." Her voice held sway, it wasn't going to be easy to convince her of anything other than what she had already decided on.

These words were why he was on the floor; his legs could no longer bear his weight as her words had set in. This was the second time she had uttered them. The first one had brought home a feeling swelling in the pit of his gut all night: something was different in her, and for the worse.

She hadn't looked at him, she had kept her replies to a minimum, and she had flinched away from him at every opportunity.

And all that had been happening before he had even mustered the courage to tell her she could no longer stay here.

He screamed.

"You're not safe here anymore, Kiv. They're coming, rest assured, they're coming." Garrett hoped his voice was steady enough to be convincing and quiet enough to only reach Kivran's ears, who was seated on the bathroom floor across from him. The door held open with an outstretched swollen ankle adorned in a tattered sock. She was stubborn if nothing else.

"Who are 'they' Garrett?" Her voice quivered.

"Keuhl, people like Keuhl probably."

"Now is the part you tell me you're just trying to do the right thing, yes?"

That wasn't lost on him, she was mirroring their last good-bye. The last time he had pulled her away into another corner of the world to hide in.

The island. He realized that's what his father had been doing to him: hiding him in a corner of the world.

Good luck with everything, kid.

Garrett sunk his head deeper into his chest. Maybe he could just leave her. Let them find her. Let them experiment on her. Let them…

That little girl screamed.

No. She deserved his emotions; he needed to try.

"Please, Kivran. I'll come with you this time, if you want that, that is. But I can't in good conscience leave you here when I know what's coming. I've seen what's coming, Kiv."

"Good conscience, really? You keep dragging me around. You tore my home apart and shepherded me away." Christ, of all the words. "And like an idiot I went along." She took her foot out of way, and the door began to shut him out. "I held your bloody hands and danced for you. I don't think I want you to come with me anywhere, and I sure as hell don't want to go anywhere with you."

When had they both gotten to their feet, voices raised? The bathroom door was held open by his outstretched arm now as he caught it just before it had completely swung shut. They didn't seem to care who heard.

He watched her reflection in the bathroom mirror as she stood facing away. Cupping her belly with one arm and bracing herself against the sink with the other. He saw her eyes soften, the eyes that always gave her away. But now, he had difficulty determining if she felt sorry for him in this moment, or more sure in her own footing.

She met his gaze in the reflection illuminated beneath the yellow lights, dark circles covered both their eyes. He knew she hadn't slept the remainder of the night; he knew because he had watched her. Like he watched her through every night they were together.

It's funny, the things you remember at the weirdest of times. Not too long ago, on a night not significant in any other way, he had found her lying on the floor of her quarters. Arms and legs spread as much as possible, meaning she ended up half under the bed, unfocused, panic-stricken eyes, sweat stains along the front chest and under her arms, dirt and some dark, sticky, ointment-like substance splattered across her uniform. And all that accompanied by a hushed, yet mad, giggling bordering on a sob. Lying on the floor next to her, he waited patiently for her to make him privy to the circumstances. In time, her giggling morphed into a plead as she pulled her knees to her chest.

"I'm so tired. I just want to sleep." Leaked out of her.

This was the simplest problem Garrett had ever been presented with.

In one swift motion, he had picked her up off the cold floor and rested her on the bed, instructing her to sleep. Tugging at the collar of his shirt she reluctantly obliged with eyes already shut but not before saying, "If I seize or do anything frantic in my sleep, don't do anything. Just let me be." She had then tugged up the collar of her shirt and stuffed as much as possible into her mouth.

Even then, he had thought of that little girl tearing herself apart. But Kivran hadn't seized, she hadn't done anything frantic. He had watched the moment her eyes had shut to the moment they fluttered open.

Kivran would never tell him whether or not she had the Mutation, this was the closest she'd ever come to admitting it. After that night, Garrett didn't much care either way.

Now, standing behind her, hesitantly he stretched out a hand, giving her ample time to flinch away if she wanted. She didn't. And so, he traced the scar on her abdomen through her stretched shirt. The scar she had never offered up an explanation for, not that she had given them for any others, and not that he minded. Regardless, Garrett knew every inch of her by memory.

When she spoke finally, he felt his legs shake beneath his weight once again, a dread that made him wonder whether the feelings that had crept up to the surface yesterday were mutual or not. It's an awful feeling, wondering if something that deep is reciprocated and still somehow knowing in that depth it wasn't.

"You killed him."

Budapest, HUNGARY
Same day

The words spilled from her. Finally. Floating on her tongue all morning, she had finally let them out. This time, he flinched away from her.

He had left go of the door, letting it swing shut behind them, confining them to each other.

Kivran felt disgusted with herself. She thought of the goats under her care, in a different life, in a different time. She fed them every day, knowing they were headed to slaughter. Had they known? She hadn't known, and now here she stood, feeling as though Garrett was leading her down the same path.

Without thought, she placed her hand exactly where his had rest a moment ago. Her flesh was cold to the touch. Through the mirror, he watched his face sink under the weight of her words.

He didn't ask who. Who he had killed, who he was being accused of killing. He didn't ask.

Still, she watched his figure come closer until she felt him more so than saw him next to her. It's funny, the things you remember at the weirdest of times. This memory was of the final day she had been on her island, the day, the moment Garrett had asked her to leave. Go anywhere but stay there, he had said. She had looked out at the sky wondering how awful it would be to only have vicariously lived through others. She had watched from her peripherals as his chest rose and fell; she kept pace. It felt comforting knowing she was in time with someone else, not breathing on her own. She had wondered what it would be like to die alone up to that point in time. She was sick and tired of the thought. She was going to die regardless, did it really matter where?

Watching his reflection, she instinctively closed her eyes for what she already knew was coming. Leaning over, he kissed her right temple, a lingering touch that lasted a little longer than any other time. In turn, she found herself leaning into him. An instinctive reaction induced countless times.

As he began to pull away just enough to speak, and as his stubble continued to tingle her skin, she already knew once more what was coming. She was already forging tears behind those closed eyes. In nothing more than a whisper you could have missed in the slightest noise, he spoke just as Kivran realized she was going to miss Garrett.

"Good-bye, Kivran."

Budapest, HUNGARY
19 years, 302 days after Mutation 4

A leader leads by example, not by force.

You'll recognize that quote from *The Art of War*, it also happens to be the personal mantra of one Albano Silnor. Though it's intended to carry gravitas, to instill an ethical concept in the reader, the abider, this quote wasn't quite interpreted as one would hope by Albano. What he saw in those words was the following: I have to initiate a war between the common folks and those rigging the system, no one else is going to do this.

The mantra bubbling up within him, coupled with an urgency to act before someone finally found him, led to this precise moment: Albano conversing with an attending nurse at the local general hospital.

"How many refugee patients do you have right now?" He hoped his Hungarian hadn't faded too much. His mother would be disappointed if it did; she had only spent her entire life trying to get him to speak to her in the dialect.

The nurse responded with the fakest of fake smiles from across the reception desk. She appeared exhausted, no care for personal grooming and appearance. How dare she have the audacity to smile back at him?

"Why do you ask?" Putting on that condescending tone as well.

"I ask because I'm curious." Albano slowed his speech, perhaps she would understand this pace better.

"Now, how many refugees are currently in this hospital?"

"None."

She had to have been playing a game with him.

"How is that possible? You are the primary medical facility in this region, and you have thousands of sick refugees just up that hill."

"Those refugees just happen to be there." Her smile had vanished, she began to fiddle around with something on the desk, Albano wasn't tall enough to view precisely what over the elevated portion in front of him. She wouldn't indulge him with much more attention. He despised people like her, people who believed they were better than him. "We don't cater to them, they have their own medical buildings up there."

This was about to place a damper on his plans. "But there's thousands of them, how can they have adequate means to…"

A group of orderlies were shouting somewhere behind him, their loud voices echoing out against the near empty lobby.

"Look, sir, damned if you do, damned if you don't, right? Hospital's empty, people like you are going to complain; hospital's full, people like you are going to complain. It's a government-funded place, there's no way they're treating any refugees down here because that would mean they're aiding the crisis, which the government definitely isn't." He was fixated on a hair peeking out of her left nostril. "So they've got their fancy aide workers up there while you get to have an empty hospital all to yourself. Happy?"

The primary thought floating around Albano's mind was: at least my Hungarian's still good, she thinks I'm a local. The secondary thought was: I won't get as many causalities, but at least an attack on a government facility would still get some attention. Besides, he couldn't get anywhere near that refugee camp without a dozen military eyes on him at any given moment.

Lead by example, Albano, lead by example.

A wave of déjà vu and nausea washed over Kivran as she saw the hospital emergency doors before her. Garrett's words were still swimming around in her head, even after all these months: you can't trust Tamsin anymore. That's why when forty minutes ago, when the labour pains had gotten so excruciating, she handed in half-filled reports for her shift and walked herself out of the camp limits hoping to flag down a Good Samaritan. It took her almost forty minutes to find a cab in the near-deserted streets and in that while, not only had her water definitely broken, she also fallen into hard fits of labour. The moment she realized what was happening, before she flagged down the cab, before her water broke, before she handed in her reports, she thought of calling Garrett. As quickly as the thought had come to her, it dissolved. She could do this just like she had done everything else. Alone.

Reaching the hospital, she had no idea why a group of men and woman appeared to be heckling a few of the orderlies by the entrance, and in this state, she didn't much care to stand and find out. Bypassing them with a protective arm over her stomach and the other out in front like a shield, Kivran found her way in. Had she been paying attention, she may have heard something along the lines of "You have to leave, that guy is serious" in the gathering.

Waddling half-way across the polished, near-deserted lobby, feeling like an idiot with this gait no less, she took a moment to catch her breath. There was no one to keep pace with.

Alone.

The panic was razing all logical thought. She was going to die alone, in this place, this insurmountable amount of pain.

She screamed.

No one in sight, unable to contain the medley of horror within, she opted to shout for all the reasons she ever wanted to. Miraculously, a nurse appeared before her.

"Doctor! I'm going to need help! Tell me your name please, love."

There were about seven different languages scattered across the camp, each of them with a common-enough English thread to hold up a conversation. Fortunately, one of them was Hungarian, and she had picked up the bare essentials in the last ten months. Hence, she understood most of what the nurse was shouting. If she was required to provide an articulate reply at any point, however, Kivran would be lost for words.

"Kiv… Kivran."

The nurse grabbed a wheelchair near the desk and guided Kivran onto it. Half in a conscious state now, Kivran saw a doctor appear from a nearby room, running towards her in slow motion, it seemed. Together, they wheeled her down the hall.

"Which room, Doc?"

"*A legtávolabbi elölr□ l, a többi már kiürítette a berendezések.*"

Somewhere along the way, another nurse joined them, but Kivran was barely paying attention now. She didn't realize when they arrived at the room or even understand she was being lifted onto the bed. She did, however, remember the doctor telling her to let him have a look.

"No, I can't! It hurts!"

Had she been fully conscious and aware of herself, she would've known in the back of her mind she was clenching every muscle tight and shut. She didn't want the baby to come out. She didn't know what kind of life she would be giving it. She came to the altogether quite late realization that she didn't want to be here.

"I know; I need to make sure everything's okay. Just okay."

One of the nurses placed a cold hand upon her forehead, and Kivran exhaled the bated breath she hadn't realized she was holding. Nodding silently and feeling sweat drip down her forehead, Kivran spread her legs. She hadn't even realized when her pants were taken off. The doctor said something to one of the other nurses, and she returned with a tray of surgical instruments. Looking at the intimidating tools, Kivran finally let herself cry.

Involuntarily, she rested a palm against her right temple, looking for a touch that wasn't there.

Everyone in the room suddenly froze at a striking sound towards the front of the hospital. Like a battering ram on a steel door, a bang. And again. The doctor returned his attention to Kivran.

"Nem úgy néz ki, mint ami sok id□t, nem akarsz kezdeni most?"

The only part of that she understood involved something about not having time. His urgent tone allowed her to fill in the blanks. Spreading her legs farther, Kivran tried to keep conscious. One of the nurses came to her side and held her hand.

"*Csak lélegezz.*"

Seeing the confused look on her patient's face, the nurse began to take short breaths and pointed at her. Kivran began to take short breaths. Looking down, she saw the other nurse hand something to the doctor, who was now out of sight over and around the hill that was Kivran's stomach. She felt a sharp pain, and then saw the doctor's face.

Something was wrong.

"*Valami nincs rendben.*"

He proceeded to speak in faster Hungarian to the other nurses. Kivran didn't understand any of it, all she knew was: the pain was getting worse, and she was dangerously close to blacking out. The nurse holding her hand said with an accent, "Push."

So that's what Kivran did. She pushed with all her might as the doctor continued to speak quickly. It put Kivran at unease, but she tried not to think about that, nor about her right temple.

Budapest, HUNGARY
Same day

Death, death, and more death with a few specks of disease sprinkled in. She couldn't take it anymore. The smell, the people, the whole situation, it was chipping away at her sanity.

The people, oh God, the people. The types of bastards that filtered in and out of this hell-hole. Mostly in. If this is what the world had come to, she was done with it. She mentally convinced herself without a doubt that that asshole's breath was still on her, alcohol and tobacco. A walking stereotype he was. And she, in turn, felt violated, violated at his presence, at his words, at the fact that he had been looking at her. Her skin was crawling as she was unable to shake the sickening feeling he had brought about in her.

This was the only thing she could do to rid herself of this, of him. Shivering in the spring breeze, she gazed down the edge of the cliff feeling dizzy at the aerial view of the waves crashing against the rocks below. There was a storm coming for sure; the river wasn't usually this violent.

Glancing once again at the hoard behind her, lost in their own world, in their own tents, their own relationships, their own conversations. She awaited someone's attention. It was broad daylight, someone, anyone would notice soon. Right? A couple walked by, looking her way for just a moment before returning to their private conversation. Fine, that's how it was going to be. She was okay with partaking in the death statistics of this damned camp then.

Camp, could you even call it that? It was a city unto itself, a lawless, disease-infested city, complete with its own brand of homegrown scumbags. Had there yet been a night when someone *hadn't* been raped or robbed?! What the hell are you even robbing people of here? No one had anything of value, anyway.

She turned back around, taking in a deep breath, ready to end it once and for all. Unable to look at the waves any longer, she lifted her eyes towards the north part of the city. From this far away, it didn't look like a despot, like hell's waiting room. It was a damn shame.

Bending her knees slightly to maintain balance, she lifted her right foot up and over the cliff, letting the feeling of nothingness below her feet become a familiarity. As though walking into a pool, she forced her body to follow through with the motion of her initial step, and before she knew it, she was off solid ground and plunging towards those nauseating rocks.

The millisecond before her body once again touched ground, a thought rang out over the screams of people above.

This place honestly wasn't that bad.

Budapest, HUNGARY
Same day

Albano pulled the van into a parking spot relatively in the middle of the entire lot. Why he even bothered to park between the lines, he couldn't say. There were less than a dozen cars in sight. If he was so rudely denied the satisfaction of a high casualty count, he was going to aim for a high volume of debris, hopefully that would be sufficient enough to attract government attention, and better yet, followers. Imagine the international community chiming in! He found himself getting giddy at the mere thought.

It should be noted that Albano is deliberately ignoring statements riddled in the comments sections of his posts implying various things regarding his actions. Comments such as: "What you're doing is completely redundant asshole, these people are trying to help people survive this mess and you're just ruining their lives;" and "I can't put into words how devastatingly idiotic this such an act would be, it's going to set back the movement by no less than three years, hope it's worth it;" and "You deserve to perish in that explosion yourself dipshit." All this, and those that were, arguably, worse rolled off Albano just like his morality. He thought of himself as a genuine revolutionary at the front-line.

Opening the back doors of the van, Albano lifted the black tarp to reveal an explosive. According to his calculations, it would be enough to cause the first floor of the hospital to implode. The man hovered his hand just above the timer and allowed himself one more moment to make sure this was what he truly wanted.

It was.

Peaceful protests can only get any given cause so far before drastic measures must be taken. Albano wanted to prove to the others he could fight for something. He wasn't a burn-out like everyone claimed. He needed to show them.

Lowering his hand, he flipped the singular switch. Red numbers flashed to life before counting down. He stood and watched, marvelling at the initiation of something grand.

00:30:59… 00:30:58… 00:30:57… 00:30:56

Proud of himself, of every moment in his life that led to this exact, deliberate moment, Albano turned his back on the van and headed towards the exit.

Rushing. That's all he heard, just blood rushing past his ears. His heart pulsed at an alarming rate, his chest tightened as he began to lose air.

He had only felt this degree of petrification twice in his life:

1.   On that bloody island, after that blast; and

2.   On that other bloody island, after *it* fell to its death.

He screamed. He prayed for the sheep to not be dead.

He saw Odeli returning from the crowd, but Garrett couldn't tell you the expression the man wore nor what he said. He could tell you, however, that a crowd was gathering just ahead of them, all leaning towards the edge of the cliff, mesmerized by a singular act. He could tell you he saw a curtain of light brown hair fall, a woman fall. He could tell you she had casually taken a step where no solid ground stood.

But he couldn't tell you what she wore, or what her face looked like. He couldn't even be sure it was *her*. Hence the petrification.

The crowd shouted for someone to come help. Odeli had strolled nonchalantly off to the military trailer before medics arrived at the location, leaving Garrett on his own.

He couldn't go over, that wasn't how he wanted to find out. Taking a shallow breath, he wiped both palms over his eyes before turning around. He headed towards the primary medical building to the south.

He was going to find her in there, he was going to get her out of here, he was going let *that* feeling consume him.

If he had, in fact, found the answer to his lifelong question, if he had, in fact, finally immersed himself in a world his father never wanted him to be a part of, then he knew he would also have to feel the pain of having to give it all up. Within the motion of his long strides away from the commotion, he concluded two things:

1. Of all the people in said world, he only cared for one of them; and

2. Those sheep were going to die regardless of if he screamed or no. It was an unfortunate inevitability.

Arriving at his destination, Garrett took a few shallow breaths again before opening the entrance. He was going to find her in there, he was going to get her out of here, he was going let *that* feeling consume him.

A woman walked by, casually glancing in his direction before continuing, only to return a few steps later to approach Garrett nervously. "Do I know you?"

He looked at her, vague sparks of recognition ignited. She was one of the women who travelled with Odeli's girlfriend. She was always on the same transport, which meant...

"Yes, I'm looking for Kivran." He heard his pitch elevate and depreciate within the small sentence as he attempted to keep calm. The calluses upon his hands rubbed against the inside of his pockets, agitated. Sweat trickled down his back against the chilly lobby, awaiting the reply that seemed to take an eon to come about.

Eventually, with a puzzled expression, the condescending tone came forth. "Oh, you haven't heard."

Why was it a statement? *No, I haven't heard, that's why I'm asking you.*

It took a fair amount of control to not retort. "No, I haven't. Heard what?"

"She's not here."

He screa—

"She's at the general hospital, she went into labour."

It's what he wanted to hear, and yet he couldn't quite believe it. Whoever that woman was, walking off the edge, she wasn't Kivran.

Nodding frantically in appreciation, Garrett stepped out of the building, unaware of anything further the lady was babbling about. The commotion of the crowd was far away now. Turning his body east where countless flights of stairs meandered down towards Kivran, he inhaled deeply and set off in a flat-out sprint.

It's funny, the things you remember at the weirdest of times. Though right now, this memory might be quite a fitting one. Feeling a stitch in his side, Garrett thought about the first time he'd met Kivran. On that bloody island, in that bloody humidity, on that bloody beautiful night. She had been standing in the threshold of that make-shift hospital, pushing herself against the door frame, slouching, trying to occupy the smallest space in the universe she could. He'd watched her, petrified look across her face, shaky limbs and all, trying to lend a hand. When she'd finally come closer, he took her in.

Skin a tinge of brown, hazel hair haphazardly tied back, goose bumps running down her neck, eyes swollen and bloodshot, four finger-length scars running from her right temple to jaw-line. Her facial features told him she wasn't native to this region, and her nervous demeanour told him she wasn't native to this work. And then he observed the shirt of her light blue uniform, towards the bottom of which was a damp section clinging to the skin beneath, it carried a red hue.

She sat down beside his slouching figure and gazed at his abdomen, which he'd been sitting there clenching. The pain had become excruciating. As she moved his clothing to observe the wound, she pulled what he later found out was his burned flesh, unknowingly clean off. He was still looking at the blood expanding on her shirt. Who was he to flinch?

Their eyes met as though they had been seeking each other out. Grey eyes. Mountain grey. She was gorgeous.

Garrett dug deeper, mentally clenching his scarred hip, and sprinted faster.

The noise outside began to swell, ricocheting between Kivran's ears. At least she believed it was originating from outside. Amongst the chaos, someone continued to should "Push!" somewhere above her head, and out of simple frustration at the woman for puncturing her eardrums, Kivran pushed with every muscle left in her body still responding to neurons.

That was until the fearful whimper at the back of her skull silenced every other rattling: *you're going to pass it on.*

Kivran stopped pushing, she stopped everything with the exception of panting. Beads of sweat plunged down her cheeks every time she blinked, the hair caked to her face was irritating, but she didn't have the nerve to move her hand up—she didn't want to open the gate to movement again. She was about to change her mind. She was about to make herself physically so ill that it would take a miracle for this baby to come out alive. She was about to abandon hope.

It's funny, the things you remember at the weirdest of times. Kivran had barely registered this memory when it occurred, there was much else happening that day. For instance, her mother's death. But now, for whatever reason, the memory was boiling inside her to the point where she felt that agonizing August sun blazing against her already scorching flesh. Hopping along on one foot whilst shaking the other, Kivran had been trying to dislodge a pebble wriggling around in her sandal. One hand had held a small canvas bag gifted by her mother earlier that day, Kivran pretended it was a handbag carrying prized possessions: her favourite scarf, her butterfly clips, and a set of dice she had snuck out of her brother's pillowcase—she wanted to know what all the fuss was about. Her other hand was clasped in the gentle grip of her mother's. They were on their way to visit Aunt Ines at the clinic before it got too busy; they were hoping to confirm good news. Mommy was going to have another baby. It was just the girls' secret; they hadn't told Aydin anything yet, only because they didn't want to get this hopes up. That's what Mommy had said.

"Are you scared, Mommy?" Kivran had absent-mindedly inquired, not comprehending the weight of this conversation until nearly twenty years later.

She heard her voice now, as though she spoke from the very hospital room. "Scared of what, love?"

"Of losing a piece of you. It's going to come out of you. Won't it take some of the stuff inside you when it comes out?" There, she had finally gotten the pebble out, and that's when she let go of her mother's hand: bending down to pick up the pebble and investigate it. This had seemed so much more important than holding her mother's hand.

Mommy's warm laugh came from a few steps ahead. "Of course the baby will take something from my insides with it, but I'm not scared. You know why?" She had stopped and turned back to wait for Kivran. When she was finally done with her investigation, the little girl looked up at her mother. "Because I'm going to give it all the best stuff! Every brilliant, lovely thing inside me, I'm going to let the baby take it all. Just like I let you take the wonderful stuff, silly billy."

Kivran opened her eyes to search the visible corners of the room. Her mother wasn't there, she knew better but that feeling...

The nurse above her slammed a palm to Kivran's forehead before shouting "Push!" once more. Easing her breathing, she gently began to oblige. She felt exhausted, with every muscle now blaring pain sensors, her stomach in intolerable agony, and her nails digging into her palms. Kivran concentrated on the event happening around her. She was about to pass on the wonderful stuff.

After what felt like an eternity, especially with the commotion outside no longer present, she finally felt her skin return to its normal state, the baby was out. But it wasn't crying. Lifting her head slightly to see what was wrong or even catch a glimpse of the child, she wasn't successful. However, oddly enough, a feeling of relief was still washing over her. Although her muscles persisted their throbbing, she allowed herself a moment and she began to take down her mental walls, inhaling deeply one last time.

Blinking, attempting to clear the remaining haziness and sweat in her vision, she rested her head against the bed and tilted, she was now facing the door-way.

As though on cue, she found him standing there. Silly smile spread evenly across his face, amber eyes focusing on nothing but her, hair matted down with sweat, hunched over heaving, hands on knees. He'd sprinted here. She could have sworn she could feel the warmth of this forehead pressed against hers and his thumb rubbing the scar on her right temple, as Kivran found herself instinctively reciprocating his joy.

A moment was all it took for the oblivion to seep in. Thus, before she could see her child's face or even know if it was alive or not, before she could tell Garrett not to worry, Kivran was overcome with an indescribable wave of nothingness and shut her eyes to the world once and for all. But not before one final spark of a thought flickered within her:

She felt loved.

www.ingramcontent.com/pod-product-compliance
Lightning Source LLC
Chambersburg PA
CBHW031129120726
47905CB00006B/1624